SOUL SEARCH

Dr Vivian Blake's three-year-old son has recently died in a car crash, leaving her life shattered and her marriage under strain. On her first day back at work she meets Stephen Daunt, a young teacher who is suffering constant nightmares, has nearly caused the death of a pupil and has attempted to smother his wife in her sleep. Treating him under hypnosis, Dr Blake is shocked when Stephen starts to describe being a factory owner in Victorian times ... and even more taken aback when he apparently starts to communicate with the soul of her dead son.

SOUL SEARCH

SOUL SEARCH

by

Kathy Picard

Dales Large Print Books
Long Preston, North Yorkshire,
BD23 4ND, England.

British Library Cataloguing in Publication Data.

Picard, Kathy
  Soul search.

  A catalogue record of this book is
  available from the British Library

  ISBN   978-1-84262-835-5 pbk

Published in Large Print 2011 by arrangement with
Working Partners Two

Dales Large Print is an imprint of Library Magna Books Ltd.

Printed and bound in Great Britain by
T.J. (International) Ltd., Cornwall, PL28 8RW

CHAPTER ONE

'Welcome back Dr Blake.' At the look of dreadful sincerity washing over the kindly, worn features of Jean, UCL's psychology department secretary, Vivien almost took a step back onto the busy streets of Bloomsbury.

'Thank you Jean,' she murmured, looking down as she examined the bundle of post she'd just pulled from her pigeonhole. Little had changed in her absence; large tubs of glossy-leaved plants still stood on either side of the reception desk and the same smell of industrial polish wafted up from the marble floor. Unlike most of the surrounding buildings, this one was bright and modern and the early morning sunlight splashing through the large plate glass windows gave it the air of a thrusting city bank rather than a teaching hospital.

'We were all so very sorry about what happened. I can't imagine what these past few months have been like for you...'

However hard Vivien Blake had rehearsed for this moment, it had done nothing to prepare her for this feeling of awkwardness. Embarrassment, even. As if she should apologise for placing her colleagues in the position of having to struggle to find the right words. She only looked up again when she heard Jean clear her throat

Fortunately, they were both spared further discomfort by Dr Sebastian Nicholls breezing into the office. Draped in a teal-blue suit that accentuated the colour of his eyes and with dark stubble just this side of being *designer*, he looked as though he had been out all night clubbing. Vivien suspected that he might well have been; although a few years shy of 40, he was a man who wasn't ready to give himself up to a pipe-and-slippers-respectability quite yet. And with his slim figure and boyish charm, there were plenty of young women around to ensure that he really didn't have to.

'Jean, have you had a go at trying to find those papers yet? I need them for this afternoon.'

Vivien smiled at his mock efficiency. He'd tried this tack on her too when they'd first worked together: it hadn't fooled her then, and it didn't fool her now. Seb Nicholls was a victim of his own disorganisation and by lunchtime would be admitting sheepishly that the papers had been on his desk all along.

'I see you haven't been brushing up on your desk-side manner while I've been away,' she said. 'And who appointed you the office slave-driver, anyway?'

'No need for official titles. Just because I've left the tedium of psychiatric practice behind doesn't mean I've abandoned all notions of self-importance; someone has to keep this lot in order. Do you know, only last week when I was researching some new case studies, I found my notes for *Wade* filed under *Wilde?*'

'It's your fault for having such appalling handwriting,' countered Jean.

'They spent years trying to teach us that at medical school, and it's a positive advantage to an author; everyone always assumes you've written something especially intelligent when they can't make head nor tail of it. Anyway, off I trot to my first interview only to have to spend most of the time trying to persuade the woman that she wasn't a fifty-year-old agoraphobic at all, but a twenty-something hotshot lawyer with a burgeoning Napoleon complex.'

Vivien joined in the laughter. Seb had always used gallows' humour as a way of dealing with the stresses of psychiatry but now he had crossed over into the commercially successful world of self-help books, he seemed to positively relish sending himself up as well. He could be irreverent but they all needed to find a way to cope with the pressures of their profession and remain mentally healthy themselves. She wondered what mechanism she would adopt from now on.

'Step into my parlour, Vivien, and I'll give you the low-down on what's been going on in this madhouse.'

'You've got a supervising session with Dr McFraser at the end of the day,' Jean said as Dr Nicholls put an easy arm around Vivien's shoulders and led her through the waiting room and into one of the adjoining offices.

Vivien dumped her briefcase and pile of post on the cabinet just inside the door and perched on the edge of the desk. She didn't want to have to scrabble up out of one of the low chairs and make an undignified exit if there was to be a repetition of the scene outside; the discomfort she'd felt on Jean's behalf hadn't quite left her. She tried to put it out of her mind and scanned the book-shelves opposite. Once piled high with tatty-cornered copies of *The Journal of Psychiatry* and thick clinical textbooks, Seb's own books now took pride of place with their blood-orange ('such a hopeful colour' he'd said when he'd shown her the mock-up) covers: *The Happiness Principle* and its sequel *It Could Be You: How to Win in the Happiness Lottery*. It was cheering to know that her friend had made a successful second career for himself without having to conform and lose any of the subtleties of his own brand of irony.

She took a moment to reach down and tug

the hem of her jacket flat. She had spent longer than usual this morning on her appearance – choosing a softly-structured linen suit in pale green and blow-drying her hair until it framed her face to perfection – and was glad she'd done so. At 42, being around slim-hipped and glossy-haired students all day could sometimes be tough on the ego.

After a lengthy silence, which she suspected Seb found easier to relax into than she did, Vivien decided that she had to take the initiative. She folded her arms and adopted the look of a stern schoolmarm.

'Come on, tell all. What's been going on while I've been away? Someone will be sure to spill the beans of what you've been up to, so why don't you get in first?'

Seb Nicholls assumed an exaggerated look of defeat. 'How I wish I could say the lunatics have taken over the asylum at last but that would only give you false hope. First thing Friday morning you'd come crashing back down to earth. Fat Man McFraser has instituted a new round of pointless meetings he calls team briefings. "An opportunity for us all to be open and honest in a spirit of mutual cooperation and run up the flagpole any issues the cat sicks up".'

Vivien's snort of laughter surprised even her. It had been a while since she'd laughed.

'Don't be so mean, he can't help sounding

as if he's swallowed the latest management textbook.'

'Any more than I can help having to listen to the pompous fart.'

'Just try being nice for a change and imagine he's doing his best to make everyone feel supported in their work.'

'And what about you?'

'What about me?'

'Do you feel supported?'

The muscles in Vivien's cheeks began to ache with the effort of keeping her smile in place.

'Of course. Everyone has been very ... very...' her voice dropped; the amusement entirely gone from it now, '...understanding.'

How she wished she could understand what had happened; why it had happened to her.

Seb looked for a moment as if he was going to reach out and touch her arm and Vivien involuntarily stiffened at the prospect of such intimate concern. She was finding it difficult enough to mask her vulnerability as it was.

'Don't be delusional, my dear,' Seb intoned in a music hall version of a Viennese accent, 'your paranoiac tendencies are getting the better of you once more. We neither can, nor care to, even try to understand anyone here; don't you see? We'd all be out of a lucrative little earner if we did.'

Vivien allowed herself to release her grip on the edge of the desk. She'd been ready to push herself towards the door in a second if Seb had picked up on her unguarded moment.

'I've not been here myself much,' Seb continued easily in his normal voice. 'Being a popular author isn't all it's cracked up to be. The publishers had me traipsing all over the country to the most out of the way places imaginable on my latest book tour. Wick. Do you know where that is? I didn't. Went there and still don't. It must've been chucking out day at the local library because the only people who came to the bookshop were three bag-ladies and an old man who snored the whole way through my pitch. You won't be surprised to learn that none of them shelled out for one of my books.'

'Perhaps they know the secret of happiness already.' Vivien smiled to show there was no bitterness or self-pity behind her remark.

'Well, you'll be pleased to know that the trip wasn't entirely wasted. I took a little friend as a travelling companion. They have very early and long nights up there in Scotland.'

'Oh, Seb. Not again. I still remember the tears and tantrums from last year; I'm amazed they haven't started issuing all the new PhD students with a written warning about you.'

13

Seb looked across at her and grinned. 'Can I help it if these good looks lure all the innocent young things into falling in love with me? I wish they'd just play it for laughs, I really do, but is it my fault if they're just dying for an older man to worship?'

Vivien was forced to agree. Seb was undeniably handsome – if you liked strong cheekbones, a chiselled jaw and baby-blue eyes – and had a knack of speaking to a woman as if she was the most special person in the world; she'd seen him in action. But he was more vulnerable than he liked to admit (and much, much more than any of his young admirers could possibly ever see); if there was a victim in this perpetual game of chase and conquest, it was probably Seb.

She jumped as her friend clapped his hands.

'Right, enough of dissecting me. Come on, let's go into your office and I'll show you what I've done with your case notes.'

Vivien gathered up her things and walked next door with him.

Her office wasn't entirely as she'd left it. Everything was still in the same place but someone had done their best to make it look – and feel – as if it hadn't just been abandoned. All the surfaces in the room were spotless and the sharp-edged leaves of a spider plant spilt out of a blue glazed pot beside her telephone. She suspected that had been Jean's touch; she would have to take over the watering of it herself if it was to fair better than the one on the radiator shelf in the outside office.

Much as she welcomed Seb's efforts to ease her gently back into her work, Vivien suddenly wanted to be alone so that she could connect again with the atmosphere in the room. This space was part of her and it contained her persona even when she wasn't there: her framed qualifications – the degree from Columbia University and medical qualification from Yale – hanging on the wall; the row of books all making reference to her clinical case studies or containing acknowledgments to her; the award on the coffee table presented at the last symposium she had attended: all outward symbols of her dedication to the scientific pursuit of healing disturbed and fractured minds. She was proud of all this but it had come at a price. When she'd first come over from the States ten years ago to be with Jerry, she hadn't just been able to walk into such a senior position. She'd had to work hard to adapt to the different professional culture and it had been tough at first. *Sacrifices are the stuff of life, honey, and they'll always be worth it in the end,* her mother's words rang in her ears once more. Smiling as she recalled her Minnesota twang, Vivien supposed that she might just believe that again herself, one day.

She walked a little further into the office and caught sight of something she had missed with her first glance. There, tucked beside the computer monitor on her desk, was the family photograph they'd posed for last year. She side-stepped Seb and moved forward to snatch it up and slip it into the top drawer before he could spot it too. Maybe it was just as well that she hadn't come in here on her own.

Self-absorbed as ever, Seb didn't seem to have noticed as he indicated the files stacked neatly in front of her. 'There are two piles,' he said, 'the *hopeless*, and the *helpless*. I thought that was as good a distinction as any.' The telephone rang. 'Ah, the lovely Jean must've thought it was time you started working for a living. I'll leave you to it.'

Vivien picked up the phone and asked for a moment before the call was put through. 'Seb,' she said as he strolled towards the door, 'thanks for not mentioning the obvious.'

He held his hands up as if defending himself. 'Now, now, that is way below the belt, Dr Blake. Since when have I ever been accused of doing anything so banal? However, far be it from me to admit to being the sort to offer a shoulder to cry on but,' he paused as he pulled the office door open, 'if it ever gets too much for you here then there's always an open invitation to join me on my next book tour. I've a feeling we'll both be able to make the most of the distraction.'

Vivien laughed at his roguish grin. 'Thanks for the offer but I think I'd be better off trying to grapple with whatever they throw at me here. Now, get out and leave me in peace; I've got work to do.' She turned her attention back to the telephone as Seb closed the door behind him.

CHAPTER TWO

For the rest of the morning, Vivien immersed herself in the familiar routine of reading through files, dictating letters, and checking her diary appointments with Jean. Her immediate workload wasn't too onerous but contained enough things of interest to pique her professional curiosity. One such was the first consultation with a new patient booked for that afternoon. Seb had obviously dealt with the initial enquiry and had opened up a file ready for her. She picked it up and tutted at his characteristic scrawl; she could only feel sorry for his editor and wondered if they'd sent him to the northern tip of Scotland out of some sort of revenge. Luckily, Jean had seen fit to slip in a typewritten copy of his notes.

CASE STUDY NOTES
NAME: Stephen Daunt
AGE: 25
OCCUPATION: Maths Teacher
MARITAL STATUS: Married
REASON FOR REFERRAL:
Stephen has started behaving erratically at work and the school authorities have insisted that he seek psychiatric help. They appear to be being supportive (he is a good teacher and they don't want to lose him) however he believes this course of action unnecessary. He has already demonstrated a marked hostility towards his headmaster over his referral, wanting to be given the opportunity to work out any problems by himself. This appears unlikely as the inciting incident for his dramatic change in behaviour seems to have been a boating accident on a school trip. A boy nearly drowned.

Vivien felt a surge of conflicting emotions. Empathy for the man's crippling guilt but also something that she reluctantly identified as jealousy that her own recent experience couldn't have turned out so well. The minute the thought entered her head, she shook it away. Ashamed. Envy and snap judgements were unlike her and wouldn't help either of them to deal with his problems.

18

A snatched sandwich for lunch, and a couple of hours catching up on a request to be the keynote speaker at a series of symposia being run by the British Psychological Society, and then it was 4.30 and time for her appointment with Stephen Daunt. She retrieved her shoes from under the desk, slipped them back on, and walked over to the mirror to check her hair and that she hadn't accidentally transferred any ink, or newsprint, to her face.

She reached out and flicked the light switch. Her initial glimpse of herself under the unforgiving fluorescent glare wasn't heartening. She wondered if anyone else had noticed the extra lines around her mouth and eyes, which didn't come from laughter; the seemingly permanent tenseness in her jaw; the slightly puffy eyelids from too many nights of broken sleep. Had Seb recognised the signs but just been too tactful to point them out? She fingered her right earlobe. It was red and sore from not wearing earrings for such a long time but she didn't want to take them out; they were essential to her image of being a capable woman who paid attention to detail: but a woman all the same. The fact that the emeralds complemented her green suit beautifully only added to the overall effect. She continued looking at herself for a moment or two longer, placed a smile on her lips and smoothed her skirt over her thighs.

Vivien opened the door and scanned the small waiting room. There was only one person there. He was slumped in his chair with his elbows resting on his knees. Vivien coughed gently to attract his attention.

'Hello. I'm Vivien Blake, and you must be Stephen Daunt. Do please come in.'

He didn't offer a response; only a slight twitch of his eyebrows, and the fact that he stood up, gave any indication that he'd heard her at all. She watched as he made his way towards her and took the opportunity to size him up professionally. He had a lean, almost scarecrow physique but his erect bearing gave him a presence that she would imagine his students would find commanding. His face, although closed to all expression, was interesting. The lower half was slightly pinched with a small chin and thin lips, but he had a prominent nose, large ears and a high forehead. It was as if his parents' genes had been fighting it out for supremacy and the more dominant had come out on top. Vivien made eye contact and smiled but his gaze remained determinedly blank.

'After you,' she said and stood aside to let him enter the office. Even that small courtesy went unacknowledged. This was a man who would demand every one of her skills to get him to open up to her.

She closed the door behind them and

indicated which of the chairs Stephen should occupy. But he had already taken the other one; her seat. Had he done that deliberately? It was obvious that he resented having to see her, his body language was even more eloquent than his hostile silence; his hunched shoulders over his folded arms and the way he thrust out his legs as he leaned back in his chair as if waiting for the interrogation to start. It wasn't unusual for patients to exhibit such an attitude but most tried to hide it initially with an attempt at humour or in nervous chatter. This man was just staring at her with his direct gaze as if daring her to begin.

Her cursory assessment over, Vivien picked up a notepad and pen from her desk, and sat down.

'Thank you for making this appointment, Stephen. I know that not many people relish the idea of seeing a psychiatrist but, if it helps reassure you, I'm not here to label but to identify some ways in which we can work through whatever's at the root of your recent problems.'

Vivien felt the air between them vibrate with a tension that came off him like body heat. Was he now feeling patronised? Or could it simply be that he wasn't used to someone else taking control. She injected a note of deeper warmth into her voice.

'Why don't you start by telling me a little

about yourself?'

'Born in Devon; uprooted to London at an early age but didn't become a bed-wetter – that sort of thing?'

His voice was unnaturally loud and had a hard edge to it. He was clearly determined to make this as difficult as possible. She wrote the information down anyway; every contribution – however sarcastic – would reveal something of his current state of mind.

'Let's bring things a little more up to date.' Vivien spoke with a deliberate slowness to contrast with his clipped response. 'Your headmaster has some ... shall we say "issues" ... with your recent behaviour; I understand he described it as "erratic".'

In the silence that followed, Vivien sat with her hands folded over her notepad. When the waiting stretched to over a minute, her fingers moved towards her wedding ring and she started to twist it slowly.

'What's the matter, doctor? Your frustration getting to you?'

Vivien relaxed her hands once more. This man may be surly, but he was astute.

'Frustration is a good word, Stephen. Are you sure it's not you who's feeling that right now?'

'Ha! Don't tell me I'm being accused of what you shrinks call "projection"?'

She let the slur on her profession go.

'If that is what's taking place, then it's nothing to be ashamed of. It's very common and very...' she sought carefully for the right word, '...understandable. We all do it in moments of stress in order to deflect the attention away from ourselves. From our feelings.' She thought back to her encounter with Seb earlier that day; wasn't that precisely what she had been doing?

'So you're telling me you know what I'm feeling already? It must be very comforting to know you have such remarkable powers.'

'I'm good at my job, Stephen, and so are you. That's why you're here. Because it appears that something has been going on with you lately that seems to be interfering with your professional abilities. Challenging your competence, maybe.'

'Now you're telling me I'm incompetent. Thanks very much.'

Vivien winced a little inside. She had asked for that.

'I'm sorry. A bad choice of words. That isn't what I meant at all. I'm not accusing you of anything. I merely want to try to help you get to the bottom of what's upsetting you – because something clearly is.'

Stephen grunted and flexed his jaw. The skin over his cheekbones stretched and made the dark circles under his eyes stand out even more.

Vivien leaned slightly towards him. She

23

had never failed to make a connection with a patient yet: Stephen Daunt was clearly going to be a test case in more ways than one.

'Tell me about your headmaster; why do you think he has found it necessary to call your recent behaviour "erratic"?'

Stephen shifted in his seat but his shoulders relaxed a little. 'The old fool's exaggerating. OK, I might have been late for a class a couple of times but it's a large school and there isn't always enough time to get from one end to the other.'

'Have you ever missed any classes?'

'One or two. Not many. That hardly qualifies me as a candidate for the nut-house, does it?'

'Is that why you think you're here? Is that your fear, Stephen? Do you think you're going mad?'

He barked out a mirthless laugh. 'I'm obviously that already; they always say you have to be mad to teach. Perhaps I'm just a late developer.'

Vivien thought that last comment very apt. He did look a little like an overgrown schoolboy with his tie jutting out of his trouser pocket and his wispy flyaway hair. They betrayed his vulnerability, and brought out her compassion. He was a man who had been – and most probably still was – frightened by something in himself that he had yet to come

24

to terms with. It was her job to overcome his resistance and help him to do just that.

'Has anyone else said anything to you about any changes they've noticed recently?'

'Oh, a couple of the other teachers – but they can hardly talk. One said I was "distracted" and asked if I was "going for the absent-minded professor routine". I wasn't distracted, only bored with having to listen to him bleating on. Just because he's got a little seniority over me, he thinks he can tell me how to do my job. But I'm a bloody good teacher.'

'That's something everyone seems to be agreed on, at least. What about at home, Stephen? Has your wife picked up on anything?'

'Only that I don't sleep as well as I used to. But I know that already. She thinks I should put lavender oil on my pillow or some such nonsense. Started making me hot milky drinks too; I feel like I'm about to be pensioned off with a nice soothing cup of cocoa.'

He smiled and Vivien saw the first indication of gentleness in him.

'She meant well, though.' His face resumed its closed expression. 'But I'll sort this out on my own. I don't need anyone telling me what's best for me. Including you.'

Vivien looked down at her notepad for a moment to distance herself from the hostility in his gaze; and to cover up the fact

25

that she'd had her fill of being told what was best for her recently, too.

'Tell me a little more about your sleeping patterns. Is it that you have difficulty getting to sleep in the first place, or do you wake up in the night?'

'I don't see what difference it makes, but both as it happens. And you'll love this: I get violent nightmares.'

Vivien felt a shiver of recognition. She wondered if, as in her case, they were related to the accident and his role in it. But it was too soon for her to probe him about the actual events of that day. He wasn't ready yet. Maybe the dreams themselves would shed some light on what had happened.

'Why don't you tell me about them?'

'God, you're not going to go all Freudian on me, are you? Tell me that I'm really in love with my mother or something.'

Vivien simply held his gaze.

'Okay, okay, I can see you're going to do the silent treatment on me until I cough up. Want to hear my dreams, do you? Learn about all my dark and dirty secrets? Well, here goes ... you asked for it...'

He looked around the room briefly and then back at her.

'They always open with children screaming and running down the school corridor. I can't see what they are trying to escape from but I can sense a malevolent force. Then, above their terrified shouts, I can hear the cracks of intermittent gunshots. Some of the children bang on the door to my classroom, crying for help and begging to be let in. But I've barricaded myself in with a dozen of my students and daren't open the door in case whatever's out there gets in and attacks them too. You see, I already know that I can't save them all. And I can't tear my eyes away from the glass panel in the door and the scene of carnage going on in the corridor. I'm forced to watch as every child in turn crumples as a bullet hits them. It's too much and I collapse to the floor. But I have to stay strong for the children in the classroom with me and I turn around to reassure them that everything's going to be alright. But the room is empty. In the end, I've managed to save no one's life but my own.'

There was a long silence while Stephen seemed to wrestle with himself about whether to say something else. Vivien noticed his blink-rate increase and the colour flood to his cheeks; if he decided to unbend a little more, then this could be the most telling moment of the whole session. He finally locked his gaze onto hers.

'Whatever else you can accuse me of, it's not lack of imagination because I seem to have developed several variations on the theme – each more unpleasant than the one before.'

He sat up slightly and crossed his legs. His free foot twitched his anxiety.

'Sometimes, I'm in the corridor and I hear the children screaming and shouting as before but I can't see them. I know they're around the corner somewhere ahead of me, so I walk towards them. I have to get to them to put an end to their suffering but for some reason I don't understand, my legs are heavy and I can't run. I call out to them that it's okay and that I'm coming to get them but they just scream even more. I turn the corner. The children see me. I hold my arms out to them but they stare back at me in horror. "It's him ... it's him ... it's him," I hear one of them yell. He is pointing at my legs. I look down and notice that my trousers are stiff and dark with dried blood and I realise that the child is right and that it is me. I'm the monster they're all so afraid of...'

His voice broke a little but he covered it up quickly with a cough.

'And here's the best of the lot. I warn you, it's a real humdinger. I'm back in the class-room again. The children in the corridor are pounding on the door and screaming to be let in. And this time I do open the door and they come pouring through. Their little faces turn towards me, all tear-stained and naked with trust. I smile back. And the smile turns into laughter. I laugh ... and laugh ... and laugh ... as I raise the gun in my hand and shoot every single one of them through the head.'

He unfolded his arms and put his hands behind his head as he pushed himself even further back on his chair.

'What do you make of that, Doctor Blake?'

Vivien heard the challenge in his voice but refused to rise to it, despite the fact that this man was pressing all kinds of buttons in her. She tried to remember what her mother had said about always having to wait for a grub to turn into a butterfly before it could come out of its cocoon. It helped her focus her professional detachment.

'Dreams aren't always literal, Stephen,' she said. 'They're the way our subconscious processes our experiences, feelings and thoughts. Sometimes it can conjure up all sorts of outlandish and bizarre scenarios to help us understand some of our everyday anxieties and fears.'

'I realise that; I'm not stupid. But you try having dreams like these every night and see how you like it.'

Vivien knew what this man was going through only too well, but to tell him so wouldn't move them any further forward. She felt sure that he'd only use it to shore up his belief that she was incapable of helping him. She picked the notepad off her lap and placed it on the floor beside her chair. Then she crossed her legs, placed her hands over her knee, and laced her fingers together. It was almost a sign of submission and she wanted him to interpret it as such. This man was intent on engineering a confrontation but she wouldn't let him; he was only destroying himself further in the process.

'I think we'll call it a halt for now. We've covered quite a bit of ground for a first session but I think we need to see if we can do something about your sleep deprivation before we can take this any further. I'll give you a prescription for some sleeping pills but, if you're willing, I'd like to try something next time that should help to relax you on a much deeper level. It's a vicious circle: your anxiety stops you sleeping and your tiredness feeds the anxiety.'

'Tell me something I don't know... What's the big idea, then? Are you going to brainwash me?'

'Nothing of the sort.' She spoke more sharply than she meant to. 'Merely hypnosis. It is firmly rooted in the science of the brain and has a good track record of uncovering the conflicts leading to inner tension and, once we can begin to tackle those, I think you'll find your insomnia improving.'

'An attempt at dream analysis, and now hypnosis? My, but you're pulling out all the stops to get me back on the straight and narrow. How do I know you won't plant some memories of child abuse or some such nonsense while I'm under the 'fluence?'

Vivien was relieved to see he was smiling.

'But OK, I'll give it a go – I'll try anything if it means I can get a decent night's sleep for once.'

Vivien stood up and walked over to her desk. She made a few keystrokes to pull the prescription screen up on her computer. She typed in Stephen's details and the dosage, and pressed *return.*

'These will be waiting for you in the pharmacy on the ground floor if you stop by there on your way out. Take one an hour before you go to bed. They should see you through until our next appointment.' She turned to her open diary. 'It's May Bank Holiday next week so I'll see you again in a fortnight; is the same time good for you?'

Stephen got up and started to walk towards the door. 'No time's good for me,' he said, 'but I'll be here.' He let himself out.

Vivien closed her computer screen and then walked over to the window. She un-latched it and pushed it open a crack. The hum of the traffic on Gower Street dis-turbed the silence in the room but provided a welcome distraction as she organised her thoughts. It had been a tough session for all sorts of reasons – not least the feelings that it had provoked in her. But she knew that she had to learn to forgive herself her subliminal reactions; she was human, after all.

CHAPTER THREE

Vivien checked her watch. Time for her supervisory meeting with her departmental head. It was standard practice when starting with a new patient. She walked down the corridor to his office.

Jim McFraser met her at the door. He smiled and waved his arm to usher her into the sleek and barely furnished room.

'Come in, come in, take a seat. I can't tell you how pleased I am you're back on the team again, Vivien. Fighting fit, I trust?'

He was a large man who spoke loud and fast as a way of further increasing his presence. He was more sales manager than psychiatrist but liked to play up to the stereotype by sporting a range of flamboyant bowties. It was easy to see why Seb could never resist mocking him; she always wondered if his wife spent her days ironing sets of matching polka-dot pyjamas.

'Of course you are or you wouldn't have re-entered the fray again so soon, would you?'

Dr McFraser patted her awkwardly on the shoulder as she sat down and then retreated behind the safety of his desk. He cleared his throat noisily.

'I know you're not the sort to want a fuss made but I want to tell you how much we've all been thinking about you.'

'I know, Jim, thanks. I got the flowers. It was very kind.'

It had been but she suspected that it hadn't been his idea. And he certainly hadn't picked them out; red carnations were too subtle a gesture of sympathy for such a blustering man: *my heart aches for you* in the language of flowers; they'd had Jean's fingerprints all over them.

'You've gone through a very difficult time and, as you're undoubtedly the most competent and perceptive psychiatrist we have, I'm sure I don't have to tell you that there may well be worse to come?'

Vivien folded her hands in her lap. Jim McFraser was not known for either his tact or his small-talk.

'I knew you'd want to get straight back in harness,' he continued, 'so I arranged for you to pick up that new fella, Stephen Daunt; has all the makings of a very interesting case.'

'Yes, I've just met him. A bit prickly but that's all part of the challenge.'

'Indeed. The defences we throw up, eh?'

Vivien had to smile. Jim McFraser was as transparent as a child in wanting to test her reactions to her new patient as a way of probing her current emotional state. It was partly because it was his job to check on her introduction to Stephen Daunt but it was also because – like so many in their profession – he was faintly embarrassed by the discussion of personal feelings: scientific exploration was the most impenetrable defence of all.

'Seb Nicholls left me some sketchy notes. I've got the presenting problems – erratic behaviour, insomnia, and an inability to concentrate – but I don't know much yet about what's behind it.'

Jim McFraser puffed out his cheeks and then released a large sigh. 'Why doesn't that surprise me? No slur on yourself intended. I know I'm not telling tales out of school when I say that Dr Nicholls has a well-earned reputation for appealing to the lowest common denominator, and the sensationalist approach. I suppose he told you that a boy nearly drowned?'

'Well, yes, the event does seem significant in this case.'

'Pertinent, I'll grant you but I suspect our Dr Nicholls made it all sound very lurid.'

'Hardly. In fact he merely made reference to it in the notes.'

Why did she feel she had to defend Seb all

the time? He was more than capable of looking out for himself. A part of her was habitually flattered that Jim McFraser trusted her enough to speak to her openly about her colleagues but his confidences never failed to leave her feeling placed in an awkward position. And it was particularly bad with Seb because it was as if she was a go-between in his never-ending battle with their head of department. Seb's weapon was subversion and Jim McFraser's was ... was ... pragmatism and conservative acceptance. Theirs would never be a meeting of like minds.

'I wanted him on your case list, Vivien, because I accepted him as a sort of personal favour and I know he'll be in safe and reliable hands with you – unlike some I could name.'

Vivien acknowledged the compliment with a faint nod, and ignored the jibe at Seb's expense; this really was all beginning to get a little tiresome. Jim McFraser picked up a pen from his desk and started to twirl it between his fingers.

'I'm sure it's crossed your mind how he came to us in the first place.' His eyes were riveted by the movement of his hands. 'Call it the Old Boys' Network, if you like. The headmaster of Fairway and I are members of the same Lodge – you won't believe how many opportunities those meetings have furnished for me to raise the profile of this department – and when he mentioned the recent difficulties he'd had with one of his teachers – I suggested he refer him here.'

'Ah.'

That certainly explained why Stephen Daunt had been under such pressure to agree to receiving treatment.

'An accident happened on a school trip. The police did investigate the matter – as they must of course – but decided that it was probably just a case of boys being boys and not doing what they are told. Your guy's been behaving oddly ever since and everyone at the school is getting worried. The head wants everything back to normal and to stop him doing anything silly to ruin his previously impeccable reputation. Seems he quite fond of the young man. If you want my opinion–'

'No.' The word came out more harshly than Vivien intended. She held up her hands to stem the tide of information. 'Jim, I'm very grateful for the background but anything else has to come from Stephen himself. You know how important it is for a patient to tell his own story in his own words. I'll come to you if I think there are gaps that he can't – or won't – fill, I promise. But I think that's enough for now.'

Jim McFraser patted his bowtie flat. 'Point taken, Vivien, point taken.'

'If there isn't anything else?' Vivien began

to stand up.

'There is, actually.'

She sat down again.

'You know that paper you're going to be presenting at the British Psychological Society symposium? I wondered if you'd had a chance to jot down any ideas yet.'

'Give me a chance; I've only just got back.'

'I know, I know, and I don't mean to put any undue pressure on you but there's a lot riding on this.'

'If that's your idea of undue pressure, Jim, then I'd like to hear what you say when you really want to turn the screws.' She was smiling but she really could do without his nannying interference; she was very experienced at presenting papers. Besides, she liked the buzz of working up to the wire on deadlines and the date for this one was a least a month away.

'It's just that it's a great opportunity. With you as the keynote speaker there's even a chance we might get to host the return match. Academic kudos, Vivien, and a high profile; that's what this department needs.'

'I appreciate your faith in me and I won't let you down.'

'I know you won't and that's not what I'm scared of.'

Vivien looked at him more intently. She had never heard Jim McFraser admit to being scared of anything.

'You know I'm due for retirement soon, don't you?'

Vivien nodded. Jean had even started sounding them out about what to buy him as a parting gift. 'End of the next academic year, isn't it? Got any plans?'

'Only to leave this department in safe hands. I don't want it going down the same slippery slope as Seb Nicholls.'

'He's not Lucifer, Jim. And, believe it or not, his books have done a lot of good in popularising some of the more hard to understand theories. He has a real gift with words.'

'That's as maybe but it's not the common touch we need around here. Scientific rigour and hard facts to back up hypotheses are what's called for. Having a media celebrity on the staff distracts from all the hard work I have done to build up the reputation of this department. And that's where you come in.'

He stood up and walked around to the front of his desk. He parked his ample buttocks on the edge and leaned towards Vivien.

'When I go, there will be a real scrap over my position. Now, of course there will have to be a proper selection procedure but my recommendation will carry a lot of weight. It's no secret that I'd like to see you sitting in my chair, Vivien. Were you to apply when the time comes, then I'll back you all the way.'

'Thank you, Jim, it's very good of you but I'm not really ready to make any commitment right now.'

'I know you're not and I wouldn't expect you to. But I want you to be aware that if you are interested then this symposium could help your application enormously. A rock solid paper would pave the way, as it were.'

Vivien was flattered by his support but she knew that he wasn't being entirely altruistic. He would be sure to take on some private patients in his retirement – probably cabinet ministers or minor aristocracy knowing him – and would want the endorsement of having left a university department at the height of its reputation in the field.

'I'll tell you what, why don't I run it past you beforehand?'

'Capital idea, Vivien, capital.' Jim McFraser levered himself off the edge of the desk and virtually spun back to his seat. 'Not that it won't be perfect coming from your pen but, who knows, I might just be able to add a little something from my not inconsiderable experience. Now, I'd better let you get back to the coalface. Pop in anytime. Open door policy and all that.'

Suitably dismissed, Vivien left Jim Mc-

Fraser humming to himself and walked back down the corridor to her office. Amused as she was by her boss's flagrant manipulation of her opportunity to shine, she couldn't help feeling an underlying disquiet that she hadn't made the most of the opportunity to talk with him in his supervisory capacity about her new patient. Maybe she shouldn't have cut him off so quickly and should've voiced her concerns. Because she did have some. Deep ones. After all, Stephen Daunt was a teacher and was having nightmares about killing children. Although feelings engendered by dreams of violence didn't always cross over into waking life, it did happen on occasion. She may have chosen not to express the question but that hadn't made it go away: just how much of a danger was Stephen Daunt? She only hoped she'd be able to remove any potential threat through analysis before anyone ever had to find that out for certain.

CHAPTER FOUR

The taxi dropped Vivien at the top of Haverstock Hill. The fare from Bloomsbury to Hampstead was extortionate but her first day back had been a long one and she hadn't had the energy to cope with the claustrophobia of the underground for the return journey. She walked the short distance up the path to her elegantly proportioned house. The early evening light glinted off the glass of the large bay windows and seemed to make them wink in greeting. She scrabbled in her handbag for her key and opened the front door. The stained-glass of the panels threw a brief pattern of blood-red and blue onto the hallway tiles. She stifled a shudder and closed the door quickly. Dumping her briefcase by the umbrella stand, she kicked off her shoes and then padded into the sitting room. Jerry wasn't here. The big house always felt so empty now without him. She slid into the embrace of one of the brown leather armchairs and reached down to massage her aching feet. That was another thing she'd have to get used to; no more days schlepping around dressed for comfort.

Vivien dragged herself up again and walked through into the kitchen. It hadn't been so long ago since they'd had it gutted and a pair of french windows inserted into the back wall to make the most of the small London garden and the backdrop of the heath behind. She flicked her eyes away before she caught sight of the apple tree tucked up in the corner with its ridiculously bright swing hanging forlornly down. Her hand reached towards one of the bottles peeking out from the wine rack beside the sink. No, that wasn't the way. She hadn't resorted to drowning her memories in a glass all this time, and she wasn't going to start now. Life was about rolling up your sleeves and just getting on with it; she'd learnt that from her parents and the cold Minnesotan winters. Wood still had to be chopped and brought in for the fire, however deep the snow.

Back in the hallway, Vivien picked up her briefcase and took it through into the dining room. Once there, she pulled out the notes she'd made after her meeting with Stephen Daunt and proceeded to write them up in his file:

CASE STUDY NOTES

NAME: Stephen Daunt

CONSULTATION DATE: Monday 23rd April

INITIAL DIAGNOSIS: Possibility of the patient possessing a childhood memory that he either can't – or doesn't want to – access. Perhaps deeply buried physical or mental abuse that took place in his early years. **EVIDENCE:** He displayed a fear about there being such a thing when he joked about what might be revealed under hypnosis. Although nothing specific at this early stage. However his dreams – which are obviously troubling him deeply – concern children and could point to there being a childhood memory that he is having difficulty letting go of. His occupation as a teacher would only exacerbate this tension within him; hence his excessive anxiety. **CONCLUSIONS:** His behaviour appears to be unpredictable and his moods volatile. The sedative drugs I have prescribed should help with the sleep deprivation and heightened anxiety, and result in a less aggressive attitude to the world around him. **FURTHER ACTION:** Second consultation in two weeks. Use hypnosis to attempt to uncover what it is that lies at the heart of his problem.

Vivien put down her pen and rubbed at

the gritty feeling in her tired eyes. She could do with a long hot soak in the bath. She hauled herself up the stairs and into the bathroom where she poured some essence of roses into the tub and turned on the taps. She lit the row of candles on the shelf at the foot of the bath while the room filled with fragrant steam. She felt the warmth seep into her shoulders and relax her neck muscles. She stripped but couldn't summon the energy to hang her suit up so left it in a crumpled pile on the washing basket, turned off the taps, and slipped into the inviting water. She sighed and stretched out until she was up to her neck in bubbles. The light from the flickering candles danced on the pale peach walls and she watched the ethereal movement for a moment before closing her eyes and giving herself up to welcome oblivion.

But it was too soon and not enough. Relaxed as her body was, Vivien's mind wouldn't let go that easily and she was powerless to stop the images playing like a well-worn film on the inside of her eyelids. A picture came into focus of her lying in bed with Jerry, limbs still soft and heavy from sleep. She'd been snuggling into him as he lifted his arm and tucked her up against his side. She loved their early-morning cuddles; they had none of the passion of their love-making but were just as satisfying.

Her husband was a large well-padded man and lying beside him made her feel safe and secure and daintily feminine. She reached out and slipped her hand between the buttons on his pyjama top to steal her fingers into his chest hair. He pulled her tighter against him.

'I think we'd better have a little less of that if you expect me to let you get out of this bed any time soon.'

Vivien pulled her head back and looked up at him.

'And you can cut out gazing at me with that sexy half-closed-eyes look, too, or neither of us will ever get up.'

Vivien head butted his ribcage lightly and sank back into lassitude. She felt desired and lazy and cocooned against whatever the day was going to throw at her. She became aware of a flurry of energy in the doorway. A moment's hesitation, and then Jerry's voice:

'Come on in then, Jimmy.'

She felt the duvet being lifted off her shoulders as Jerry picked up their son on his flight towards their bed and hurled him into the downy space he'd created between them. Dmitri's little legs kicked against her with delight and she threw her arm out to embrace the two of them. 'Tell me a story. Tell me a story.'

'You've got the wrong end of the day there, little man, stories are for bedtime.'

45

Dmitri turned towards his father, his round cheeks flushed with seriousness. 'But we're in bed now.'

Vivien laughed. She couldn't fault her son's logic. Jerry chuckled too. 'So what's it to be,' he said as if it had been his idea all along, 'The Three Bears or Little Red Riding Hood?'

'The one about how I got my name.'

Vivien and Jerry looked at each other and smiled. Their son was as egotistical as every three year-old and liked nothing more than to be reminded that he was the centre of his own world. Jerry pushed his floppy hair away from his eyes and adopted a serious expression.

'It was long ago and far, far away in a cold, cold land of snow and ice.'

'Where the bears come from.'

'That's right. Your great, great grandfather wanted to go on a ship across the sea to America.'

'Where mummy was born.'

'Who's the one telling this story, you or me?'

Vivien could see the laughter lines crinkle around Jerry's eyes as he fought to maintain his mock authority. 'But he didn't have enough money to buy the ticket.'

'He was poor.'

'So he went to his elder brother and asked him for a loan. But the brother said no. And your great, great grandfather was very sad and disappointed. But the next day, his brother came to his house and tipped a hatful of money on the kitchen table. He had sold his favourite horse and cart.'

'Not the cart, just the horse,' Vivien corrected.

'Now that's what I get for being married to a psychiatrist who's a stickler for the truth … so, he sold the horse – but it *was* his favourite,' Jerry added with a wink, 'and your great, great grandfather was able to sail across the sea and start a new life in America. I bet you can't guess the name of the kind brother.'

'I can. I can. It was Dmitri, like me. But I couldn't say it when I was a baby, could I, mummy? So I said Dimmy.'

'And that's why we call you…'

'Jimmy!' they all chorused and Dmitri dissolved into satisfied giggles.

'What's the betting one of us will have to go through all that again tonight?' Vivien said over Dmitri's head. Jerry shrugged and looked delighted at the prospect.

Vivien closed her eyes again. 'What time is it, darling?' she said as she felt herself start to doze. She heard Jerry pick up his watch from the bedside table. 'Seven-thirty.'

'God, I wish we didn't have to get up. Why don't we all just stay here and pretend it's Sunday?'

She felt Dmitri wriggling with excitement. 'Yes, mummy, yes,' he said, 'Mrs Hill says I have to learn to be as quiet as a mouse.'

Vivien yawned and stretched. 'Oh yes, it's the rehearsal for your play today, isn't it? Sorry, Jimmy, mummy was only joking. We can't have you missing dressing up in that mask you made especially, can we?' She ruffled her son's dark hair and then shrugged herself reluctantly out of bed. 'Come on, beat you to the bathroom. First one to the toothpaste gets to squeeze the tube...'

Forty minutes later and they were almost ready to leave the house.

'You got a busy day ahead?' Vivien asked as she stacked the breakfast plates in the dishwasher.

'Couple of routine procedures but I've a big one this afternoon. They brought a five-year-old girl over from the Royal Free yesterday. Skin grafts, I'm afraid. Pretty serious.'

Vivien stroked his arm as she passed to collect Dmitri's lunchbox.

'Damn! I forgot. Darling, I'm sorry,' Jerry said, 'but we've a meeting about this child before surgery starts this morning. I won't have time to take Jimmy into nursery.' He tossed back the remains of his coffee.

'Oh, Jerry, not again.'

'I'm sorry but I can't be late.'

'Neither can I; I've got an early appointment, too.'

'What do you want me to do? Phone in and tell the team that they'll have to work out what needs to be done, without me?'

'Of course not.' Vivien slammed the dishwasher door shut. 'But I wish you'd told me this earlier.'

'Well, I forgot. I've a lot on my mind.'

'And I haven't? I can't just keep changing my arrangements at the last minute. This happened the other week, too, remember?'

'I know; what can I say? I'm sorry.'

'My patients rely on me as well.'

'Look, Viv, this isn't helping. I've got to go. We'll talk about it tonight. I'll bring my diary home and we can plan out the school run again.' He crossed the kitchen, pecked her on the cheek, and left.

Vivien took a second or two to calm down and then walked through into the front room to find her son. He was sitting on the floor, his brown eyes large with tears.

'My mouse is broke.' He trailed the mask from his fingers.

'Oh, Jimmy, I told you to hold it carefully and not keep playing with it. Give it here and mummy will mend it for you.'

Vivien took the mask, rethreaded the elastic through the hole and tied it in a knot again. 'There. Now go and find your thick coat. It's snowing and I don't want you catching a cold.'

'Where's daddy?'

'He had to go in to the hospital early. Mummy's going to take you in this morning.'

'But I want daddy.'

'Now, Jimmy, don't start. And get a move on or we'll be late.'

Dmitri went out into the hall and re-appeared a moment later dragging his blue duffle coat behind him.

'Can I wear my frog wellingtons?'

'If you're quick...' Dmitri scurried out again. 'They're in the porch,' Vivien shouted after him.

The car windscreen was taking longer to demist than usual. Vivien pulled away from the curb anyway and into the stream of traffic heading down the hill and into Belsize Park. The pavements on either side glittered with ice. She watched out of the corner of her eye as a woman in unseasonably high heels nearly slipped over. A song came on the radio. It was Dmitri's favourite of the moment. Vivien turned up the volume and they both sang along. She pressed on the brake gingerly as the car in front of her skewed slightly as it turned left. The lights at the bottom of the hill were in their favour and the traffic surged forward and picked up speed. The silver SUV up ahead belched out black diesel smoke as the driver put their foot down.

'Play it again. Play it again,' Dmitri

chanted from the back.

'I can't, honey, it's the radio.'

'I want my song.'

'Why don't you sing it yourself, then? You know the words.'

'But I can't sing the music.' Dmitri was getting unusually fractious. Maybe he missed being in his father's company for the short journey or perhaps he was nervous about performing in his first Christmas panto. She hoped he wasn't suffering from full-blown performance anxiety; it was something that had always plagued her as a child – the pressure to be the best. It didn't matter what: hall-monitor; first in class – first in school even; classmate; friend; sister; daughter. And it hadn't stopped there; she'd also had to excel as a medical student. She felt a bleak stab of self-recognition as she realised that it was the driving force in her adult life, too. Wasn't she always striving to be the best doctor, colleague, wife, lover, mother? It was one of life's burdens that she could lay at no one's feet but her own. It would be awful if she'd unwittingly passed on those expectations to her son.

She glanced at him in the rear-view mirror. Dmitri was squirming in his car seat and had somehow managed to wriggle an arm out from under one of the straps. She was sure she'd done them up tightly but maybe in her hurry to get him settled and with the bulk of the duffle coat... She would pull over the moment she could. It would make her even later, of course, but it couldn't be helped. She could always take the opportunity to ring Jean on her mobile and warn her. If she was even in the office yet.

Vivien twisted around for a moment and stretched her hand out to try to prevent Dmitri from pulling his other arm free. A darted look ahead. The lights were changing again. She turned back to the road. The brake lights of the SUV snapped on. Vivien slammed her own foot down. But suddenly the car was bucking and then sliding along the icy road, and the back of the SUV was filling her entire windscreen. And then, amazingly, the car stopped six inches from the massive bumper up ahead. Counting their blessings, she was dimly aware of Bing Crosby warbling some Christmas song on the radio when the real smash came. Lurching, she could do nothing as the car spun into the stream of traffic coming up the hill.

There was a second sickening jolt and finally the tearing of metal on metal. For a moment, even with all the noise and movement outside the car, everything inside the vehicle was ominously still. Vivien had time to register that the car behind hadn't been able to stop and skidded them into a side-on collision, as she wrenched herself around. It was only then that she screamed.

The back passenger door was crumpled in. Dmitri was slumped in the child seat next to the buckled frame; his free arm hanging loose.

'Dmitri! Dmitri!' She tried to lunge between the gap in the two front seats but her seatbelt held her back. She punched at the release, animal cries of distress and panic pouring from her mouth. Finally able to reach behind her, Vivien's fingers touched her son's waxy cheek. She tipped his head back gently. She knew she probably shouldn't because of the risk of neck injury, the way his head was lolling forward, but she had to check on him ... see he was still breathing... His eyelids fluttered. There was blood soaking into his collar from a gash on the side of his forehead ... he must have been thrown sideways by the force of the impact ... if only she'd tightened the strap.

What followed was a merciful jumble of sounds and distorted images stretched out in time that seemed to have no pattern to its passing. The film in her head fast-forwarded to the point where she was sitting in the hospital corridor, her hands wrapped around a plastic cup of something hot. She took a sip to soothe her raspy throat. The tea was stewed and sweet. She wanted to be sick. People were padding past her; the occasional whisper, or light laughter, from the nurses filling her ears. She knew where she was; recognised the jolly paintings of clowns and animals that lined the walls. The paediatric department of the Royal London. Where Jerry worked.

She couldn't imagine what he'd felt when he'd seen his own son being brought into the operating suite. She knew that Dmitri had been badly hurt. She'd seen it in the faces of the paramedics who'd wheeled him, oh, so gently, into the back of the ambulance. At the sound of heavy footsteps, she looked up. Jerry was walking down the corridor towards her. She wanted to throw herself into his arms but there was something about the slope of his shoulders that stopped her from getting up. His large physique appeared diminished by the swing doors behind him. She tried to smile but her lips stuck to her teeth. She took another sip of the tea. He was standing in front of her. Vivien couldn't be the one to speak first. The questions were burning in her head but there was a part of her that didn't want to know the answers. Nothing in her professional life had pre-pared her for this. Jerry lowered himself onto the too-small plastic seat beside her.

'Dr Ramsay is an excellent surgeon but there was nothing she could do. Dmitri didn't make it. Our son is dead.'

Vivien knew that Jerry never prevaricated around the truth but his bluntness rocked her. She reached down and placed the plastic cup on the floor between them. She couldn't look at him. If she didn't see his face then she could believe that he hadn't said it ... or that she'd misheard ... or that it was someone else's child that he was talking about. God forgive her: she almost prayed that it was.

'I'm sorry but there is never any other way to say it.' Jerry slipped his arm around her trembling shoulders. 'You're in shock. Just take some deep breaths. Slowly.'

'Don't you have to be somewhere? Aren't there patients waiting?'

'My place is here with you.'

They sat in silence. After a while, Vivien was surprised to feel that her face was wet. It was as if her eyes were crying but she didn't know why. She felt numb. And cold. Almost icy, despite the warmth of Jerry's arm around her. The edge of the plastic chair bit into her thighs. Her brain registered the physical sensations as if they were happening to another person. And in a way they were. They were happening to Dmitri's mother; the woman sitting in the hospital corridor swinging between wondering if they'd enough food in for the weekend, and wanting to scream and punch the man sitting next to her who had uttered those cruel words. That wasn't her. She didn't recognise her. She felt Jerry's attention pull towards someone at the other end of the corridor; she had heard the whisper of tactful feet.

'Listen, Viv,' he said, 'do you think you can stand? They've moved Dmitri out of the theatre and into a side room. I think you should see him. It'll help you come to terms with it all later.'

Vivien wanted to ask him what he was talking about. Why there was any need for her to move at all.

'Come on, Viv. I'll be with you. Let's go together.'

Vivien was aware of Jerry helping her to her feet. She leant against him as he walked her slowly towards the swing doors. She didn't want to go through them. She didn't want to see what lay beyond. She tried to wrench away. If her son was there waiting for her then she'd know what Jerry had told her was true. But then she straightened her shoulders and started to walk more purposefully because, on the other hand, if she was right, then he was still at nursery and she'd pick him up as usual and he'd run into her arms and tell her about his day and what he had to eat for lunch and how he'd been a good boy and as quiet as a mouse for his teacher and...

Vivien snapped her eyes open. The bath water was cold and her skin felt clammy. She was shaking. Would it never get any better? Was she always going to punish herself like this in a never-ending cycle of regrets and recrimination? She knew the stages of grief – of course she did: it was part of her job – but to experience it like this, day in, day out, was too much. She had to learn to move on and accept what had happened. There was nothing she could do to change it.

She stepped out of the bath and rubbed herself so hard with the towel that her skin stung. The sensation calmed her a little. She felt that the soreness was justified. Once dry, Vivien blew out the candles and walked through into the bedroom where she pulled on jogging pants and a baggy sweater. The trousers hung off her hips. Once, she'd have congratulated herself on having a few less curves to worry about, but such empty vanity was beyond her now. She heard the door below slam shut. He was home at last.

Vivien walked into the kitchen. Jerry was pouring them both a glass of Merlot. She took her glass from him before sliding into a chair at the breakfast table. Jerry put the bottle down between them and sat in the chair opposite. They left the one between them empty now. It was where Dmitri had always insisted on sitting. He'd liked to be able to look out into the garden in the hope of seeing a squirrel scampering at the base of the apple tree. Vivien snatched a breath and saw Jerry do the same. They looked into each other's eyes for a moment and a pang of shared grief passed between them.

'How was your first day back?' Jerry said into the silence.

'Not as bad as I thought it might be. Seb was his usual self and made it all a little easier. And I've got an interesting case to get stuck into; it's good to be working again.'

'Of course it is. Something else to think about.'

Vivien took a sip of her wine. 'Not that Jimmy is ever out of my mind,' she said quietly. In the background, the kitchen tap dripped relentlessly. It was one of the many things that Jerry had been getting around to doing. Before their lives had been put on hold. 'What was your day like?' Vivien wanted to take the words back as soon as they'd left her mouth. It had been an automatic response. She hadn't wanted to ask that; didn't want to know about the other children he'd been able to work miracles on.

'Oh, the usual. Busy.' He took a deep glug of his wine before he spoke again, 'Sandra rang again, asking us if we could join them Saturday fortnight.

'Oh Jerry, I'm not sure.'

'They're family, Viv. They care. I've said we'll go.'

'Oh well, if you've said.'

There was a sarcasm in her voice unusual

to her ears. Before, she and Jerry had been so much in sync. Now she could see his jaw set a little tighter.

'Of course we'll go.' Vivien twirled the stem of her wine glass in her fingers. 'Did she say how Oliver was? Has he got over that cold yet?'

'Fit as a fiddle apparently; bouncing around as ever.'

She heard the crack in his voice. When she looked up, Jerry was gazing at the swing in the apple tree, his face unreadable. For a moment she wanted to hug and soothe him as she'd done so often to their little boy. But they'd established some time ago that Jerry found such attempts at comfort distressing. Vivien thought it was because it made him feel too vulnerable. She was scared he was trying to stay strong for her, to be the rock on which she could lean whenever it all became too much. The effect was that he'd grown withdrawn; as if to protect himself from any further hurt. Clinically, it made sense. Except she wasn't a psychiatrist now: she was Jerry's wife. Dmitri's mother.

Vivien couldn't stop the memory coming back of the day when she'd first told Jerry she was pregnant. It was their second gruelling round of IVF treatment. She'd never seen him so happy, before or since. They'd always planned on having two children – she came from a family of four and Jerry had two sisters – they'd never wanted Dmitri to be an only child; wanted him to have someone to play with. She remembered when she and her brother would dig out her great grandfather's canvas duffle bag – the one that had held all his possessions. Her mother had kept it in the attic and she'd climb into it, and her brother would carry her over his shoulder. They'd called the game 'arriving in America'. It had never crossed her mind then what courage her great grandfather must have been forced to summon up in order to face such an uncertain and frightening future. But she knew it now. It was becoming her story, too.

'Shall I make a start on supper?'

'I'm not very hungry, actually. I think I'll go up to the study and catch up on some paperwork. I'll probably be at it for hours; I'll use the spare room tonight so you can get a good night's sleep.'

He topped up his wineglass and scraped back his chair.

Vivien watched him leave. Was it only the loss of her son that she was going to have to learn to live with?

CHAPTER FIVE

Stephen came to their second session together looking even worse than before. His eyes were bloodshot and his cheeks sunken with exhaustion. Nervous energy was making his body twitch and tiring him further. Vivien wanted to get him hypnotised as soon as possible; the poor man needed to relax desperately.

'Isn't your insomnia any better? I could prescribe you something stronger.'

'God, no. Not on your life. I'd go off to sleep quickly enough but found I couldn't wake up when I wanted to. I flushed the things down the toilet.'

'Are you still having the nightmares?'

'Yes ... no... I mean, yes. I keep having the same ones ... but I think there's something else I should tell you about...'

He paced around the room like a caged animal. When he passed by her desk for the second time, he glanced down at the framed photograph beside her computer.

'This your family?'

Vivien cursed herself for not putting it away in the drawer. It wasn't just that she didn't want to discuss her private life with a patient, it was also that she didn't want him to pick up on any convenient distraction just now.

'Yes.'

'Nice looking boy.'

'He is ... he was...' Even she heard the crack in her voice. She prayed that he was too wired to notice.

'What happened?'

Vivien had yet to lie to a patient, and she wouldn't start now.

'He died.'

'Sorry to hear it, I–'

'Let's get back to you, Stephen. What were you going to say to me? Why don't you sit down and take a moment to get your thoughts together? Tell me when you are ready.'

Vivien waited as Stephen slumped into the chair. He began to tap his fingers on his knees. She had the feeling that he was struggling with how much he should reveal to her. His voice, when it came, was soft and tinged with a complexity of emotions that Vivien couldn't quite identify.

'Last week, I was having the nightmare as usual but this time I was pushing at the door to keep the monster out of the classroom. I could feel my arms grow stiff with the effort. I didn't know if I could hold out and I could feel my heart pounding and my breath rasping in my throat. There was a muffled scream in the corridor and I wondered if it had turned the gun on itself. I considered opening the door to find out but then it sort of went soft under my hands and seemed to melt. I was falling through it. Then I woke up.'

He looked down at his outstretched hands. They were shaking. He folded his arms again and tucked them away.

'You won't believe what I found I was doing ... pressing a pillow against my wife's face. It was bloody awful. She was struggling and trying to stop me smothering her.'

Vivien forced her face to remain composed; if she showed any sign of shock then he would never open up to her again.

'What's the matter, don't you believe me? I'm not making it up. Here, I've the marks to prove it.'

Stephen undid the button on his right shirtsleeve. When he rolled it up, Vivien saw three thin scratch trails just below his elbow.

'I don't know what would have happened if I hadn't woken up,' he said raggedly as he pushed the material back down.

Vivien didn't know either. It took her a while to decide what to say.

'I'm very glad you opted to tell me, Stephen. I know how hard it was for you. It's really important that you keep nothing hidden – however distressing – it's the only way we can make any real progress together.

But I don't think that it would be particularly helpful for us to discuss what happened right now; it would be better to come back to it later at the end of this session when you've had a chance to relax a little. Do you remember I mentioned hypnosis? Would you be willing to try that now?'

Stephen shrugged in a way that reminded her painfully of Dmitri when he was reluctant to be coaxed out of one of his sulks.

'Take your shoes off and slip up onto the couch. I want you to be as physically comfortable as possible.'

Stephen did as he was bid and Vivien moved her chair to where she could sit by his head. In a soft but authoritative voice, she took him through the initial relaxation exercises. In less than ten minutes, he was in the altered consciousness of a hypnotic trance.

'I want to think of a moment in your childhood, Stephen. The first one that comes to mind. Then tell me about it.'

She waited until his eyes, under their closed lids, began moving rapidly from side to side. 'Where are you, Stephen?'

'Up a tree. We've gone out for a day in the country. Dad said the pub could manage without them for once and that we all needed a holiday. We're playing hide-and-seek. Dad's *it*. I can feel the sun on my head. It's hot and I'm sticky from running all the way over here. But it's a good place. He'll never find me. Mum's gone behind the gate but that's stupid because even I can see her. Bet it'll be the first place Dad looks. We'll be having fish fingers tonight and it's Dr Who on telly. I'm allowed to stay up and watch after my bath. Mum says it'll give me bad dreams but Dad and I just laugh at her.'

He had entered into the trance so easily that Vivien decided to risk asking him to recall something a little less pleasant. Maybe even a touch threatening. Everyone had an incident like that somewhere in their past and it was often a clue as to what was going on in the subconscious.

'It sounds like a perfect day, Stephen. Let's leave it there with you undiscovered up your tree and bring you forward a little. You're at secondary school now. I want you to find a memory of that time and to make it one when you weren't quite so happy. Maybe it's one that you haven't thought of in a very long while. You'll know when you've found the right one because you'll feel a tingle of recognition in the pit of your stomach. Take a moment to retrieve the memory and then tell me what happened. Remember what it was like and what you were feeling and thinking. Remember the smells and the taste in your mouth and what you could see and hear all around you. Can you do that for me, Stephen?'

Stephen shifted a little on the couch. Vivien reached out and picked up his wrist. It was still limp and relaxed. She hadn't pushed him too far too soon and he would still co-operate. She laid his hand down gently by his side.

She had time to write a full page of notes before she noticed a shy smile twitch at the edge of his lips.

'That's good, Stephen. Can you tell me how old you are?'

'Twelve.'

'Where are you?'

'At school, in assembly.'

'Why are you smiling, Stephen?'

'I've just been called up on stage. The Head's going to give me a prize for coming top in maths.'

'That sounds a nice memory, Stephen; are you sure it's the one you want to tell me?'

'Yes, because it's games straight after assembly. I hate football and on Thursdays we have to play with some of the older kids. I'm in the changing room. The teacher has gone out to the pitch and there's just me and some of the boys from the top class. They've got a packet of cigarettes and they're trying to make me take one, but I won't. Now they're calling me names and pushing me around.'

Stephen's breathing had turned shallow and under his closed lids, his eyes were moving rapidly.

'It feels as though it is happening to you again, Stephen, but it's not. It's a memory and a memory can't hurt you. Just stay with it a while longer. Remember that you're safe here in the room with me. Breathe deeply. Feel your chest rising and falling and the air moving in and out of your lungs.'

She watched Stephen's breathing pattern change as his diaphragm took over.

'That's better ... now tell me what happened next.'

'They begin to push me in a circle from one to the other like I'm a Frisbee or something. Now one of them turns away as I'm shoved towards him. I think he's going to hit me and I duck my head but he's reached behind and opened one of the lockers. He pushes me in and slams the door.'

'What does it feel like, Stephen? Can you describe it to me?'

'It's dark and honks of sweaty trainers. And there's not much space. I can't even lift my arms to bang on the sides. I want to shout for them to let me out but I remember reading somewhere that you use up all the oxygen that way. And I begin to think how sorry they'll be if I'm found dead in here and how much trouble they'll get into and how the school will probably have to have a special assembly for me...'

'Aren't you scared, Stephen?'

'Nope ... not at all ... well, only a little bit... But I know they can't have locked me in because there's only one key for all of the lockers and the teacher carries it around his neck – he thinks the big boys will hide drink in them or something. And it's not so bad in here and at least they're not pushing me around anymore but then I feel like I need to have a pee and the more I think about it, the more my tummy begins to hurt. It's just got so I think I can't hold on any longer and might piss myself, and I hear the teacher come back in. "What are you lot doing hanging around like a fart in a lift?" And the door opens and I fall out. And I know he wants to ask me what I was doing in there but I run past him into the bogs and I hear him telling the others off and giving them detention but then he shouts at me to "hurry up and get changed". And all I can think about as I do my zip up is that I haven't even missed the kick-off.'

Vivien made some brief notes. It had obviously been more distressing at the time than any twelve-year-old boy was ever going to admit to, but he'd patently been secure enough in himself to ride out the experience. And, once he'd got used to the vivid nature of memory recall under hypnosis, he'd spoken about it easily enough which proved that there were no lingering after-effects. She would try and take him further back once more and see if the root to his present psychological state lay there.

'Thank you, Stephen; that was very good. Now I want you let that memory go and to wipe it clean from your mind. Put it back to where it was before, along with all the other long forgotten things of your past. Count backwards from seven once more, Stephen, and when you reach one, your thoughts are free and empty.'

She gave him a moment to comply; then resumed speaking in a voice that was even softer than before.

'Now concentrate again on finding a memory of when you were unhappy. Really unhappy. And I want it to come from an earlier time than the last one. Go back as far as you need to. I want you to go with the memory and to live it exactly as if it is happening again to you now with the same feelings and sensations. Can you do that for me, Stephen?'

'Yes.' A thin voice barely louder than an exhaled sigh.

'Where are you?' Vivien said gently.

'Where I never wanted to be.'

'Just relax and breathe normally ... that's it ... slowly, in and out. You are quite safe, Stephen. Nothing can happen to you. Now, tell me what you can see.'

There was a moment's pause as Stephen's features rearranged themselves into a mask of disgust.

'Those infernal chimneys.'

'What are you feeling?'

'Wretched.'

'Why, Stephen? Can you tell me why?'

Stephen shuddered.

'Remember to count, Stephen. Count backwards from seven and feel the tension drain away. When you reach one, there is none left. Your mind is free to go where it wants; let it take you there. You have a picture before you and it is vivid and as real as if you were living it. Describe it to me, Stephen. Tell me what you can see.'

'Smoke. Black clouds of it hanging over the roofs of the houses. The horse is one of my father's best and the gig, light. I am driving my companion back into town and we are descending more rapidly than I would desire. I have a fancy that the gates to Hades have opened before me.'

Vivien was intrigued by the sudden change in his language and speech patterns. She scribbled a note on her pad.

'You're being presented with a dream, a fantasy, Stephen. It often happens under hypnosis. Our sub-conscious experiences something outside the constraints of our rational mind and we believe it to be true. It's your memories we're trying to access, not your imagination, and it's part of my job to help you to distinguish between the two.

Take a moment and then clear the image from your mind.'

Stephen's eyelids flickered.

'I want you to go below that world you have created for yourself and keep searching for some memories. You'll know when you find them because they'll give you the same feeling in the pit of your stomach as those others did.'

A car horn honked on the street outside. Vivien had to steel herself not to jump: this was about Stephen's memories, not hers.

'Now tell me what you can see.'

'Blast you, woman! What is it that you want from me? I answer your questions truthfully – even though it pains me – and still you are not satisfied.'

Vivien swallowed the rebuke. There was a chance he would co-operate again eventually; she wouldn't abandon the session quite yet. Besides, it was noteworthy the way he was inhabiting his dream so thoroughly; it was a testament to his intelligence, as well as his creativity. Stephen was speaking again:

'The bottle ovens are not the stuff of dreams but of nightmares.'

So his rational mind wasn't completely absent after all. He'd heard what she'd said and had incorporated it into his fantasy. There was still hope of a genuine memory resurfacing.

'The closer I get, the more the stench of

burning coal-tar envelopes me and tightens my chest. A whistle blows and a little while later the air is full of a poisonous yellow vapour. My nose prickles with the tang of sulphur and my eyes begin to stream. The kilns to the north are firing salt-glaze; I can taste it the same as when father would bring home the reek from the factory.'

But she'd already ascertained that Stephen had been born in Devon and lived in London; also that his father had been a publican. However, the facts of his life aside, smell was a powerful evoker of memories – even false and transplanted ones – and she wondered if perhaps he was trying to interpret something that he had smelt at an early age and hadn't been able to put a name to: car-spraying perhaps or even the laying of a new road surface. She made a few more notes. She would encourage him in his fantasy a little while longer; if he could embroider his olfactory memories with such detail then he was getting close to being able to uncover what it was that really lay behind them.

'Where are you now, Stephen? What's happening?'

'I am in the narrow streets. My throat has closed against the vicious smog; and my mind is oppressed by what is being asked of me. I am like a child who fears he cannot live up to the expectations placed on his shoulders. My companion touches my arm.

I look to where he is pointing and I see that the area of our destination has more of the flavour of the fires of hell about it than they did before we repaired for luncheon. We have reached the river and the breeze from the water soothes my eyes somewhat, but not my agitation. Where are the women in their yards pegging out their linen? Where are the men going about their business? We are drawing close now and I sense a ripple in the horse's muscles; he too would turn and flee back to the Manor if he could. We alight outside the warehouse to walk the rest of the way on foot. A man rushes out of the factory courtyard and urges me to make haste in my father's name. You see, they all know who I am and everybody but me knows where my duty lies.'

'And who do you think you are, Stephen?'

'Why the devil do you persist in calling me by that name? Have you not been listening to a word I have said? I am Edward Houghton, the son of Charles Houghton of Stoke on the Trent.'

CHAPTER SIX

Acrid black smoke billowed out of the windows of the upper floors of the main factory building. Edward stood in horrified disbelief as, all around him, men, women, and children ran out of the surrounding workshops. Their shouts and cries bounced off the walls of the courtyard.

'Fire!'

'Douse the flames!'

The woman nearest the yard pump started to fill up a dipping basin.

'That'll not be enough to put out a spark! Get to the river!'

All at once everyone was rushing around and bumping into each other in their panic to find pails and jugs or whatever else would hold water, and run with them down the path to the Trent. Edward grabbed hold of the man nearest him.

'How did it start, man?'

'I don't rightly know. Happen in the packing shed with all the straw and that. George Bentley reckoned he could put it out his self but it took hold and spread to the moulding room.'

Edward let him go and looked across at

the gaggle of women and children gathered next to the pile of misfired pottery shards. Their faces were smutty and they were crying and coughing. A capable looking woman was tending to the knees of a blubbering young lad who had obviously fallen over in his haste to get out of the building.

The first of the men returned from the river. Wet with splashes from their heavy pails, they disappeared into the maw of the factory entrance only to emerge seconds later wreathed in veils of steam that strung out like ectoplasm as they ran back the way they had come. Edward watched their efforts with a growing sense of anger. They were doing their best but they were not nearly organised enough. Where was the foreman? He should be ordering them into teams or some such.

'Where's Crossly, blast him?' he shouted at a man lumbering past with two full pails of water.

'He was here earlier by all accounts. Like as not he's in there,' he nodded towards the office tacked onto the end of the burning building, 'happen he's trying to save them ledgers of his.'

'The Devil he is! Precious use they'll be without a factory.'

The partially enclosed yard echoed with the sounds of roof tiles cracking and half-baked pots exploding. Every now and then a retort as loud as pistol shot set Edward's eardrums thrumming as some of the flints used in the manufacturing process blew apart.

'Get out! Get out of there, now!'

Edward waved his hands frantically and ran forward until he could feel the heat from the brickwork sear the skin on his forehead. But the men had come to the same conclusion themselves. The last two emerged from the building, coughing and gasping; their arms, faces and hair filthy with soot, and their aprons singed. They threw their empty pails to the ground and went over to douse their heads under the pump.

Suddenly a piercing scream went up. Edward looked to his left to see a young woman pointing to the third floor of the burning building.

'Daniel!' She shouted in a smoke-hoarse voice. 'Daniel! My son!'

Everyone in the yard stopped what they were doing and followed the direction of her arm. The ghostly shape of a boy was framed in one of the windows. He began to move with a ghastly slow deliberateness and then started to pound his fists silently on the window. As one, every face in the yard turned towards Edward, as if looking to him for answers. They were his responsibility, after all. The look of fierce anger in their eyes was more eloquent than words. It was his fault this had happened. He felt it too.

Every muscle in Stephen's body had gone rigid. Vivien could hear his teeth grinding together. This was obviously affecting him deeply. It was rare for a subject to react so physically under hypnosis but not unknown: it was a sign of trauma.

'Stephen. Listen to my voice. You are here with me in this room. You are safe and nothing can hurt you. I want you to let the tension go. Count backwards from seven again like you did before. When you get to one, you will feel it all drain away.'

Vivien watched as Stephen slowly relaxed until his body resembled that of a sleeper once more. She reached out and touched his wrist; his skin was cold and clammy.

'I'm going to bring you back to your normal state of consciousness, Stephen. Listen carefully to my voice as I count to five... One... Two... When you hear me say five, Stephen, your eyes will open and you will wake up feeling relaxed and refreshed... Three... Four...'

Stephen's eyelids flickered.

'On the next number your eyes will open and you'll feel relaxed and refreshed... Five. Eyes open feeling relaxed and refreshed.'

Stephen blinked a number of times. He ran his hand over his face and appeared to not know where he was. He levered himself upright on the couch, looked across at her and, cleared his throat.

'What's going on? What are you doing to me? That was the most horrible experience of my life; it was so real.'

Vivien could feel his anxiety threatening to tip into hostility. She sought her words carefully; many patients coming out of hypnosis for the first time found the process disorientating and she wanted to bring his rationality back to the fore.

'Everything in the mind is real, Stephen,' she said gently, 'we just don't always have control over how we experience it. That's the point of hypnosis, to temporarily relax our conscious self so we can see what is there underneath.'

'But why would I have all that inside my head? It just doesn't make sense. Why would I imagine a fire and a little boy trapped? It was as if I was there. I could smell the smoke and feel the heat and everything.'

Vivien judged that now was the right time for full disclosure; it would help bridge the distance between them.

'I have to be honest and say that I've no idea of the significance. But there is always a logical explanation for everything and we will get to the bottom of why your mind has so thoroughly confused fantasy and reality in the coming weeks. It's very early days.'

She planted her hand over his as a small sign that she was beside him in this. For the first time, there was no resentment in his expression. He seemed as surprised as her by this development, and as curious to get to a logical explanation for it.

'We don't have much of this session left, Stephen, so I'd like to suggest that we leave the mystery of what just happened, and why, until the next time. I want to take our last few minutes together to talk about what happened with your wife. The nightmare. Can you tell me, did it feel any more or less real than what you experienced just now?'

'About the same, I'd say. But that was a dream. So is that was this was too? Because if it was, then you can stuff your bloody hypnosis; I've had more than enough nightmares to last me a lifetime without you putting more in my head.'

'I've not put anything there, Stephen. Whatever is going on is the work of your subconscious and the hypnosis will help us to uncover what is at the root of it. Because, rest assured, something is and once we can get it out in the open then we can examine it and remove some of its power to affect you so deeply. It's a process of uncovering, Stephen. In every one of us, our mind keeps something hidden from our rational selves but it is only this rational, logical part that can understand it and transform it. It's about making things discussable. And to that end I'd like to suggest that you bring your wife along with you to the next session. I think it would help if we explored what happened and your reactions to it, together.'

Stephen levered himself off the couch and slipped his shoes back on. He kept his face turned away as he made a show of doing up his laces.

'You don't know how much I wish I could do that.' His voice was thick with yearning. 'But she's not here. She's gone to her parents' house in Normandy until I get myself sorted out – thinks some space between us is a good idea – and I'm not surprised after what I tried to do to her.'

Vivien thought so, too. She still wasn't entirely sure how far Stephen would've gone if he hadn't woken up. His disturbing fantasy under hypnosis only seemed to confirm that he really had no conception of his own limits.

'And how do you feel about that?'

'I hate being apart from her – especially now. We've always been each other's best friends and I can talk to her about anything. Except why I have become this monster. I don't know how to even begin explaining that. I just don't know what to say. I want her back here with me desperately but I can understand why she felt she had to go. She must've been so scared.'

He finally looked across at her and Vivien

could see the naked hurt in his eyes, and something else? A hesitancy. Was there something else? Something Stephen was keeping back from her. Before she can follow that thought process, Stephen was busy questioning again.

'Can you imagine what it must have been like for her to be terrified of her own husband?' He glanced down at his hands. 'How could I have done such an awful thing? I love her.'

Vivien nodded slowly and gave him a moment to compose himself. She was sure that there was something he wasn't telling her; his body language was leaking clues: his shoulders hunched in defence and the set of his jaw. The red light above the doorway flicked on; Jean signalling that her next patient was outside. She would have to wait to find out what Stephen was hiding; she had to spend the last few minutes making sure he didn't leave her office feeling too vulnerable.

'Your wife probably made the decision to go away not out of fear but because she thinks that is the best thing for you. It's what we do when we love someone: we try to give them what we think they need. And her instincts are right. Much as you miss her, you need to focus all your energies on keeping up your teaching standards as much as you can, and the work we are going to be doing together here.'

'I'd be able to do that better with her by my side.'

'Perhaps. But the main thing is you're not alone in this Stephen. I'm here. And don't forget, there's email and you can always call Hélène. There's no need to isolate yourself here.'

It was only then that she glanced down at her Cartier.

'Now, I'm afraid we really have run out of time.' She smiled reassuringly. 'Have a word with Jean on your way out and tell her to give you the earliest possible appointment for next week. And don't worry. Everything will be fine.'

She watched Stephen walk with head bowed from the room, and hoped that was true. She was at the stage where she didn't even know if she believed it herself.

CHAPTER SEVEN

It was the Saturday before Vivien got to spend an evening with Jerry. But it wasn't one that they were due to share alone. Anne, Jerry's sister, had arranged a family dinner party. Vivien felt duty-bound to make an effort – they went out so rarely these days –

and dressed carefully in a royal blue silk dress that showed off her waist and skimmed her hips, and high-heeled shoes that she would just about be able to walk in the couple of hundred yards to Anne's house. Jerry looked handsome, if a little aloof, in a dark suit. He had washed his hair with some of her shampoo and it had turned fluffy and slightly flyaway. She wanted to smooth it down with her hand.

They were met at the door by Sandra, Jerry's younger sister.

'Anne and Mike are through in the kitchen,' she said after she had given them both a kiss. 'Some mini crisis with the starters, apparently. Mike's bought himself one of those celebrity chefs cookbook full of recipes that involve lots of drizzling and split-second timing and he would insist on using us as guinea pigs. Stick with what you know is my motto. Can't go wrong with a good prawn cocktail.'

Vivien and Jerry looked at each other and smiled. Sandra's cuisine was firmly routed in the 1970s and had been a family joke for years. It was comforting to be sharing in it again.

The kitchen was full of delicious smells. The room was large with an artfully dis-tressed pine table that had never seen the inside of a farmhouse, and a huge dresser adorned with some highly collectable Clarice

Cliffe and Susie Cooper plates. Vivien envied the style of this couple; it was made up of throwing everything together that they liked and although much of it was incongruous, it all worked because of the confidence with which they carried it off. *No such thing as bad taste,* her mother had loved to say, *only the lack of courage of convictions.* She accepted a glass of wine from Sandra and wondered if her home would ever have such a relaxed atmosphere. She doubted it; she was too much of a perfectionist to allow it to.

She slid gratefully onto a chair; her feet were hurting already. But it had been worth it. Anne – who, with her trim figure, would look a million dollars in a pair of her husband's jeans and Wellingtons – had already noticed her shoes and given her the thumbs-up. It was nice to be complimented. Jerry hadn't said a word.

'Mike, leave it. Stop fussing. They won't cook any quicker just because you're staring at them through the oven glass. Come and sit down.'

Anne made a "men: they always have to pretend they know what they're doing" face at Vivien. She smiled back as her sister-in-law plopped herself onto a chair.

'So,' she said, 'how's things?'

There was a slightly brittle brightness in her voice that Vivien recognised as genuine, but restrained, concern.

'Where's Peter?' Vivien asked. 'It's not like him to get behind on the wine so early on.'

'Ah, but that's where you're wrong,' Sandra answered with a smile, 'my connoisseur of a husband has already tasted this bottle and pronounced it unsuitable to accompany whatever it is Mike's cooking up-'

'Goat's cheese tartlets with roasted vine tomatoes.'

'-and has gone down to the cellar in search of something that will be "less astringent to my palate".'

'Well, it tastes fine to me,' Vivien said.

'It does to everyone but Peter. Never mind, we'll just have to finish it up amongst ourselves before we eat.'

'I guess we're basically coping. But it's hard.'

Vivien was surprised that Jerry had chosen to answer Anne's earlier question. And a little annoyed. It was natural that the others would want to know how they both were but she didn't feel that it was right to start to talk about it quite yet. She hadn't had the time to find the right words. She shot Jerry a sharp look and then cursed herself as she saw Sandra catch the edge of it.

'I know it should be obvious,' Jerry continued, 'but it's all so very different when it happens to you. I see tragedy at the hospital almost every day and naively thought that would sort of inure me to it a little but it's almost as if it makes it worse somehow. Renders the dreadful loss of our son almost commonplace.'

Vivien scrabbled around for something to say that would shut him up. It was all very well for her patients to spill out their vulnerabilities – it was her job to encourage them to, after all – but to have it all laid out on such public display was almost unbearable. The irony was, of course, that it had been Jerry's openness about himself and his feelings that had been one of the things that had made her fall in love with him in the first place. But now? Now, it felt as if he were violating their grief in some way. She knew she was being unreasonable as she filled the silence by topping up their wine glasses. They had barely been here ten minutes and she was in danger of ruining the evening already.

'Is that food nearly ready, Mike?' she said, 'I'm starving.'

Mike bent down once more to peer into the oven.

'The pastry's not as brown as it is in the picture and the filling still looks a little wet but I guess we could give it a go once Peter gets back. But don't blame me if the tartlets collapse in a soggy mess after the first forkful.'

'They won't.'

Anne stroked the back of his neck as she

walked past to fetch the balsamic vinegar. The kind reassurance of the gesture made Vivien's eyes prick with the prelude to tears.

The moment passed in a flurry of activity as Peter returned with a bottle of wine that he announced 'not really adequate but the best I could find', and Mike fussed with setting the tartlets to one side to cool slightly and moving the other dishes in the oven up a shelf.

A child's voice, fuzzy with sleep, stopped everything. Emily, Anne and Mike's six year old, stood in the kitchen doorway looking flushed.

'Mummy. I had a dream and can't go back to sleep.'

'Are you sure you've tried hard enough, honey? I'm sure if you snuggle down again and think nice thoughts then your eyes will soon close again.'

'But I can't.' Emily's voice was close to a wail. 'I need a hug.'

'Not now, pumpkin, give me two ticks and I'll come on up. Your daddy has been slaving over this all afternoon and we don't want to spoil his big moment, do we?'

Vivien watched in disbelief as Jerry held his arms out to his niece. Emily didn't need a second invitation and scooted over to him. Jerry kissed her sleep-tousled hair as he scooped her up and onto his lap. The sight was so achingly familiar that Vivien thought for a moment that she was living in a parallel life where time had turned back. She had to look away but, in doing so, caught the looks on Anne and Sandra's faces. Both women's eyes were about to overflow with tears.

It was Peter who rescued the situation. He stood up and stretched out his hand.

'What say you let your old uncle tuck you up again? I'll even read you a quick story if you like.'

Emily slid off Jerry's lap.

'Thanks, mate,' Mike said, 'I'm not sure you'll be missing much anyway. These tartlets are a disaster.'

Eventually, the meal got underway. Vivien made an effort to eat but the scene with Emily had distressed her. No, that wasn't accurate. It had hurt her. It was almost as if Jerry had been disloyal in his palpable love for another child. As if he had betrayed Dmitri. She should never have come.

The conversation flowed around her as she picked at her food. A tapestry of snippets of gossip from work, criticisms of the latest films, and less than flattering comments about the new teacher at Oliver's school. Vivien contributed little but nodded and sympathised in the right places. The wine was helping the evening to mellow into something like an ordinary family get-together by the time Peter rejoined them and they were all ready for the main course.

'It's Emily's birthday soon, isn't it? Jerry asked. 'If there isn't anything particular she wants, then I've got an idea. I was passing by a toy shop on my way from the hospital and saw this doll's house in the window. You know, one of those old-fashioned ones where you can open up the whole front and move the furniture around. What do you think?'

'Oh, Jerry,' Anne said, 'she'd love it. You've always been so good at picking out the perfect presents for both of the kids.'

'It'll sound silly, but that's one of the things I miss most of all. Planning little surprises for Dmitri and then seeing the look on his face when I brought them home.'

It was too much. With a mumbled excuse about needing to wash her hands, Vivien got up and left the room. In the downstairs cloakroom she held her wrists under the cold tap to try to calm the trembling that was threatening to suffuse her whole body. It hadn't just been the poignancy of what Jerry had said that had affected her so deeply. It wasn't even the look of isolation that she'd seen on his face when she'd walked out. It wasn't really about him at all. It was her. That she could never give him what he so obviously wanted more than anything in the world: to be a father. Not in order to replace Dmitri – that would be impossible – but to complete him as a person; to make him more of who he already was. It made her feel so inadequate. Even if the doctors decided she wasn't too old to undergo another round of IVF, how could she ever go through all that again knowing that it might only end up in more heartbreak if fate decided to step in and snatch it all away again. She would not be able to endure it.

The worst of it all was that she could never tell Jerry any of this. They were locked in their own private hells of grief and didn't understand where to find the key that would let each other in. It was a pattern she saw in her patients all the time and knew, once established and entrenched, was next to impossible to break out of. Was the slow and painful dawning she saw on their faces what she would see one day when she looked at Jerry: love replaced by incomprehension? The thought made her feel sick and lonely. And afraid. For them both.

Back home again, Vivien let Jerry go up to bed without her. She knew she wouldn't be able to sleep and she'd spent too many nights laying beside him in a cocoon of misery just waiting for the morning to come. Maybe if she did a little work first then she might be able to drive some of her worst thoughts away, and tire herself in the process. But a part of her knew that the real reason was that she wanted to be alone. Didn't want to be with Jerry. It was a devastating thought: but it was the truth.

She picked up her briefcase from where she'd left it in the hall and walked through into the dining room. She sat at the table and pulled out Stephen Daunt's file. She had a feeling that it was likely to end up being very thick by the time she had finished with him. She uncapped her fountain pen and began to write.

CASE STUDY NOTES
NAME: Stephen Daunt
CONSULTATION DATE: Monday 14th May
TREATMENT SUMMARY:
The patient was unusually susceptible to hypnosis. However this was only the first time he had undergone it and, as his anxiety begins to lessen under treatment and he subsequently re-establishes his sleeping pattern, he may well exhibit some reluctance to co-operate in the future.

Various periods of his childhood were explored – no obvious evidence of abuse or lingering trauma. However, when I attempted to take him further back he adopted a different persona and answered my questions in that guise. He was consistent in his use of language and speech patterns and seemed to believe that he was recounting a real life experience. His apparent memories were vivid – interesting to note that he engaged all his senses.

CONCLUSIONS:

He is a highly imaginative, and intelligent, man. This may go some way to explaining the adoption of the persona called Edward. There is no reason to consider Multiple-personality Syndrome. Neither is it likely that he possesses the damaged neural pathways that could lead to identity confusion. It may well be that his subconscious is operating to protect itself from revealing whatever it is that is driving his current behaviour.

The ease with which I was able to hypnotise him and his recurrent nightmares suggest that he may be fantasy prone. The important thing to remember is that HE believed at the time that he was truly experiencing the world he created for himself.

FURTHER ACTION:

Despite his disorientation on re-emerging from his hypnotic state and obvious confusion about what occurred in the latter part, he appeared to be more physically relaxed – unburdened almost. Continue with hypnosis.

CHAPTER EIGHT

Vivien had noticed the difference in Stephen the minute he had walked into her office. In this, their third session together, it was obvious that something was shifting. She felt a frisson of professional pride; her approach was working.

'How's the sleep, Stephen?'

'Can you believe that I'm actually getting some? No dreams, either.'

'That's excellent. I hope that continues but don't be alarmed if they start to come back. We've a lot of work to do to get to the bottom of what it was that caused them in the first place and we might come to a point where something triggers them off again. But if you've been free of them for the last week then at least you know that they need not be a permanent feature of your life. What about your wife, have you been in touch with her?'

'Yes. It's a little strained between us. I've tried to explain what we've been doing here but it's all so confusing. And I don't want to worry her – she really needs to take care of herself right now – so we end up chatting about small things. But at least we're talking, right?'

'It's good that you can think of her welfare when you are going through so much yourself. It bodes well for your relationship ending up being much stronger once this is all over.'

How she wished she had the same confidence in her relationship with Jerry. Nothing there seemed to be going right these days.

'Let's talk about what happened last time when you were under hypnosis. Now you've had some time to reflect, how do you feel about it?'

'How do you think? Confused. A little baffled about where it all came from. If I taught English or history then maybe I could understand it – all that immersion in Gothic horror and murky pasts – but I'm a maths teacher for God's sake. You can't get any more strait-jacketed in rationality than that.'

'Except maybe in the world of psychiatry.'

Vivien smiled at him and was rewarded with a flash of genuine warmth back.

'So I suppose,' Stephen continued, 'that if all that stuff didn't get into my head by absorption, then it must've been in there in the first place. You're the shrink; do you reckon that it could be my subconscious trying to tell me something?'

'That's a very astute conclusion to draw, Stephen, and probably as accurate as any I could make at this stage.'

'Do you mean to say that even you don't know what's going on?'

'Much as I would like it to be, psychiatry is rarely about certainties, Stephen. A lot of it comes down to educated guesswork.'

'Now you tell me. You want me to spill my guts out so you can have a stab in the dark?'

'I didn't say that. It's just that I don't think it will help if I simply reverted to a checklist of symptoms and came up with the most obvious answer.'

'Which is?'

'Frankly, Stephen, that is what we're here to discover. Together.'

'So there could be just about anything lurking at the back of my brain waiting to explode? Hardly a comforting thought.'

'Although all our minds work in the same way, they are unique. How we process information and experiences is different in every single one of us. My job is to try and find out how you go about it and what it says about you.'

'Are you telling me that this has never happened with any of your other patients?'

'Not precisely, no. Certainly not this detailed. But Stephen I can assure you there is a rational explanation for this and we will get to the bottom of it. I think therefore the most productive thing we can do now is to try another session of hypnosis and see what else we can uncover. Are you okay with that?'

'Yes. I suppose so. The sooner we get on with it, the quicker all this will be over and I can be back with Hélène. I can't wait to get back to normal.'

Vivien resisted the urge to comment on the relativity of the term 'normality' and watched as Stephen removed his shoes and lay down on the couch.

She took him through the preliminary relaxation stages as before and was surprised that, despite no longer being in the grip of acute physical exhaustion, Stephen still slipped into a trance-like state with ease. It was further evidence – if she needed it – of the imaginative qualities of the man. She waited until his breathing was relaxed and regular, and then picked up her pad and pen from the coffee table by her side; she would make as many notes as possible this time. Now that she knew the sort of thing to expect, she had to concentrate on his thought patterns; on what he did – and didn't – say.

'Stephen, I want you to go back to the same place in your mind as you were the last time. Remember that tingle in your stomach when you thought you'd found the memory? Keep flicking through the pictures that flash in front of your eyes until you feel it again. Can you do that for me, Stephen?'

'Edward. My name is Edward.'

The speed of his transformation took Vivien by surprise. Maybe his subconscious was even more ready to let go than she had imagined.

'Hello, Edward. I'd like to ask you a few questions if I may? Nothing complicated. Would that be all right?'

'I have no reason to refuse any reasonable request for information.'

'I'm very pleased to hear it. How old are you, Edward?'

'Twenty-five.'

The same age as Stephen. Nothing remarkable in that; they were one and the same person, after all.

'Where are you?'

'At home, where else? I suppose that I must call the Manor home now. Although it brings me no joy to say so.'

'Can you tell me what it's like?'

'Large. Imposing. Soulless. There are few comforts here and too many memories. Once, I thought I had escaped this place for good but now I know that it was only a fool's dream to believe that destiny had something better to offer.'

'What's brought you back to a place that you obviously dislike so much?'

'Duty. Always duty. It was my father's watchword and it would take a man with more courage than I possess to turn my back on the dictates of my upbringing. I was in training to be a lawyer when the un-expected burden of inheriting my father's potbanks fell to me. I had no choice but to return to Stoke on the Trent.'

'How long have you been back there?'

'Too long. Months that feel like years.'

Vivien imagined that Stephen felt the weeks since the accident on the school trip which had precipitated him coming to see her, probably felt like years too.

'And will you stay there since you are so unhappy?'

'What choice do I have? Life has dealt me this fate and I must endure it.'

Was this what Stephen's subconscious was trying to tell him: that he must remain the person he had recently become forever? She hoped not. It was a bleak thought to have to live with. And it was one that she knew only too well. The parallels his fantasy were throw-ing up were not only between Edward's future and Stephen's.

'Thank you, Edward. I've no more questions for now. I want you to relax and take me into your world with you. Show me what it is like to be Edward...'

Edward stood up from his writing bureau and stretched his shoulders as he walked across the room. He found it hard work studying here; the space oppressed him and the moulded ceiling high above seemed to press down on the top of his head and make it ache. How he longed to be back in his cramped quarters at the university; there all his books were within reaching distance of his desk and he did not have to give a fig about spilling ink any of the furniture.

He supposed that all this was his now but it hardly seemed that way; this room had been where his father had always received his visitors and, even now, it felt as though he would hear him clearing his throat with disapproval at any moment. He couldn't stop himself from looking up at the portrait hanging on the wall. His father glared back in return. Edward wondered why he hadn't removed it; had it taken up to the attic or wrapped in hessian and stored in one of the outbuildings for the mice and damp to corrupt. But to make even such a small change as that to his surroundings would be to accept that he was there to stay and he was unable to face the truth of that quite yet.

His footsteps sounded hollow on the floorboards as he paced towards the fire. At least there was one thing in the room that gave it a sense of homeliness – even if it was surrounded by a floor to ceiling marble edifice that would not look out of place in a mausoleum. He held his frozen fingers out and felt them tingle back into life as the warmth seeped down to his bones. He folded his hands behind his back under the tails of his frockcoat and watched a trail of sparks drift like burnt-out stars up the chimney.

A respectful knock on the door pulled his attention. Horwood, his butler, stepped into the room. It seemed to take an age for him to traverse the space between them and arrive in front of Edward. He combined a discreet cough with a nod of his head before speaking.

'Sir. There are visitors.'

'I am not expecting anyone. If they are from the town after patronage, you can send them away.' The blankness in Horwood's eyes sent a shiver of apprehension through Edward's chest. 'Not from the factory, surely? Tell them I am otherwise engaged and not at home to enquiries concerning commerce.' His father's voice rang in his head: *Business may be troublesome, but idleness is pernicious.* He would be instructed to that effect at least once every school holiday as he was handed a long list of unnecessary chores that had to be performed in strict order. A blow over the knuckles with his father's cane was all he could ever expect as acknowledgment of his efforts. He clasped his hands together as if he could feel the stinging even now.

Horwood coughed again; a little louder this time. 'The gentlemen in question inform me that they are acquaintances of yours from the university.'

Edward felt a bolt of pleasure. 'Why did you not say so in the first place, man? Send them in. Send them in. And have Cook prepare tea for us. The best silver. And something to eat. They will be famished after their long journey. Well, what are you waiting for? Go and get them.'

Horwood retreated and Edward's heart sang with excitement. He had not been abandoned to his fate after all. He had not been cast out from his former society because he had been unfortunate enough to have his father and brother die and the running of the business to fall on his shoulders. Once more he would be able to laugh and gossip with like minds and be stimulated by the violent discussions over principles of law that he had loved so much and been wrenched away from in such an untimely fashion.

Edward could barely contain his impatience as he stared at the open door and through into the hallway; as it was he bounded across the room and nearly tripped over one of the rugs the moment Horwood ushered his guests in. He felt a rush of joy to see their familiar figures; Richard, short and wiry with his fair hair sticking out in all directions; Henry, built like a farmhand rather than a student, thick-limbed and broad of chest, and Jonathan. Jonathan, a head taller than the other two, dressed as if for an evening at the theatre in his velvet-collared frockcoat and boots that had never so much as brushed up against a speck of dirt.

'Welcome. Welcome. How truly wonderful to see you.' He shook their hands, slapped their backs in quick succession, and stood grinning like a monkey.

His friends seemed equally pleased to see him; their smiles made their cheeks, already red from the cold, apple-shiny. But there was an air of formality that had never accompanied their meetings before. Edward realised that Horwood was still hovering awaiting any further instructions. He sent him away with a flick of his hand. Stupidly, the dismissive gesture made him feel uncomfortable. Here he was at twenty-five – the same age as his friends – with the power to give orders to a man older than their tutor had been. He let the thought go with the click of the door behind him.

'What kind and thoughtful fellows you are,' he said, 'to come to this godforsaken place to see me. The coach journey must have been hell. Come to the fire. Come and warm your bones. And tell me the news.'

The four friends gathered in front of the huge fireplace – there was room enough for them to stand shoulder to shoulder and still not out span the curved basket of flaming logs.

'Tea will be along soon. And you can smoke if you would like. There is no need to stand on ceremony at the Manor.'

Jonathan reached into the pocket and brought out a pipe and pouch of tobacco. He filled the bowl and held a taper into the fire to light it as the others took in their surroundings.

'I had no idea your old man was so ... so ... well-appointed,' Richard said with a trace of awe in his voice.

'Or was so spectacularly afflicted with bad taste,' Henry added. His comment was light enough but there was a touch of distain around the edges. 'Not everything worth more than the sum on the collection plate is worthy of admiration, Mouse.'

Edward laughed. Richard was the son of a country clergyman and his faded black coat had earned him the nickname of Church Mouse the very first day they had all met.

'Henry. It pains me to hear you speak ill of the dead. Edward's father has the right to have his home respected.'

'But it is his home no longer. It is our fine friend's here. And he should rip out the most grotesque of its trappings this instant.'

Edward shrugged. 'I hardly think it worth the effort. For now, my only wish is to continue my studies and come back to the university to sit my examinations. The manner of my surroundings are of nothing to me.'

He waved his hand around airily but did not dare to raise his eyes to the portrait glowering down at him. Maybe if he voiced such blatant untruths often enough they would, in time, diminish the oppression he felt when he was alone. *Liars begin by imposing upon others, but end up by deceiving themselves.* Was his father's voice never to leave him? He would not let this visit be ruined.

Jonathan looked up from his pipe. 'Edward, dear thing, you have to admit that the drapery would be better suited to a brothel. How about I take this taper and remove them from your sight this minute?'

Edward had to stop himself from reaching out to snuff out the thin flame. Student pranks were all very well but not in his own household. Besides, the thick curtains that kept the wind from whistling through the ill-fitting shutters reminded him of his mother. When she died ten years ago, his father immediately had the house redecorated but, finding himself unequal to the task of choosing furnishings, had reluctantly invited his wife's sister to advise. Edward knew that the muted greens and reds had been his mother's favourite colours and that his aunt had chosen them for his benefit as much as for the victory of taste over money.

Jonathan's smile was soft through the curls of grey pipe smoke. 'Ah well, no matter, it is you we have come to see after all, not the grandiose follies of an outmoded generation.' He tossed the taper into the fire. 'Where is this tea you so gallantly promised us?'

Edward stepped to the side of the fireplace and tugged at the tasselled bell-pull that hung down beside the outer marble column. His friends had seated themselves gingerly on the delicate balloon-backed chairs by the time Horwood entered with the tray. They had been chatting happily up until this point but now they all fell into an awkward silence as Edward's butler poured the tea and handed around the cream and sugar. Jonathan made a fuss of preferring lemon. For once, Edward wished he would resist playing the fop so thoroughly. It was embarrassing to have the gulf between the social standing of his friends and his servant underlined. But it was not his butler's feelings he was sensitive to – even if he did now have to fetch and carry for a boy he had once admonished for sliding down the banisters. No, it was his new status as a man of commerce that he felt was being drawn attention to. In a few short months he had been elevated unwillingly from impoverished student to rich factory owner and he felt that there must surely be one person in the room – apart from himself of course – who resented the change.

The silver had been cleared away and they were relaxing with their legs stretched out in front of them before Edward thought to ask his friends to what he owed the honour of their visit.

'To check that the air this far north of London has not totally ruined your constitution,' Henry ventured.

'And to tell you how wrong you were in the last essay you submitted; the tutor read out your conclusions in your absence and took inordinate delight in highlighting the folly of your logic.' Richard grinned. 'It was the talk of the ale-house all that evening.'

Edward blushed. He knew that he was only being teased but no one had done that for such a long time that he felt ill-equipped to simply laugh it off. 'I fear that I have lost the capacity to make any judgements, Mouse, flawed or otherwise.'

'But therein lies the real reason we have braved the potholed roads.' Jonathan stuck his fingers in the pockets of his waistcoat. 'We felt it incumbent on us to check that you have not become corrupted by your position and been transformed into a wicked factory owner and oppressor of the common man.'

Edward felt his stiff collar chafe and the flush on his cheeks, deepen. Was Jonathan to be the one who would try to cut him back down to size? It was certainly well within his character. He leapt up to gaze into the fire before his friends could see the depth of his discomfiture. Luckily, Richard spoke into the silence.

'I think you are being very unfair. Not every rich merchant is to be banished from the Kingdom of Heaven. Our Lord even allowed a tax collector to accompany Him there.'

'But first he had to repent his many sins and give up all his worldly goods. Is that what you intend to do, Edward, climb up to the top of this edifice and throw your coins to the huddled masses below?' Jonathan blew a smoke ring and watched it wobble to the ceiling.

'Ignore his sour grapes; his father is set to cut him off without a penny and forestall the huge gambling debts that he knows will ruin the family fortune.' Richard placed his hands on his knees and leant forward in his chair. 'Tell us a little of your business. We are eager to know. I have never counted a factory owner amongst my circle before. What is it that you do exactly?'

Edward was about to make some flippant remark and change the subject but Richard really did look interested. Henry too had stopped cleaning under his nails with the small knife he had attached to his watch chain, and had raised his eyebrows inquiringly.

Edward took two strides across the room and picked up a plate from one of the small side tables. 'We make these,' he held it up for them to see, 'and other wares – cups and teapots and the like. The clay is taken and made into shapes, fired, decorated, and then sold. That is all there is to it.'

'But you make it sound so mundane,' Henry said, 'there must be more involved in the process than that. If it was that straight-forward then we would all be making our own china and cooking it in our own fireplaces. We would not need factories.'

'That is as maybe, but that is all I know. I have a foreman who runs the place and keeps me informed as to the state of the balance sheet; that is all I concern myself with. I spend my days here studying the law.'

'This foreman; he has a name, I take it? Please tell me you know what it is, dear thing, or I will remain forever convinced that you are the despot I fear you may have become.'

Edward could no longer tell if Jonathan was teasing or not. 'Crossly. Archibald Crossly. Not that it will mean anything to you.'

'But that is where you are wrong because I have to know what to call him whilst he is showing us around that hive of industry of yours. It just would not do to address a re-mark with a click of the fingers, now would it?'

'Oh yes, Edward, yes. Take us to your factory.' Richard was fairly buzzing with excitement. 'We have come all this way after all and it would be of great interest.'

'We would be able to astound our tutor when we return to the university with our knowledge of working conditions. It would mean extra marks, I am sure of it.'

Edward turned to Henry. 'He will only be astounded that you would wish to spend any of your precious time away from your books up to your ankles in wet clay.'

'Is that what it is like then? I thought you said you knew nothing about what goes on?'

Jonathan was beginning to rankle him. It was almost as if he was trying to catch him out. But he would show the factory to them; he made money there, that was all, and there was nothing to be ashamed of in that. Edward spun the plate to land on his tormentor's lap and then reached for the bell-pull once more.

Horwood entered the room almost immediately.

'Tell the stables to get the brougham ready. I will drive it myself.' He waited until the butler had left to do his bidding. 'Well, you shall have your wish. Never let it be said that Edward Houghton does not accede to his guest's whims and fancies. But I want to hear no complaints from you when it transpires that you are as bored as I know

109

you will be.'

Edward led the way out of the drawing room, his good humour almost restored.

CHAPTER NINE

The weak sun was obliterated by the smoke from the chimneys as they alighted from the carriage in front of the factory. Jonathan held a handkerchief over his mouth and nose as he skipped sideways to avoid a sludgy puddle. Edward laughed. The visit would be a short one; his friends' London sensibilities would see to that.

They were met in the courtyard by the burly figure of Archibald Crossly. He was dressed in a black serge jacket and trousers and his face was florid as if he had just stepped away from the kilns. Almost ten years older than Edward and his friends – and a good deal shorter – his muscled arms and thick neck made him look as if he belonged to a different species: a crow amongst sleek songbirds. He scowled at Edward.

'Mr Houghton. This is an unusual occurrence. Is there something you want?'

'Only a tour of the pottery, Crossly. My friends here are eager to see exactly what goes on.'

'May I remind you that this is a place of work and not one of entertainment.'

Edward was taken aback by his hostility. He could understand it in part, he supposed, it must feel to Crossly that he was checking-up on him. But that was no excuse for his speaking to him so in front of his friends, and in such a parody of his father's manner too; it was his factory, after all, and he had every right to look around it whenever he pleased.

He looked at Crossly's fixed expression in an attempt to stare him down but saw a flinty determination in his eyes that caused him to turn away. He had momentarily forgotten that his foreman was a formidable opponent. He remembered back to the great pottery strike of 1836. His brother had written to him about it. Crossly had been a stoker at the factory – the perfect job for a man of his strength and bulk – and, after several weeks of cold kilns, his father had called him in to organise a group of men to start up the factory again. His father was not in sympathy with his workers' demands and, more to the point, feared bankruptcy. It seemed that Crossly went about his task with great enthusiasm and, once the bottle ovens were belching smoke once more, was rewarded with promotion to foreman. Edward wondered what sort of a man would betray his fellows and turn strikebreaker and concluded that it was one who did not seek popularity. Which was just as well; he was someone neither to be liked nor trusted but had now made himself so essential to the running of the factory that Edward had no option but to rely on him. Even if he did rule the place with fear – that much was evident in the sideways looks the workers scurrying across the courtyard were giving him. However, he had to concede that such an approach was undeniably effective; the place was as productively busy as an ants' nest.

'It is alright, Crossly,' he said eventually, 'I will conduct the tour myself. We will start with where the clay is prepared. It is the room over there, I believe?'

'No, Mr Houghton. You want the Slip House. Last building on your left.'

Edward blushed and his façade of confidence cracked a little.

'Mind you do not hold up any of the process. We are firing every kiln today,' Crossly started to walk away, 'and I would watch those fine boots of yours, gents, if I were you. A pottery is no place for Dandies.'

Jonathan bowed a little from the waist and doffed his top hat. Edward took a little courage from his friend's sarcastic gesture and led his little party away.

The contrast between the smoke-blackened courtyard and the interior of the Slip House couldn't have been greater; at first glance, everything seemed to be covered in a luminous off-white gloss. A man in a caked apron was stirring a long, low tank of sludgy water with a wooden plank.

'That looks like an amusing little job,' Henry remarked, 'I wonder if he will step aside for a moment and allow me to try my hand at it?'

He took a step forward and his feet slid from under him on the slippery floor. Only Richard's outstretched arms saved him from falling.

'God's teeth, it is like walking on a frozen pond.' Henry looked down. His legs were splashed with congealing clay.

'It takes a steady gait to work in here,' Edward said, 'as it does in the whole pottery. I remember marvelling as a child when my father showed me the men carrying great mounds of pots on their heads up and down ladders. I defy you to want to try that, Henry.'

His friend held his hands up in instant acquiescence.

'What is through there?' Jonathan asked, indicating a doorway on their right, 'it looks altogether drier.'

'As it has to be.' Edward was beginning to get into his stride now and enjoy himself. He may not have remembered where the Slip House was but he did know what went on in it; his father had insisted on many a tour such as this when he was young and he knew the processes of the first three rooms off by heart. It was only after them that he had got bored and ceased to pay attention.

'It is where the alchemy proper begins. The earthen sediment this fellow is leaching is mixed with other ingredients to form china clay; the raw material that will make the cup you will one day drink from.'

'I swear I will not be putting any product from this place anywhere near my lips, dear thing, not now I know how mucky everything is.'

Jonathan had walked ahead and was half-way through the doorway. He took a step into the room and then retched out a gut-heaving cough. He was doubled over and spluttering by the time he was able to raise his handkerchief for protection.

'Ye gods, what is that stench?'

Edward laughed. It had caught him that way too, the first time. 'Heated, crushed, and powered cattle bones. It is one of those magical ingredients I alluded to.'

'I thought the atmosphere resembled that of a charnel house. Are you sure it is animals you pulverise and not the skulls of recalcitrant workers?'

The others smiled but Edward chose to ignore him. 'Henry, Mouse, just peek in a little but try not to breathe too deeply or you will suffer the effects as Jonathan did.'

The two men did as they were bid.

'They all look like they are covered in hoar frost; this place is altogether too like a winter landscape for my liking.' Richard shivered.

'That is the flint dust. We pulverise the stones too. I will wager that you would never have guessed how many different things went into that little plate I showed you at the Manor. Come on; come out into the air before the dust catches in all our throats.'

Once back out in the courtyard, the four men brushed themselves down but their attempts only left them with white streaks on their clothes.

'Is it not bad for them to be breathing that foul air all the time?' Henry asked. 'I caught a glimpse of a young child in there; he could hardly have been more than ten or twelve.'

'Their lungs are used to it. Their fathers would have worked in the Slip House and they would have been breathing the dust off them, as infants. Now, let me show you what I consider to be the best sight of all. In here, I think.' Edward shepherded them towards another opening off the courtyard.

Jonathan coughed again. 'The smoke really is getting quite intolerable. Is it always like this?'

'Only when the kilns are firing.'

'And how often is that, pray?'

'All the time.'

Edward was gratified to see Henry and Richard enjoy his little joke at Jonathan's expense.

'Here we are, the Throwing Shop. I will lead the way. Mind you do not touch anything and keep your wits about you for wet clay on the floor. Henry has already tasted how treacherous it can be.'

The room they entered stretched almost one entire side of the courtyard but was shrunk to almost coal-hole proportions by the floor to ceiling stacks of freshly-thrown pottery, and the number of people crammed up against workbenches. A few looked their way; the men touching their caps and the women dipping a quick courtesy, before returning to their work. The air in the room was fetid and the light was cut to that of a grimy twilight by the clay dust on the windows.

Edward grasped Henry's arm and pointed to where a hunch-shouldered woman, her once-black skirt a pallid grey despite a protective apron, was cranking the handle of a four-foot wooden wheel.

'A veritable wood-cut of the goddess turning Cicero's Wheel of Fortune. Please tell me that what she spins off the end determines whether one's life is full of prosperity or disaster?'

Edward slapped Jonathan's back heartily. 'You have got it in one; my fortune rests in her hands and all of the others anywhere along this chain. But it all starts with her; if she fails to get it right and the ball of clay that leaves her contraption is not centred sufficiently on the potter's wheel, then he cannot form it into a useable item and it will have to be scrapped.'

'What is that man doing over there?'

Edward followed Richard's gaze. He felt a momentary stab of embarrassment that he was not able to enlighten him; he had been doing so well up until now. He grabbed the shoulder of a boy of about six who was running past and nearly caused him to drop the load he was carrying.

'Can you tell me what that man is doing?' he said in his friendliest voice. He was surprised to see that the boy looked terrified to be stopped in his tracks.

'Him be the jigger, your lordship. Him's doing what we calls "jollying". Pressing out plates and that.'

'Hook it into that drying room afore that mould be cracking!'

The disembodied voice was heavy with anger. Edward cringed and patted the boy on the top of his cap.

'Off you go and do as he says.' The boy scurried away. 'And thank you for your time,' Edward shouted after him. He found it hard to credit that so brief an interruption had produced such an outburst. The man was at the other end of the room in any event so how could he see that the boy had paused in his running? And surely he could not have realised to whom he was speaking? Edward tapped each of his friends on their shoulders and beckoned them to follow him out; his erstwhile excitement lying sour in the pit of his stomach.

They came across Archibald Crossly in the courtyard directing a stream of men and young boys who were carrying stacks of moulds on their heads. 'You gents had enough yet?' His voice was loaded with patronising scorn.

'I am about to show them the kilns,' Edward said, choosing to ignore the trapped expressions on his friends' faces.

'I will accompany you,' Crossly said, 'I was going that way myself to see these pots get loaded properly.'

The five men walked together across the courtyard to the nearest of the bottle ovens.

Jonathan had his handkerchief out again and was mopping his sweating brow. 'Is it always so deuced hot?'

Crossly laughed. 'You wait until you get inside. It gets to 120 degrees Fahrenheit – hotter when the oven doors are opened. The fires are attended to day and night. That is a real man's occupation; not sitting all day with his nose in a book.'

Edward screwed his fists into balls to stop

from responding. The man was damned impertinent but he could not be seen to confront him in front of the others. They would only interpret it as his weakness which, of course, it was; he was the factory owner and should have earned the respect of his workers by now.

The atmosphere inside the bottle oven was close to unbearable. The thick brick of the outer skin trapped the heat and coal-dust and felt like a paralysed chest wall preventing them from catching their breath. Incredibly, there were men – and boys – working inside this hell-hole. Edward felt a little sick. From beside them a man shouted for them to stand clear and the air was suddenly full of eyeball searing heat and blue-black smoke. Edward forced himself to watch as the fireman, his head and body draped in steaming wet towels, hoisted shovel loads of coal into the hungry furnace. A ball of angry flame licked out of the open door and missed the man's arms by inches. Edward felt his own skin pucker in sympathy. A running boy darted between them and the treacherous oven and, as he skipped sideways to avoid the end of the fireman's shovel, he tripped. The large earthenware tub he was carrying was full of cups and the sound of them smashing echoed around the hellish chamber.

Crossly took a step forward and hoiked

the lad up by his collar. The boy's face was tearstained – Edward didn't know whether from the smoke or fear.

'I will give thee a strapping for that, the like of which you will never forget.'

Crossly dragged him out into the court-yard and over to where more of the earthenware tubs were being made. The others followed and watched as Crossly picked up a thin rolling pin from a bench and set about beating the boy across his back and shoulders.

'Stop him! Can you not stop him?' Richard shouted.

'This is barbaric!'

'You see I was right all along,' Jonathan joined in, 'Houghton here runs a place not much better than a slaughterhouse.'

CHAPTER TEN

Edward shuddered with horror and indecision. There was a group of workers looking on – Crossly had obviously brought the boy out into the courtyard so that the punishment would be witnessed as a lesson to all – and he felt sure that any interference from him would be inappropriate; he had left his foreman to his own devices and surely had therefore forfeited any right to say how the place should operate.

He was saved from his dilemma by a young woman dashing out of the Throwing Shop – no doubt alerted by the boy's cries – and pulling the boy out of Crossly's grip.

'This here be my son,' her voice was strident but respectful, 'tak' it owt the brass I am owed for my piece making.'

'Happen I will that,' Crossly said, 'and the young'un's too. He'll not be getting nowt for the coming week.'

The woman shrugged her acceptance and Edward saw a defiant nobility in her face the like of which he had not encountered since he had first embarked on this ill-advised and nightmarish venture.

He had to run to catch up with the others who were already striding out of the courtyard. None of them said a word. He knew they blamed him for what had just happened; Jonathan's jibe about him being a wicked factory owner and oppressor of the common man suddenly didn't seem so far removed from the truth. They stood together awkwardly by the brougham.

'It is getting late,' Edward said at last, 'come back to the Manor for dinner and I will have Horwood make you all up beds for the night.'

He caught the edge of exchanged glances.

'I think it is fair to say that we would

121

prefer to return to our lodgings.'

'Jonathan's right,' Henry said, 'we have plans for the morrow that we must attend to.'

Richard looked disappointed. 'Must we really leave already? We so rarely venture out of London and I was looking forward to spending the night in a country house again.'

'Mouse, your origins so often betray you. A bed for the night is a bed for the night, wherever it is taken.'

Richard waited until Edward had stepped away from them and then inclined his head towards Henry and Jonathan. 'But he will have gone to much trouble. I heard him tell his servants to cut down the venison they had been hanging. Could you not also do with a decent meal?'

'I would not eat in that museum of a house if they were stuffing peacocks for us. I half suspect he may well have an army of little boys to do just that for him.'

'That is unfair and unkind. We are Edward's friends. You saw how happy he was to see us. We should treat him to our company a while longer.'

'And get treated to a display the like of which we just witnessed, under his own roof? I think not. You stay if you want, Mouse, but Henry and I are returning forthwith.'

'Do not judge, lest ye be judged.'

'And does not the Good Book say something else about the company you keep? I for one will endeavour to choose my friends more carefully in the future. I intend to ensure that there is not a whiff of commerce about any of them.'

But Edward had only been on the other side of the carriage lowering the steps, and had heard every word. He would not press them. He knew they no longer wanted to spend one minute more in his company and he had no arguments to persuade them. Even Richard was only tempted to stay because it was not in his nature to exhibit rudeness.

He escorted his friends on foot to the town square where the London coach was about to pull out. They exchanged polite, but distant, words of farewell and he was left standing in the square feeling even more isolated and alone than he had been before their visit.

His anger finally crystallised as he struck back for the pottery. He should have been stronger in refusing their request to visit; his father should never have contrived for him to have such a poisoned chalice for his inheritance; Crossly should be denounced as a blackguard and a bully. He was seething with all the things he would say to his foreman about his conduct when he became conscious of a light step falling in beside him. He looked across. A pretty young woman was smiling at him.

'Hello, Edward.'

He scowled in return.

'Do you not remember me?' she persisted.

'I do not believe that we are acquainted.'

'You have been away too long.'

'Then that is one other thing we do not have in common because I do not feel that I have stayed away long enough.' He rammed his hat back on his head. 'And I am not in the habit of dispensing patronage on the streets to those who make free with my name so if you would be so good to leave me alone, I will bid you good day.'

He stalked away without a backward glance.

Edward strode away from the town square and headed back towards the potbank. The day had turned sour and with it, his mood. To make matters worse, it had begun to rain. Fat droplets that found their way under his collar and stained the front of his britches with damp smuts from the chimneys.

He turned into the courtyard of Houghton's to find it empty. At least something was going his way; he could not have faced the sight of any of his workers drenched and shivering as they went about their business. He ducked into the packing shed. It was dry and smelt comfortingly of straw. He picked up a handful and brushed the worst of the rain off his shoulders.

Edward was contemplating making a dash across the yard when the very person he had come to see walked in. He would have it out here and now and then send him to bring the brougham around. He was damned if he was going to risk contracting a chill by venturing outside again when there was someone else paid to do his bidding.

Crossly unbuttoned his coat and pulled out the ledger he had been sheltering. He had walked across to the first of the barrels packed with wares ready for dispatch, before he noticed Edward.

'Your father always had a fancy to do the checking, too. Reckoned more pots found their way into the miserable houses around here than on the road to London.'

Unbelievably, the man was smiling. It was a ghastly sight, his red cheeks scrunched up under his eyes and the tip of his tongue poking out between his teeth.

'And did he also like to stand by and watch you beat a boy for making a simple mistake?'

'On occasion.'

'Hell fire, man. I am not my father and you will never do it again in my presence.'

'Happen it is alright with you if I do behind your back, then?'

Edward was astounded at the man's impudence.

'We both know that my father would have had you dismissed if you had spoken to him in that fashion.'

'I never would. He was a man who commanded respect.'

'Unlike me, you mean?'

'Them's your words, not mine.'

Edward held his foreman's stare for as long as he could but eventually was forced to turn away. The hostility was too strong. God knows, he did not expect the man to like him but he did deserve the courtesy of being treated as any gentleman of his class and position should be. But Crossly – like his own father had been – was a bully and men like that only understood one thing. Edward was ashamed to realise that he was shaking. He wanted to believe that it was from the cold or anger, but it was fear that had provoked it. He was afraid of his own foreman. Or the memory of his father. Or both. Perhaps if he sought to prevent Crossly from punctuating everything with violence then he would dilute some of the power they had over him.

'This is my factory now and I will not have the people in it subject to beatings. I scare think that they work any better for the feel of a stick across their backs.'

'That is how much you know.'

'Do not be insolent. Any halfway decent foreman should be able to run this place without having to put the fear of God into those who are producing the goods that pay his wages.'

'What would you have me do? Hold their hands and dry their eyes when they drop all your profits on the floor? This is a business – though how you would understand that when you never see fit to poke your face inside these premises, I do not know.'

'Money is no excuse for downright brutality.' Edward was aware that he was shouting but he could no longer control himself. 'I am here now, and for the first time in the whole of this dismal day, I am glad that I am. I will not have my workers subject to such a degrading spectacle as being beaten in front of their companions. Damn it, man, oft times it will be some of their own children who will be looking on.'

'Your workers?' Crossly's voice was every bit as loud as Edward's and there were balls of spittle at the corners of his mouth. 'You *and* the government commissioners will have them turned into charity cases between you. I know your sort. It is your conscience that grieves you but you are willing enough to live on the money their toil brings. Close this place if it offends you so and then you can visit your erstwhile charges in the poor house. Or down the mines if you can stomach it.'

'Any change will be an improvement. They

are treated no better than animals.'

'That is because they are animals. You think you know them because they touch their caps and hold their tongues in your presence. I will show you what they are really like; the lives they lead when there is no overseer around to ensure that the worst sides of them are tempered. If you are man enough, that is?'

The challenge lay between them as impossible to skirt around as one of the fully laden barrels. Edward could not – would not – back down now. *You'll never be a real man until you face the facts of life and get your nose out of your books.* Although his father had never said that to him with anything less than a sneer and the intention of belittlement, Edward chose to interpret his words now as a challenge to be faced. He would show him. He had already exhibited more bravery in his words to Crossly than he had thought himself capable of. But to take up the gauntlet and risk the humiliation of his courage failing at the last minute? It was not as if he would be spurred on by the righteous anger that had fired him a moment ago; he did not even know if he truly believed the words that had come from his mouth. The fear of appearing a fool would have to be enough to carry him through. It was not much but it would have to do. He took a step towards Crossly. He could see the corners of the man's mouth twitch. If he so much as dares to smile...

'Happen you have some of your father's blood in you after all. Meet me in the town square at six of the clock. And do not come wearing those fancy clothes of yours; where I am taking you they will only draw the sort of attention that even I might not be able to protect you from.'

Edward glared at him for one long minute and then nodded curtly. Then he stalked past him and out into the rain.

The beginnings of a light summer shower pattered on the window of Vivien's office as she waited patiently for Stephen to regain his composure after taking him out of his trance.

'Stephen, can you remember everything you've just told me?'

'Of course.' He slipped off the couch and resumed his place in the chair opposite her. 'It felt even more real than the last time, if that's possible.'

'That in itself is interesting. It could be that your subconscious is embroidering more detail because there is something going on that you have failed to recognise. Sort of like placing clues. What about the people in that world, are there any of them that you can identify as being significant to you here and now?'

'I don't think so. I seem to know them all pretty well but I can't say that I actually know them – if that makes sense. No, wait. The young woman in the square. There was something about her. She reminds me of Hélène, my wife. Not in looks or anything but more like in her actual soul.' He gave a little embarrassed laugh. 'Now, I'm truly sounding barking.'

'Far from it. You can't be with her right now and it's inevitable that your feelings for her will crop up somewhere in the workings of your subconscious or your imagination.'

'But that's just the thing. Edward was horrible to her. Totally dismissive as if he didn't want anything to do with her. So does that mean that's how I deep down want to be towards Hélène? Because I don't. I love her too much.'

'It could be a reverse expression of your fear, Stephen.'

'That she doesn't want to know me? That I'll never be truly forgiven for the way I behaved? God, I never thought of that. Thanks a bunch for planting that little seed. Now you've gone and given me something else to worry about.'

'Obsessing about how Hélène may or may not respond to you in the future isn't going to help, Stephen. You haven't seen her for a while and it's obvious that you are experiencing some separation anxiety, but you can't possibly extrapolate from that the possibility that your worst fears will come true.'

'Mine have a horrible habit of doing just that sometimes. Don't yours?'

Vivien's fingers groped for her wedding ring. She had experienced every mother's worst nightmare but she knew that even though she bore a responsibility for what physically happened to Dmitri, she had in no way influenced on some precognitive level. However, if Stephen thought that was possible then it raised the question of just how well his ego was assimilating his recent experiences. Separation, loss, and then death was the classic Jungian triumvirate. Was it mortality – his own, or someone else's, that was at the heart of his neurosis?

'How do you feel about death, Stephen?'

'I'll admit I've thought about it more in the last few weeks than I've ever done before but I can't say that I've got any particular theories – religious or otherwise. I suppose that if I had to say something then it'd be that when you're dead, you're dead. End of story.'

Vivien was relieved at the simplicity of his answer. Even though it had been the perfect question to ask, she had been dreading that he might have said something that would've provoked an inappropriate response in her. Because although logically she shared

Stephen's rational approach to death, she couldn't package up her feelings nearly so tidily. She worked hard to switch her thoughts back to her patient and away from such dangerous ground.

'Tell me how it is going at work these days. Is it any better now you're sleeping again?'

'So, so. I'm not as tired but still can't seem to make myself concentrate. I find my thoughts wandering off all over the place and many of them are pretty grim to be honest. Pointlessness, hopelessness; that sort of thing.'

'It's a natural step in the process, Stephen. When they happen, go with them but don't dwell on them. It's inevitable that our sessions will bring up all sorts of things and make you ask questions of yourself and of life.'

Stephen nodded as if he understood and Vivien was happy to leave it there. It was probably just as well that he had no idea that things were likely to get far worse before they got better.

'One last question before we finish. You said at the beginning of the session that you knew little about history and didn't think that you could have absorbed any aspects of Edward's life through reading. But your fantasy is remarkably detailed; I'd hazard to say, too detailed, to have come simply from your imagination. Have you ever been to

Stoke on Trent?'

'Never.'

'Seen a programme on television about the potteries?'

'Not that I remember. Sport's more my thing.'

'Studied the industrial conditions of the 19th-century? Even in your schooldays? You will be amazed at how much information we can retain and how it can come back as freshly as if we were learning it all for the first time.'

'The only period I remember studying was the Enlightenment. I was never very good at history. In a strange sort of a way I've a good brain for numbers but not for dates. Told you that maybe I was wired up wrong.'

Vivien returned his smile and put down her pen. 'That's enough for now. Our time is up. I'll see you again next week, Stephen. And don't worry. We're making good progress.'

'I suppose I've no choice but to take your word for that.'

He let himself out.

CHAPTER ELEVEN

Vivien walked the hundred yards or so from her office and, leaving the tail end of the rush hour traffic behind her, entered the university library. She swiped her staff pass through the turnstile and made her way to the second floor. She knew that she should really have gone home. Home. It was hardly that anymore, just a house in Hampstead where she ate and slept and tried to find things to keep herself busily distracted through the long, lonely evenings. And things weren't much better when Jerry did manage to tear himself away from the hospital in time for them to have supper together. It they weren't eating in silence, then one or other of them would say something that would inevitably lead to a row. It was as if they were both simmering just below the surface and in each other's company couldn't help boiling over. She couldn't face that again; not tonight. Besides, she wanted to see if she could do a little research into the origins of the mysterious Edward Houghton. She would write up her notes and then search the on-line catalogue to see what books might have sourced Stephen's fantasy.

The history section had a comforting air of hushed reverence about it and wasn't too crowded at this time on a soft early-summer evening. Vivien walked past the banks of regimented study desks and found herself a cosy niche at one of the tables set back amongst the stacks of books. She seated herself with her back to the window and, as she opened her briefcase, tried not to look enviously at the young couples pouring over books together and holding hands. She opened Stephen Daunt's case file before the envy had a chance to turn into anything worse.

She sat for a while, tapping lightly on her front teeth with her pen and staring unseeing at the pages, as she thought back to their recently concluded session. To say that the turn it had taken had perplexed her was an understatement. Years of listening to patients had resulted in almost perfect recall and she hadn't missed out anything, she was sure of it. But still no new insights came to her. She decided to write up what she did know in his file.

CASE STUDY NOTES
NAME: Stephen Daunt
CONSULTATION DATE: Monday 28th May
TREATMENT SUMMARY:
The patient is curious about where his

135

fantasy under hypnosis comes from and is willing to explore further.

In this session there appeared to be some cross-over with his real life as he has incorporated his wife in the scenario in the person of a young woman. His reaction to this character was also significant; he was irritated by her presence and dismissive of her. As for the other characters, do they represent real people or are they all aspects of Stephen's own psyche? For example: Is the foreman, Archibald Crossly, his headmaster or father, or is he the part of Stephen that is critical and judgemental – and ultimately destructive?

CONCLUSIONS:
He clearly has unresolved issues with his wife. Pay careful attention to his treatment of women should they appear again in his fantasy.

The complexity of the fantasy and his thorough immersion in it suggests that Stephen's subconscious has constructed it in order to avoid some deeply-buried trauma that he is not yet ready to openly face. If there was a real Edward Houghton, maybe there was something in his past that links to Stephen's own past and present. If so, being able to pinpoint it and confront Stephen with the patterns it reveals will undoubtedly be the way to returning him to a healthy and balanced mental state once more.

FURTHER ACTION:
Continue with hypnosis. Actively encourage the patient to indulge in his fantasy. Look for any patterns of attitude and/or behaviour that emerge. Engage Stephen's rational mind when out of the hypnotic state to facilitate his active co-operation in his treatment and help him to identify and confront his issues for himself.

Vivien jumped as she felt a hand on her shoulder. It was Seb Nicholls. He pulled up a chair and bent his head conspiratorially close to hers.

'What's all this? Fat Man McFraser will have you for not handing that over. He's about to do "an overarching standardisation exercise" on all current cases, remember? So what's this, one of your little lame ducks that you couldn't bear to part with, eh?'

'Nothing of the sort,' Vivien whispered back as she closed the file. 'It's just that I'm at a crucial stage with this particular patient and – what with one thing and another – hadn't quite got around to writing up my notes.'

But that wasn't the only reason; she had no intention of giving Dr McFraser ammunition to query how she was handling the case. She was acutely aware that her lack of any satisfactory conclusions could make her look out of her depth – or even worse, incompetent – and that would undoubtedly make him reconsider her role as his natural successor. Let him continue to think that Stephen Daunt was a straightforward patient with authority issues. It would make her life in the department so much easier. Heaven knows, her life outside it was complicated enough.

'Falling behind on the job, Dr Blake. Tsk, tsk. That will never do.'

'You're a fine one to talk.' Vivien lowered her voice again as a student at the next table glared at her. 'I remember the days when you'd be dictating a whole lot of meaningless jargon to Jean in order to get your files up to date less than an hour before the departmental review was about to start.'

'Ah, but that's me. I like to take things to the wire. It's exhilarating and releases a sort of creative energy that's almost as good as sex.' He grinned. 'Almost.'

Vivien laughed. This man was incorrigible. But he also had a wealth of experience; maybe he could help her to fathom out just what was going on with Stephen Daunt.

'If you have a patient who, under hypnosis, lives a fantasy set in a 19th-century pottery town – one for which he claims to have no prior historical knowledge but somehow manages to describe an amazing amount of detail and live it intently for almost the whole length of a session, what conclusions would you draw?'

'Is that your boy here?'

Vivien nodded as Seb tapped the file.

'Well, it's a juicy one, I'll grant you that. No wonder you wanted to keep him all to yourself. I'm honoured that you're even prepared to divulge that little snippet.'

Vivien punched him lightly on the arm.

'Well,' Seb looked thoughtful for a moment, 'I'd start off by not assuming that he isn't telling me the truth.'

'I think that his subconscious is using his latent knowledge for its own ends and is keeping the source from his rational mind. So, in that sense, I don't think he's lying, if that's what you mean.'

'Not exactly. Have you considered for one moment that his memory might be genuine and that he really did lead a past life?'

Vivien started to laugh again at his teasing but one look at Seb's expression told her that he was half-serious.

'Don't tell me that you actually entertain the possibility that could occur? Come on, Seb, get real. There's no scientific evidence whatsoever of past lives. You know as well as I do that all the case studies and literature on the subject point to there being physio-logical causes for the phenomenon – either that, or the patient is deeply, deeply dis-turbed.'

'And is he?'

139

'Yes, but not in that way.'

'Then you have to entertain the unpalatable truth that maybe something is going on that you have no logical explanation for. The healing power of faith; miraculous events; reincarnation: followers of various religions all over the world adhere to the belief that such things exist and we have no way of even proving that they don't. I'm not saying that your patient was Josiah Wedgwood in a previous life, just that it might be possible.'

Jim McFraser's assessment that Seb was prone to lurid sensationalism flicked across her mind. There was no way she was going down the same – what did he call it? – "slippery slope". There was a rational scientific reason behind Stephen Daunt's fantasy life, she was sure of it.

Seb leaned in closer. 'I'll tell you what, why don't we get out of this dreary place stuffed with all the weight of irrefutable knowledge and I'll get you to unwind and unbend a little over a drink?'

'No thanks, Seb. I really should head home now.'

'It would be very instructive...'

Vivien slid the case file into her briefcase. 'Time with you always is, Dr Nicholls, and sometimes I just can't help thinking that I end up learning a little more about the weird and wonderful things in your head than is strictly good for me.'

She grinned at his expression of heart-broken rejection.

'There's someone over there who keeps giving you the eye. Why don't you ask her to go with you instead? She looks altogether more prone to your suggestive nature than me.'

Seb followed her gaze and gave an appreciative nod.

'You have excellent taste in my women, Vivien. I think I should hang out with you after work more often.'

'I don't know why I encourage you, I really don't. But you'd better get going before she drops those books she's so obviously waiting for you to offer to carry for her.'

Vivien shook her head in mock disapproval at her friend's back as he walked confidently over towards his quarry. The journey home shouldn't take long at this time of night and, if she was lucky, Jerry would already be in bed and she would be spared another confrontation; she had enough conflicting thoughts to entertain as it was.

CHAPTER TWELVE

'Okay, Stephen, you know the routine by now. Make yourself comfortable.'

Vivien waited for Stephen to get up on the couch and relax. She felt an uncomfortable mixture of anticipation and apprehension. The thoughts that Seb had planted in her mind about there being a possibility that past lives really existed had been haunting her these last few days. Seb's teasing of her intellect challenged her and her beliefs until she was on the very edge of her comfort zone and didn't know which way she was going to tip: towards his world of dangerous daring, or away from it. Either option might leave her exposed and vulnerable.

However, she knew better than anyone that a psychiatrist in possession of a closed mind was unlikely to be able to help in the way that was most needed. Patient-centred therapy; as he lived it, Edward's world felt completely real to Stephen and she would explore it with him as such. Then she would get down to some serious research; she knew that the facts she would glean would soon support her theory that his knowledge, although apparently convincing, was superficial. Of course it still wouldn't prove or disprove his assertion that he really had been there. But the time for confronting him with his delusion would come when she had some clues as to what to lay behind it; he was still too fragile to remove the safety of that façade quite yet.

Once she had taken him into his trance-like state, Stephen only needed Vivien to read out her notes of what he had said under hypnosis at the conclusion of their last session, and he was immediately Edward again...

The setting sun turned the smoke-filled sky a dirty orange as Edward and Archibald Crossly turned into the main street. A cart loaded with coal lumbered past them and Edward had to step back to avoid being splashed with mud. Not that his appearance could have been disfigured any further; he had borrowed some clothes from his groom under the pretence of going night-fishing, and felt as conspicuous as a play actor outside the stage door.

Small groups of miners returning from their shifts walked past them in tired silence. A gaggle of ragged children followed the coal cart, picking up any lumps that fell as the wheels bumped their way over the cobbles. If Edward had never enjoyed being in town during daylight hours, he liked it even less now. The very buildings they passed were cloaked in the gloom of dispirited defeat; street after street of small blackened brick houses. Edward had no idea where he was, his only reference the tops of the monstrous bottle ovens on every skyline.

'Where are you taking me?'

'Happen thou will'st find out soon enough.'

Edward wondered at his foreman's descent into the vernacular. Was it because he feared being overheard speaking above his class, or did he now consider himself Edward's teacher and therefore an equal? It was more than his rough and ill-fitting clothes that were making him feel uncomfortable.

They rounded the corner and Edward heard shouts and raucous laughter. At the end of the street, a group of men were entering what looked to be a public house. When they got closer, Edward could see that the building was shabby in the extreme; the dimly burning lamps outside picking out the scabby stucco and peeling paint on the window frames. He looked at the name set out in brown and cream tiles: The Potter's Wheel. Crossly spun him a quick glance and then walked up to the door. This must be where he was bent on giving him an education. It was one that, at this moment, Edward felt he could do without. He had never stepped over the threshold of such an establishment before and would have declined to do so now if it were not for the scorn such an act would no doubt engender in his foreman.

Drawing a deep breath, Edward followed Crossly inside. It was not only the name of the place that made Edward think of the potbank; the room was every bit as crowded with humanity as the workshops had been earlier. Benches lined the walls and round tables filled the rest of the available space. At them sat red-faced men and women, all feverish in their attempts to have a good time. The place smelt of tobacco, burning fat from the tallow candles, sour beer, and gin. Edward also detected the tang of sweat and unwashed clothes.

Crossly spoke over his shoulder. 'This here room's full of them that has their trade elsewhere. We will find none of your workers amongst them.'

'How do you know?'

'They has'na been paid yet. And no drink can be bought without brass. Happen we will sit and wait until the time comes.'

Crossly pointed Edward in the direction of an empty table just inside the door and threaded his way towards the high dark wood bar. He returned a short while later with a pottery jug of beer saying that, with a drink in front of him, Edward would look less conspicuous. Edward felt it was the last thing he wanted; a stiff shot of brandy in a chair beside his fire was the only thing he could think of that would restore his spirits right now. He was feeling awkward and out of place and more than a little foolish. Why had he agreed to come with Crossly? He had thought at the time that it was because he wanted to learn more about the lives of the people who worked for him, but he had a shameful feeling that pride was really at the heart of it: his foreman had issued him with what amounted to a challenge and he had not wanted to be seen to refuse. And now he was being made to suffer the consequences. His head was beginning to ache with the noise of harsh voices raised in drunkenness and his feet hurt in the too-tight borrowed boots.

He felt a movement at the table to his left. He looked across and smothered a gasp as he recognised Emily Smallthorne. She was dressed in a drab skirt and blouse but her face was shining with something like missionary zeal. She appeared to be handing pamphlets to anyone who would take them. Surely she was wasting her time; even if the men and women in this place could read, they were far too inebriated to do so now. Edward turned his face toward the table top and stared at his jug of beer as she made her way in his direction. He had realised that it was she who had spoken to him in the town square. He had been unforgivably rude then and he neither wanted to make his apologies in front of Crossly, nor explain to his childhood friend what he was doing sitting with his foreman in a public house.

But his disguise must have been more complete than he thought because, although now standing at his elbow, Emily did not appear to recognise him. She placed one of her pamphlets on the table with a cheery invitation for the two men to 'learn a little of the true state of affairs and unfair practices in the potbanks,' and left. Edward felt a rush of cold air as she opened the door and stepped out into the thickening evening.

He reached his hand out and pulled the pamphlet towards him. The dim light that escaped from the shade around the candle and the poor quality of the print made it difficult to read but he could see that it was a trade union discourse. He picked it up and shuffled his chair sideways to borrow a little of the glow from the oil lamp on the wall behind him. He flicked it open.

...and when asked "would you bring your son to work at the dipping-tub?", he replied, "on no account being as how I want the young 'un to live".

UNFAIR PAYMENT METHODS
And even those who escape a fate of slow poisoning by becoming moulders and throwers

147

are cheated out of a life that is rightfully theirs. They toil night and day at their trades to feed the ravenous kilns but much of their work goes unrewarded. A 72 hour week should result in £2 but many are paid not half that. This is justified under the system of GOOD FROM THE OVEN whereby they pay only for the pieces that are fired successfully. How can a man do all that is asked of him but have his wages cut for something over which he has no dominion?

RESTRICTIVE PRACTICES
As if poor health and remuneration were not enough, once with an employer, the workers must remain in their positions for a full calendar year or face imprisonment for breach of contract. A man has a right to take his labour where he will and ply his trade in safe and wholesome conditions but in the potbanks of this country...

Edward looked up to see Crossly eyeing him suspiciously. It was as if he were waiting for Edward to say something; well, he was not about to give him that satisfaction. He laid the pamphlet back on the table and took a deep draught of his beer. It did nothing to calm his thoughts but did, momentarily, re-move the necessity of returning his foreman's gaze. He banged his half-drained jug down just as Crossly snatched up the pamphlet and tore it into eight, precisely equal, pieces.

'That lass who left this arse-wipe is nowt

but a busy-body and trades unions are full of her like; do-gooders all, meddling in affairs and blathering on about the "oppression of the common man".'

Edward felt the sharp prick of memory. Jonathan had said those same words not six hours before. Half a day in which he had learned more about the burdens of being a pottery owner than he had even wanted to know. Opposite him, Crossly stirred as four men came in through the door. They were each carrying a wooden box clasped close to their chests.

'Happen it's time for the doings to start.'

Edward watched as the men handed the boxes over to the landlord behind the bar. They nodded at Crossly on their way out.

'Them's in your employ. Some of the longest serving. I have it arranged that they bring the wages here every Friday evening. We should remove ourselves to t'other room. The workers will be coming in through the back like as not, and you mun catch every second of what I brought you here to see.'

Stuffing the remnants of the pamphlet into what was left of Edward's beer; he stood up and walked away from the table, clearly expecting Edward to do likewise. They followed the curve of the bar around to a short and narrow passageway which led into a room almost an exact replica of the one they had just left. The bar counter re-emerged from behind the partitioning wall and had large pitchers of beer ranged along it. The boxes Edward had seen being handed over were now nestled beside the till. The barmaid finished topping up the last of the jugs and was then relieved by the landlord who sent her around to the front room in his stead. With a pencil tucked behind each ear and a notebook visible in his apron pocket, it looked as though he was expecting to have a busy time of it.

Edward and Crossly sat themselves down at a table in one of the dark and dingy corners and waited. In a short time the room was full; Crossly pointed out the trades of several of them to emphasise the point that they were all from Edward's factory. For himself, he would not have recognised them out of their clay-encrusted aprons with their faces washed clean of the sickly-hue of china clay and flint dust. The men were all wearing collarless shirts, jackets and caps, and the women were in cheap print dresses or skirts and unstructured blouses. They looked like unruly schoolchildren all dressed up in their Sunday best but determined to misbehave the minute their mothers' backs were turned. A couple of suspicious glances were thrown towards them but Edward could see from the way their eyes slid away from him that they took him to be a stranger. In reality, he was as good as.

The next few hours were filled with a never-ending pattern of movement. Men and women went up to the bar counter, were supplied with beer or gin, staggered to their tables, drank, and returned to the bar once more. All the time the landlord kept tally in his notebook seemingly never once confusing who was drinking what – although how he could tell the difference between them in their rush to never see the bottom of their drinking vessels, Edward was at a loss to know.

The air grew fuggier as the night pressed in against the windows. Crossly left the sanctuary of their corner occasionally to keep Edward supplied with jugs of beer. At first Edward was willing to sup to make it look as if he belonged in the company, but soon he began to enjoy the taste of it for its own sake. It made the assaults on his senses a little softer, too.

'Will you not join me in one, Crossly?' he asked as his foreman returned with a third refill of his jug.

'Nay. I am teetotal and never felt the need to lose mysen in the demon the way some folks do. Happen I have nowt in my life I mun forget.'

Despite the blur of alcohol, Edward felt the rebuke sharply. He had little he wished to obliterate from his life either – excepting maybe the experience of tonight, once it was over.

The noise in the room increased suddenly as if a switch had been thrown. Edward looked across at a table where three men and two women were vying to be heard.

'...thee dar'sna...'

'I dar's. It be summat that'll set your hair curling.'

'Happen not just that on your head.'

A wave of cackling assaulted Edward's ears.

'She were nak'd as the day she were born. Bubbies down to her waist, they were. All ripe for suckling.'

'Thou didn'a?'

'Took 'em in me hands, I did. Heavy as suet cobblers they were and as tasty as a...'

The comparison was lost in another gale of bawdy laughter. Edward was no prude. He had heard worse stories in his student days but that had been in male company and not screamed out across a room in a fit of drunken excess.

A steady stream of men and women left and returned by the back door. Edward thought it was probably to relieve themselves – he dreaded to think in what conditions – and he saw a woman, dressed for the night with a shawl over her head, enter the room. Her face was pale and un-blurred by drink. She stood still for a moment in the chaos surrounding her and then pushed her way towards a group of men sitting three tables away from Edward.

'What's thou doing 'ere, my chuck?' He heard one of them ask, his voice sodden with sentiment. 'Can'a wait 'til I gets home for a bit of t'other? Don'a worry. I'll be giving thee a right seeing to afore the night is out.'

Edward cringed at the look of abject embarrassment on the woman's face. She seemed to shrink inside her clothes momentarily before pulling up some reserve of courage.

'Come back to the house now. I can'a have thou throwing a week's brass away on gin. The young'uns need feeding and I've nowt left to buy even tatties and a scrap of bacon with.'

'A wife mun manage on what's she's given and not ask for more.'

The woman stood in silence while her husband tossed another glass of spirits down his throat. A trickle escaped from the corner of his mouth.

'I'm asking nicely, John. Come home with me.'

But that last drink seemed to be the one too many. The man's burly arm shot out and he slapped his wife's face hard with the back of his hand. The sound rang in Edward's ears but no one else in the room seemed to notice. He made to stand up and confront

153

the bully but Crossly caught hold of his sleeve.

'Leave it. It is nowt that she would'na taken afore and the men will have thee for meddling in their doings. There's not one of them in the mood for a showing up from their master and that one with the fists is as hard as brazzle – and I'll not be standing in his road.'

Edward reluctantly saw the wisdom of his foreman's words. He drank down the rest of his beer in the hope that it would help him swallow the double humiliation of being powerless to defend a helpless woman, and having to bow to the advice of such a man as Crossly. He held his empty jug out. He could give a silent order for another drink at least.

He watched as the woman, head unbowed but tears streaking the red of her flaming cheeks, left. The drunken exchanges were continuing at the table as if nothing had happened. Edward waited impatiently for Crossly to return with his beer. When he looked back from the bar to the table, he saw that another woman had now insinuated herself amongst the men. She was sitting beside the husband, seemingly content to have his heavy arm lying across her shoulder. She leaned forward to share a joke or remark and Edward watched as the man's stubby fingers fumbled with the top two buttons of her blouse. He slid his hand down her throat until it was burrowing under the loose material. She pressed herself against the drunken brute, seemingly to allow him to get a better purchase on her breast.

Edward felt a frisson of shocked recognition when she bent her head back in unfocused pleasure: it was the young woman from the afternoon who had rescued her son from Crossly's savage beating. He had thought her brave and noble and beautiful then but now she looked like nothing more than a whore in the worst of bawdy-houses, her hair tumbling out of her bun and her flushed features swollen with sexual longing.

Edward felt that he had seen as much as he could take. Crossly had made his point; he had no real idea of what these people's lives were like. It was late – he had heard the church clock strike midnight some time back and, although he was sure sleep would not come easily to him, he wanted to be in his bed at the Manor.

He stood up and the world spun a little. He grasped hold of the edge of the table for support. Out of the corner of his eye he could fuzzily see Archibald Crossly returning with his beer and looking at him with what could have been pity. But it was probably disdain. The man seemed to feel little else for any of his fellow human beings.

'I wish to leave now.' Edward's tongue felt thick in his mouth. 'Where does that door lead?'

'To the courtyard. Quicker that way than through the front. Happen I'll settle your tab then follow you on.'

Belatedly Edward wondered if he should have offered Crossly money; it did not seem quite respectable to have his foreman pay for his drinks but then he thought that he was here on Crossly's invitation, and therefore he should foot the bill. The experience was never going to be repeated but perhaps he could make his repayment some other way. Edward felt the repugnant touch of a few women's hands as he pushed his way past the tables towards the door. A man slapped him heartily on the back and tried to engage him in conversation. Edward did not waste any energy in thinking he was being discourteous and twisted away from him. Into the arms of a slattern who appeared to have put herself in his path deliberately. This was turning into a journey through hell. He felt nimble fingers reaching under the skirts of his jacket; for his crotch or his money-pouch? He felt his stomach lurch at the prospect of either.

The air of the courtyard was hardly a relief. The kilns were still firing and the smoke was thick and heavy under the blanket of night. As his eyes adjusted to the darkness he became aware of the smudgy glow of lanterns – held at head height – in the far reaches of the quadrangle. His ears felt blocked by the intensity and pitch of the past few hours, but he could just hear a low muttering. His near brush with robbery made him reluctant to pass by but there was no other way to leave the premises – he was not going back in that den of iniquity and out through the front for anything. He edged around the wall until he was close enough to bolt for it should the need arise.

Five, or maybe six, men stood in a circle, excitement radiating off them like heat from a furnace. In the middle, Edward could see the grotesque forms of two dogs, their jaws clamped around each others throats. There was a growl and a strangled yelp and the bigger of the two began to flail the body of the other around as life, and blood, drained out and onto the cobbles. The baying of encouragement this drew from the spectators was enough to make Edward feel that, at any moment, he might lose all that he had drunk throughout the evening.

A firm hand grasped his elbow and all but pulled him through the archway. Once on the street, Archibald Crossly released him so abruptly that Edward nearly fell. Everything was reeling.

'Why in heaven's name do they behave like that?' he said for something to say.

'Fighting curs reminds them of their daily lives and makes them glad it's not them.'

'I did not means that alone. Why do they drink so much and why do you have their wages placed behind the bar? Surely it would be better for them to be paid in the factory and take the money home with them?'

'This be the way they want it. They requested it of me when I was first overseer. Saves them wearing through their pockets as they will spend all they have in The Potter's Wheel anyway. Happen many in there'll not see their young'uns or the outside of them walls or a bite of food neither afore Monday night.'

'Hell's teeth, man. I had no idea. To think that I was feeling they were treated harshly in the pottery when they put themselves through worse on their own accord. I have not one ounce of respect for anyone who can disport themselves in such an ungodly and inhuman manner. I am beginning to have an inkling that maybe the philosophers are right and there is no helping those who choose to steep themselves in depravity.'

He was lost in miserable thought for a moment before becoming aware that Crossly was asking him if he required a carriage fetched.

'On no account. I have learned many sobering lessons tonight and would wish my

158

head cleared to a similar degree by the walk. I will bid you goodnight.'

Crossly returned the farewell and then strode off down the street. Edward stood for a moment to get his bearings before striking off in the direction he thought the river lay. If he could follow the Trent around then he knew he would reach the outskirts of the town, and eventually the Manor. Never had he wanted to put so much distance between himself and a place in all his life.

CHAPTER THIRTEEN

The university cafeteria was buzzing with students gossiping and expending the energy they had contained during a whole morning of lectures. Vivien joined the queue at the food counter and spent an awful lot longer than she should choosing between a fat wedge of chocolate cake and a bowl of fruit salad to go with her sandwich. She paid absent-mindedly and had to go back to the till to collect her change. The last few days had been ridiculously busy and her mind was whirling with all the things she had to do before the end of the week. Thank God for an hour's peace.

She smiled at a few of her colleagues but

declined their invitation to join their table and moved on to an empty one. She knew that she was isolating herself deliberately and that one day, if she wasn't careful, people would stop making the effort, but she just couldn't relax with them anymore. Every conversation was always peppered with news of other people's families and how their children were doing at school or what their plans for the forthcoming summer holidays were. Or, even worse, the holes where those topics should naturally have been were filled with inconsequential details of departmental life or a dissection of last night's television programmes. Underneath it all Vivien could always hear the sound of the eggshells crushing.

You're too sensitive by half; it's the shoots that poke themselves above the snow that grow the strongest.

'Yes, mother,' Vivien muttered under her breath just as she caught sight of Seb fast approaching.

'Talking to yourself? Not even the first sign of madness.'

'No, Seb, talking to you is.'

Her friend made an unnecessary is-this-chair-free? gesture.

'Take your pick,' Vivien invited.

Seb slid his tray beside hers and sat down.

'Where've you been the past week? I've been looking everywhere. Been all agog to know how that lame duck of yours is getting on.'

'Don't call him that; he's a patient.'

'Well you haven't told me his name and I have to call him something, don't I?'

'I'm bound by patient confidentiality, as you well know.'

'Bet you're telling all to Fat Man McFraser though.'

'As it happens, we decided to dispense with the supervisory sessions and that I'd speak to him again when I've reached my conclusions.'

'And when precisely will that be? Will I have sprouted a bowtie and be looking forward to pruning my roses by then?'

'Don't be ridiculous. Even if I was making any progress – and I'm not saying I'm not – it's none of your business.'

'I thought there were no secrets between fellow psychiatrists.'

'But you're not a practicing one any longer and I can't discuss my cases with you.'

'Maybe not but there's no harm in us talking about someone who's no longer in the land of the living is there? Do tell me that you've given in to your insatiable curiosity and dug around a little into the prologue of this little story of yours?'

'I have managed to do a little research, yes.'

'And...?'

161

'Why are you so interested?'

'Because everyone else around here is so boring and I rely on you to liven up my dull life.'

Vivien couldn't resist a smile. Every moment of Seb's existence was anything but dull.

'So, was he real or not?'

Vivien felt herself blush. Her thoughts had strayed so far from those of a psychiatrist exploring a professional dilemma.

'In fact, he was. A Mr Houghton lived at exactly the time my patient said he did.'

'Well that's pretty good evidence for them being one and the same person.'

'It proves nothing of the sort. If I'm going to tell you about this then you've got to drop this past lives nonsense and just listen.'

Seb raised his finger and crossed his heart.

'I phoned a potteries museum in Stoke. The curator told me that there was a family called Houghton who made ceramic ware in the middle of the 19th-century but – and this is where it gets interesting – the man who ran the pottery after his father's death was Matthew Houghton, not Edward.'

'Curiouser and curiouser. So, my dear Watson, if your patient was merely regurgitating the facts of the matter that he had picked up from some book or whatever then you'd think he'd at least get the name right, wouldn't you?'

'Seb, you promised...'

'But you have to admit that it does muddy the water a bit.'

'Not necessarily. Stephen could've taken a shine to the name Edward Houghton and is using it for a cipher; a blank canvas that his subconscious has invented to be a repository for everything uncomfortable and challenging that can't be handled directly. Not dissimilar to a child imagining a monster after he or she has been shouted at by a parent.'

'Okay, that's one explanation. But his Edward Houghton being real is another one. Why don't you go up and pay a visit to the museum; trawl through the archives and the like and find out for sure? Look, it just so happens that I'm going up that way Saturday fortnight on this never-ending book tour they've shackled me to. I could give you a lift if you like.'

Vivien was reminded, yet again, of just why she liked this man so much. Not only was he amusing company and took her mind off her increasingly difficult home life, but he was sensitive too. He knew that she wouldn't want to get in a car and drive all that way so soon after the accident. However, it was not going to be something she was going to take him up on.

'It's kind of you to offer, Seb, and I really appreciate it but there's no way I'm going on a field trip with you. I know your reputation with lone females remember – even if I am a bit older and an awful lot wiser than the ones you usually entice to go off somewhere with you. Besides, I'm not altogether happy about spending any more time on this fantasy world of my patient's. It's dangerously close to collusion. My best hope of unravelling whatever it is that's behind all this is to remain a dispassionate, and clinical, observer.'

'Have it your own way but you're missing the chance of a lifetime to progress things, you know.' Seb gave her a wink. 'Are you going to eat that cake...?'

The week after half-term, back once more in the refuge of a world that consisted of boundaries that she could understand, Vivien led Stephen Daunt through the usual stages of progression into deep hypnosis. She had been looking forward to their session together all through the break. It wasn't just that it had given her something to focus on as she'd drifted through the long evenings while Jerry was still at the hospital; it was also that, for the first time, she was beginning to feel as if she had some tools with which to affect a breakthrough. She could use the information she'd gained into the Houghton family background to highlight any inconsistencies in Stephen's fantasy world, thereby engaging

164

his rational mind to look under the fiction to the deeper truth that his subconscious was endeavouring to conceal. He trusted her to hypnotise him but she had to encourage him to stop hiding behind the fiction and to believe that, once it was demolished, she could help him to reconstruct the truth.

'Stephen, can you remember where we were the last time?'

A small shudder rippled through his body.

'I know this is difficult but I want you to take yourself back to that same place.'

'I can't.'

'Just relax and breathe deeply. Let your mind wander.'

'I don't want to.'

This was the first time he had attempted to resist her under hypnosis. What was it that he was expecting to happen? Did he, in fact, know what was going to happen? The disquieting thought that he was not simply making all this up as he went along entered her mind but she let it go. She should never have discussed any of this with Seb. He could afford to indulge in non-scientific speculation but she couldn't. She had a patient to treat.

'Stephen, Edward Houghton has a story to tell and he needs to tell it through you.'

It was a risky strategy but maybe a direct appeal to Stephen's subconscious persona would encourage Stephen to let go and face his fears. She looked at her notes.

'You went to The Potter's Wheel with Crossly and then you went home. What happened next, Stephen? Can you pick it up from there and tell me what happened next?'...

CHAPTER FOURTEEN

The air inside St Margaret's church was thick with the smells of incense and beeswax candles. Edward fidgeted; the Houghton family pew was narrow and he was forced to sit unnaturally upright with hardly enough room for his knees. He felt on show, too. A full congregation sat behind him. He could hear their coughs and splutters. A baby started crying; its wails of distress bouncing off the stone walls and arches and making it sound as if every child in the place was joining in out of sympathy. Just when it seemed as if the baby must be turning blue from lack of breath, the mother shuffled noisily out of her pew and carried the squalling infant down the aisle. Edward only vaguely registered the resumption of relative hush; he mind was not really on his surroundings, the events of Friday night were still too fresh and had taken on the qualities of a waking nightmare as he had replayed them over and over again.

He cast his gaze to the light coming in from the large window to his right in an effort to remain in the present. It depicted St George and the Dragon and splashed jewels of red and green and yellow on the stone flags of the aisle. His eyes settled on the bright lozenge from the saint's halo and he wondered just what it took for a man to confront his demons, and win. *Cowards die many times before their deaths.* 'Thank you, father,' Edward muttered. The minister's voice cut through his reverie:

'Do not store up for yourself treasures on earth, where moth and rust destroy, and where thieves break in and steal. But store up for yourselves treasures in heaven, where moth and rust do not destroy, and where thieves do not break in and steal. For where your treasure is, there your heart will be also.'

It was a timely reminder. But at this moment, Edward felt he had no treasures anywhere. True, he had the Manor but it came with the pottery. And with the pottery came the men and women – and children – who worked in it. He wondered if they were to be his demons: his dragon. He could not seem to get them out of his mind and he could not reconcile his thoughts about them either. On the one hand they were low lives and drunkards and scoundrels – he had seen them with his own eyes indulging in lechery and dog fighting and he was now more convinced that ever that they had tried to pick his pockets – but on the other, they were people in his charge; his responsibility. They worked hard for little money in dreadful conditions and had no prospects, no better future to look forward to. They personified all the arguments he had indulged in with his friends about the oppression of the working classes and how they had to bear the fortunes of the rich on their backs. But they would never have the luxury of being free to debate the rights and wrongs of a system that left them with next to nothing but a long, hard grind day after day: it was their lot to have to live it. If, God forbid, he were ever to find himself in their situation, could he truly say that he would be able to rise up above it all and lead an exemplary life?

Edward rose from his knees after the last prayer and, hat in hand, walked out of the church. He paused at the door to thank the minister for an edifying sermon, and then wandered down the path and into the churchyard. It was a fine sunny day and he was loath to return to the Manor just yet. He stepped into the dark shade of a yew tree and wondered at the rows of tidy headstones; a neatness in death that was never quite replicated in life. Here people were reduced to mere names and dates with no clue as to how they had spent their time on this earth, how they had acquitted themselves. Had they been drunkards or wife-beaters, saints, or just quiet law-abiding people? He wished with all his heart that the living were as easy to categorise as the dead.

His meanderings led him to the section of the graveyard where the Houghton family had their final resting place. The headstones were, not surprisingly, more elaborate than the ones he had been musing over. Urns, lilies, and angels were carved into the dark granite and the words and numbers were saved from weathering by being inset with slivers of lead. Obadiah; Joseph; Nathaniel; Clear. Amelia, his mother and, next to her, the relatively recent mounds under which his father and brother lay. There was a space just this side of the oak tree where he knew he would be buried when his time came. There was something both comforting and terrifying about the inevitability of it all.

'The rich can ever stake the best position from which to await the afterlife. Not like the wooden crosses of the poor that rot almost as quickly as their flesh.'

Edward turned around. Emily Smallthorne was not three feet behind him. She was dressed in a black skirt and jacket, a severe bonnet framing her face. She was not smiling.

'It is hardly their fault,' Edward felt obliged to defend his lineage, 'or mine. I did not ask to be born a Houghton.'

'No, but you do not have to behave as one. Those families buried one on top of the other for lack of space did not ask for the lives and deaths they had to endure, either.'

'I can hardly be blamed for that, either. You appear determined to lay all the ills of this world and the next at my door.'

He heard her sniff.

'What did you think of the sermon?' he asked when the silence between them became too oppressive.

'It was more appropriate for some in the congregation than others.' Emily looked him straight in the eye. 'There were many there who will never experience the temptation of setting too much store by earthly treasures; they will be lucky if they ever have enough to stave off hunger. I wonder sometimes if the minister even realises who it is he is preaching to. But at least I have an opportunity to redress his thoughtlessness in Sunday School. I will not have the children feeling guilty for the little they have.'

'But that was surely not the minister's intention?'

'No, it was not, but the result will be the same. The more pious amongst my class will go home and tell their parents that they will be damned to the fires of hell if they do not renounce all that they have. Children have a way of seeing things very simply – and clearly.'

Edward knew that he lacked that talent because Emily's words had now served to confuse him further. Surely the pathetic wretches that haunted the hovels of the town could not possibly follow such a refined logic of thought? He wondered if the boys who bore the brunt of Crossly's harsh treatment burned with religious fervour and righteousness when they were being beaten and, if so, if it made it any easier to endure? He tried to focus again on the woman in front of him.

'Why do you not hold Sunday School during the service? I remember that is what happened when we were young, is it no longer normal practice?'

'There are two classes. My friend takes the one we used to attend and I conduct the one for the children of the pottery workers. They have chores to do or baby brothers and sisters to mind while their parents are at church.'

Edward remembered Crossly's words and thought of how many children were having to spend their Sunday in domestic labour because their parents were still carousing in The Potter's Wheel.

'So I wait until the adults have time to

return home and then start the class. Even then there are few attendees; the poor souls are too tired or occupied to spend an hour listening to me trying to help them see that there is some good and hope in this world.'

'I will hold you up no further then.' Edward was not enjoying their encounter and saw no sense in prolonging it. He raised his hat. 'Good day, Miss Smallthorne,' he gave a little bow, 'I am sure our paths will cross again.'

'It may well be sooner than you think, Mr Houghton,' Emily said, 'there is much that we have to talk about and you are right in thinking that a churchyard is not an appropriate place for discussion. If I may, I will call on you at the Manor presently. Due to our mothers' friendship, I was always made most welcome there in the past and I trust that you will see no reason to discontinue that tradition.'

'By no means. Come whenever you like. I will look forward to it.'

Emily turned and walked away and Edward was left with a vague uneasiness as to whether he had been telling the truth or not. He and Emily Smallthorne had spent many happy hours of their childhood together but he got the impression that she would not be so easy company these days. However, that aside, he had been growing tired of his own company of late and with so little other society of any kind at his disposal, he would instruct Horwood that he was always *in* to Miss Smallthorne. He hoped he would not regret it.

CHAPTER FIFTEEN

It was three days before Emily made good her promise and paid her visit to Houghton Manor. Edward asked Horwood to show her into the library; it was more intimate than the drawing room and he felt, amongst the books, showed him off to his best advantage. He wanted to appear intelligent and thoughtful – he was sure he had displayed neither of those things during their previous meetings. He did not know why her good opinion should matter so much, but it did. Maybe it was because he wanted her to see that he had changed from the rather impulsive and shallow boy who had enjoyed splashing her with muddy puddles, into a scholar and, he hoped, a gentleman.

He was sitting at the writing desk pretending to be studying when she entered the room. He made a show of marking his place in the fat law book open in front of him, and then stood up and turned to greet her. She was dressed altogether differently from the last time they had met. Gone was the unflattering Sunday black; instead she wore a light and fresh gown decorated with springs of flowers, and a white bonnet tied with ribbon; a matching shawl over her arm. She looked like a breath of springtime in the somewhat gloomy room. In their recent encounters he had neglected to notice what a trim figure she had. He was disconcerted to find that he found her most becoming; it was so at odds with his father's strictures about governesses and schoolteachers: *Few men are admired by their inferiors; and the feeling is entirely mutual.*

'I had a very pleasant walk up from the town and through your lovely grounds,' she said by way of greeting, 'that tree we used to climb is now quite a magnificent specimen.'

Edward was absurdly delighted by her lack of need to engage in all the polite formalities of conversation; he was glad that she felt no need to stand on ceremony with him in his own home. He offered to take her bonnet and shawl from her and could not help but breathe in her soft scent as she handed them over. He laid them on top of his open books and invited her to sit.

'It so happens that I was showing it to my friends just the other day when they paid me a visit.'

He was surprised that he was able to make it sound as if it had been such a carefree

174

occasion. 'They could hardly believe that I could once reach the bottom branches.'

'But even then you had to beg me to give you a leg up.' Emily laughed. A delicious tinkling sound that made Edward think of a flowing stream.

'I hope you did not tell your mother that you used to do that. She would never forgive me for encouraging you to behave in such an unladylike manner.'

'I scarcely think that I was ever a young lady.' She laughed again.

'And how is your mother?'

Emily's brow creased. 'Her health has deteriorated greatly over the years. There is little that she can do for herself now. She is the reason that I am still here.'

'I am sorry to hear that. It must be unpalatable for such a spirit as yours to be shackled to this miserable town.'

'I cannot for the life of me understand why you speak of it so. Although I know that it is now a place tinged with tragedy for you. I have not had the opportunity to tell you how sorry I was to hear about your father and brother. To lose your last remaining family in such quick succession must be truly terrible.'

'It is not their passing I mourn so much as the burden of responsibility they have left me with.'

He saw the look on her face and immediately regretted being so free with the truth. How could he explain that after his mother had died, theirs had been a hollow sham of a family – despite his father's attempt to keep up appearances? It would be better not to risk sounding even more callous.

'It is not so bad here really,' Emily was saying, 'and, besides, there are not as many opportunities for us women to venture out and see the world as there are for you men. But I would have enjoyed spending a while in London. What is it like?'

'Busy. Noisy. Exciting. A round of dances and dinners and parties if you are that way inclined.'

An image came unbidden to him of Emily sitting beside him in an evening gown, her soft skin glowing in the candlelight. He leaned forward in his chair as an idea gripped him. 'Why not come down and stay for a visit? There is an elderly couple I know – friends of my father's – who take me under their wing whenever they feel I am studying too hard and need to get out a little and see life. They have a large house and I am sure they would make you most welcome. I could write to them today if you wish.'

'It is very kind of you to issue such an invitation on their behalf but we both have our commitments here. I have my mother and the Sunday School, and you have a pottery business to run.'

Edward's enthusiasm was suddenly as squashed as if one of the bottle ovens had fallen on him. Was every aspect of his life to be blighted by that place? He would not let it be.

'My foreman, Crossly, can run the potbank well enough. I am not needed on hand every day. Besides, once I have seen that the books and orders are as they should be, I am intending to return to London and pick up my studies again.'

'But I feel that is where you are wrong.'

'Why? I have kept my tutor abreast of my situation and he is willing to retain a place for me.'

'No, not about that; about the pottery. From what I have heard about Archibald Crossly, he is the worst possible man to be in charge of the place. You must stay and see that he changes his ways.'

Edward sat back and stared at his visitor. They had grown up together, but apart in adulthood, and she was being more than a little presumptuous to tell him how he should be conducting his affairs. He began to feel the same prickling of resentment his father had provoked in him when he had lectured him about his errant ways. This visit was not turning out to be nearly as pleasant as he had hoped.

'My time is my own and I will do with it as

I please. I am sorry that it does not appear to meet with your approval.'

Emily sat back and looked at him for a long moment, her face pale in her seriousness.

'You are wilfully choosing to misconstrue me, Edward. I never said any such thing. But the truth is – whether you like it or not – that you are no longer a man free to follow the dictates of his own desires and fancies. There are other people who depend on you.'

'Do I not know that? Every day it seems there is someone at my door beseeching me for money or patronage. Just because I have this house and a little wealth to my name does not mean that I can be expected to be tied down so thoroughly by those who cannot – or will not – make the effort to take care of their own needs.'

'But you can be expected to be present for the visit of the government commissioner. It is nothing less than your duty.'

'Duty? You go too far in speaking to me of my duty. Is it not enough that I have to be buried alive in this place because of it? My father lived and died by the tenets of duty and now I am wrapped so thoroughly in it that I no longer know what it is to breathe without its weight.'

'You become free of duty by discharging it, Edward. I cannot believe that you have studied law for so long without realising that.'

The air between them had grown frosty

and the space between their chairs, which had almost felt indecently close to him, now assumed the proportions of a chasm. Emily had two high points of colour on her cheeks. The sight was not displeasing to him; it highlighted the contours of her face.

'Were you really intending to be absent for such an important visit?'

'I ... I ... confess that it might have slipped my mind...'

She had a way with her that always seemed to force him back onto the wrong foot. He could not tell her that he left all such matters to his foreman or he would look even more irresponsible and lay himself open to further charges of neglect of duty. As would any pottery owner who was ignorant of a forthcoming inspection with regard to working practices and the law.

'He wrote to me too, you see,' Emily continued, 'he has a particular interest in the provision of education in the pottery towns. Did you know that three-quarters of the people who work in the potbanks can neither read nor write? Imagine what that must mean; a whole world of knowledge and opportunity lost to them forever. But it is not too late for the children. If we can somehow get them to labour fewer hours then they would have more time to attend school and a whole new generation would grow up with the ability to better themselves and not be condemned to work at a job just because their mothers or fathers secured it for them. They would at last be free to choose their own path in life.'

Edward looked into Emily's eyes and saw the same visionary light in them that he had glimpsed that night in The Potter's Wheel. It disturbed him. But so did the thought that the boys and girls he had seen on that terrible visit to the pottery might, in time, be disporting themselves in the same way as their dissolute parents.

'We can work on this together, Edward. Do you not see? Between us we can change these children's lives forever. You can ensure that they are no longer exploited in harsh conditions for too little pay, and I can expand my work with the Sunday School and set about teaching them properly instead of merely giving them respite to sit and just be children again without the toil and responsibilities of being a pottery worker on their shoulders.'

A picture flashed into Edward's mind: a brightly lit classroom with rows of desks and, sitting at them, well-fed and alert children; their faces clean and without the pinched pallor of the potbanks. Their eyes are all turned towards Emily Smallthorne who is standing at the front and reading to them from a book that he, Edward Houghton, has donated.

It was a heartening image but he let it slip away. Emily was expecting too much; the patterns of people's lives were not changed so easily.

'I think you have too high hopes.'

'Nonsense. You and I, with the commissioner's help, have the power to change things. We have the duty to change things.'

'Whenever you wish to provoke me, you come back to duty. In your eyes it is so clear but let me tell you that part of the responsibility I bear is the knowledge that things are not that simple. If I have any duty at all then it is to keep the pottery profitable. If I reduce the children's hours, or give their jobs to adults with their greater rates of pay, then we will not be competitive in the town and I will have no choice but to abandon the business. Livelihoods may not be much now but they will be nothing then.'

It was a simplistic argument but it would have to satisfy her. He knew that if he spent the time and trouble to learn something of his labour costs and the efficiency of some of the processes and working practices, then he could probably afford to allow the younger of the children an hour or two a day to study... But in order to do the calculations, he would have to study the workings of his factory – and in the company of Crossly. He did not see why he should undertake either activity.

'And now you sound like your father.'

Edward bristled at the accusation. Now she really was going too far. He stood up and turned his back to her in an effort to squash the anger that threatened to erupt into words that he knew he would regret; Emily might be overstepping the bounds of friendship but she was the only one left in the town who he felt could even lay claim to be in that category.

He turned back to face her again. 'My father and I had little in common before his death, and nothing now.'

'That is where I think you are wrong, Edward. I see at least one similarity: the inclination to do nothing because it is easier not to.'

Edward looked down at the floor as the harshness of the truth drew a flush to his cheeks.

'Because it is not just the education of the children that needs addressing. All your workers have to endure insufferable conditions. You have visited the potbank, have you not? Seen how they have to live – day in, day out – with your own eyes?'

Edward gave a weak nod.

'Then how can you not grasp the opportunity that is being presented to you to make improvements? Profits are not the most important thing at stake here. People's lives are. Not only do your workers have to breathe in the clay and flint dusts that will claw at their lungs, they have to swallow more if it when they eat their midday meals in that shed next to the moulding room. The workers in the kilns suffer from such extremes of temperature that their hearts are weakened and they are forever struck down with fevers; the women in the decorating shop work with pigments as bright as jewels but as deadly as poison; the dippers suck in lead through their skin until their wrists go weak and they are slowly overtaken by paralysis and can hold a cup or a jug no longer – some are even affected to such a degree that they go insane. Asthma and consumption are rife. Your workers are four times as likely to die from bronchitis as those in other trades. Women miscarry or have stillbirths. There is a greater incidence of...'

'Stop!' Edward's voice bounced off the wooden shelves surrounding him. 'I have listened to more than enough. I am not so well-versed in these matters – not seeking the company of the trades unions as I know you do – but am thoroughly aware of some facts of my own. I have witnessed them and they leave me at a loss to understand why, when everyone is so concerned about the health and welfare of the working people, they are allowed – no, encouraged – to spend their weekends rotting their insides with cheap gin and poor beer.'

Emily looked at him with a pitying, but tolerant, smile and Edward almost felt ashamed at his outburst.

'You have to understand,' she said softly as if she were addressing her Sunday School class, 'that for many of them, hours – and sometimes days – lost in the deadening embrace of alcohol is the only freedom they will ever have from a life of drudgery. It is not the best escape, I know, but sometimes it is the only one on offer. Besides, believe it or not, the Corn Laws have made bread so expensive that gin and beer are the only sustenance some of them can afford.'

Edward's stab of shame was real now. Isolated in his comfortable Manor, he had not realised that life was such a constant struggle for so many. But he was acutely aware that if he agreed to her request then it would not be because he cared about the fate of the workers. He would only be doing so to please her. In the same way that he had put a stop to Crossly's beatings merely to undermine him and not to save the skin on some poor boy's back. He was a marionette having his strings pulled by others with no viable will of his own. An emasculating pattern that had been established at the hands of his father and was continuing even after his death. But he did have a conscience: that was his, at least.

'When did you say this government commissioner was due?'

'In two days time. He is coming to me and then plans to visit the potbank. Please say you will be there to meet him, Edward. Listen to what he has to say and let him guide you in making the changes that you know in your heart you must. You owe it to yourself as well as your workers.'

She stood up, retrieved her bonnet and shawl from the writing desk, and held out her hand. Edward shook it briefly.

'I will think about it.'

Emily's smile was deep and open and he sensed an air of victory about her.

'But I am making no promises,' he said as he escorted her to the door.

'I know, Edward,' she said sweetly, 'but I also know that my visit has not been wasted. You will do what is right or you are not the young boy I once knew.'

Edward saw her out of the front door himself and, as he raised his hand in farewell, he wondered just what that young boy had done to be placed in his current dilemma.

CHAPTER SIXTEEN

Edward sat in what had been his father's office. He had not been in it for more years than he cared to remember. Little had changed. The large desk inlaid with ink-stained green leather still dominated the room and the muted-coloured globe that he had loved to spin as a boy was in its place on the stand by the door. A cabinet containing examples of the pottery's finest wares stood against one wall and beside it, two shelves on which were ranged pieces from some of their more illustrious competitors: Wedgwood, Davenport, Spode, Minton. The only things that were missing were the heavy leather-bound ledgers that used to sit in a teetering pile on the corner of the desk. Edward knew that Crossly had them now in his office at the factory. From out of the window he could just see the workshop roofs and of course the bottle ovens; always the bottle ovens.

Edward flicked his attention back to the man sitting opposite him. Mr Wharburton, the government commissioner, was already tall but his long black coat and stovepipe top-hat made him look as if it only had to unfurl himself a little more to touch the ceiling. He had grey whiskers and a face so cadaverous that he appeared to be already halfway into his grave. But beneath his thick eyebrows, his gaze was kind and patient and as alive as that of a man a quarter his age. He removed his hat then crossed his long legs and banged his knee against the desk front. He grimaced.

'An occupational hazard in my line of work. You would think I would know better having been a servant of the State all those years but I can never get used to not having quite enough space. Now, where were we?'

'I was telling you that these are my warehouses and the factory is not one hundred yards from here. Would you like to go and see it now?'

'Nay, lad. I am in no hurry. It is pleasant just to sit here and talk awhile. There will be plenty of time for inspections later. I like to get to know the proprietor first; it helps me to judge exactly what I am working with and, having met you, I get the feeling that you and I will rub along very nicely together.'

Edward let down his guard a little. Here at least was someone who did not regard him as an ogre for the mere fact of owning a pottery. Unlike his erstwhile friends. Not that he felt as if he really owned it anyway, more had it foisted upon him. And how could a person be blamed for the circumstances of their birth? It was hardly as if any of them could do anything to change it.

There was a perfunctory knock on the door and Archibald Crossly breezed in. He was dressed in rough serge jacket and trousers and had obviously hurried around from his duties at the potbank. He carried a piece of paper in his hand and was staring at it intently.

'Seeing as you are here I thought I would ask your say-so to go ahead with this order.'

'Not now, can you not see I am busy?'

Crossly looked up for the first time. 'It can'a wait. I mun see to it afore we load the next kiln.'

Edward felt a flash of irritation. His foreman had seen he was not alone and had lapsed into dialect purely to impress – or intimidate – his visitor. He began to wonder just how much manipulation his foreman engaged in. He remembered back to the last time he had heard Crossly speaking like this. The dreadful scenes he had witnessed in The Potter's Wheel had been real enough but had he contrived to take him there on the very same evening that he knew Miss Smallthorne had been handing out her leaflets in order to somehow alienate him thoroughly from his old associates? Although he pretended not to have recognised her, Crossly knew well enough who she was; he was sure of it. Edward fired a glance at the portrait of his father hanging over the fireplace. Between them, the old man and the foreman were doing their best to bind him to the pottery for life.

He became aware that Crossly had thrust the piece of paper he was holding in front of him. Did he expect him to deal with it there and then just because it was demanded of him? Well he would not. He would not be dictated to in his own place of business.

'Leave it. I will let you know my decision when I come down to the factory; need I remind you that we are being paid a visit by a government commissioner today? Or had it slipped your mind; as it has appeared to escape your notice that you should have drawn my attention to it in the first place?'

He glanced across at his visitor and received a nod of understanding in return.

'Mr Wharburton,' Edward said after a silence in which he felt his point was well made, 'this is Archibald Crossly, my foreman.'

'Pleased to meet you.'

'Happen. I hasn'a time to show you around now.'

The man was really doing his damnedest to be obnoxious.

'That will not be necessary, Crossly, I will conduct Mr Wharburton around the works myself.'

Edward pretended not to notice his

foreman's look of surprise.

'Now leave us. And I want no further interruptions.'

Crossly's face flushed an ugly magenta and he stalked out of the room. The window panes in the door rattled as he all but slammed it shut.

Edward realised he had been holding his breath. He let it out under the disguise of a cough; it would not do to let the man opposite see how easily he was intimidated.

'I am sorry about that,' he said, 'he can be a surly man at the best of times and resents all interference in what he considers his domain.'

'Think nothing of it. I am only too well aware of the difficulties of finding the perfect employees; you want someone who knows their job but if they have the wrong attitude then people assume that it is a reflection of the owner.'

'And that is the least of the many unjust accusations I have to live with.'

Against his will, Edward heard his father's voice in his head: *strength of character, boy, that is the only thing that counts for anything in this world.* Crossly had strength all right, he had seen him wield it. Because he abhorred cruelty did that make him, Edward, weak? His father had thought so. He shuddered a little.

'Let us get on with this. I take it that you

have some questions that you wish to ask me.'

'I see you are a man who likes to get down to business. Very well. As I am sure you are aware, I am visiting a number of potteries in my task to produce a report on child labour in the industry–'

'Can I enquire why you have seen fit to include Houghton's when there are so many others in the area you could have selected?'

'A pertinent but somewhat delicate observation. Your father – and your brother during his brief incumbency – earned themselves a reputation for ... shall we say ... keeping an eye on the profit margins above all else.'

'And what may I ask is wrong with that?'

The words had come out without any thought. Edward wondered why he had been so quick to leap to their defence. Was it because he felt that no outsider had the right to criticise his family, or was it because he knew that he had been happy enough to have his studies funded by the proceeds of their single-mindedness? And if the latter, did that make him as selfishly ruthless as them?

'Please, Mr Houghton. Edward. Do not take offence. If you ask me a question then I am honour-bound to tell you nothing but the truth. But I do not want us to be adversaries in this. I see you very much as a new broom and together we have the opportunity to sweep some of the most evil practices from this little corner of the industry. Rest assured, lad, I do not take you to be your father's son.'

But there was no getting away from the fact that he was. He had been making a pretence of running a factory and now, when about to be called to account for his laissez-faire approach to his responsibilities, he felt his father's blood beat in his veins as it had never done before. He did not share Wharburton's faith that he could emerge from such a deep and domineering shadow. The government commissioner was looking at him with something closely akin to compassion. Did he have an inkling of some of his thoughts and tortuous feelings?

'Let us establish ourselves on firm ground, Edward. Although each pottery is inherently the same in the processes they must use, each is different in the problems of production they encounter. Can you tell me what it is that you face here at Houghton's?'

Edward had no objection to answering this. Even his cursory examination of the books had revealed that there were some problems that had to be overcome to increase the profitability of the pottery. Maybe this man could help him to resolve them. After all, studying the law was an expensive occupation. He suppressed all emotion from his voice and answered in as matter of fact a way as possible, like the businessman he thought he ought to be.

'Many of the people who work here have done so since my father's day but it seems to me that, however expert they are, we have difficulties in achieving a consistent result. Some days the number of pots produced are much lower than others. I can only assume that a large amount are misfired.'

'That is not uncommon. And often the fault lies not with the workers but with the systems employed in the production. I will take careful note when on my inspection and see if I can help you by pointing out where I think improvements can be made. Be aware though that it might require you to invest a little capital in new machinery and suchlike.'

But had not his brother purchased that throwing wheel he and his friends had witnessed in operation, when he had first taken over? It had been listed in the accounts as costing a handsome amount of money. If the workers could still not produce decent enough pots for firing then the fault must lay with them. Squandering more of their profits on equipment that none seemed to possess the wits to use effectively was surely not the solution. His father had resisted changes and his production had remained consistently high. His brother had instituted one, and the quality of the finished product had diminished. If he were to introduce more would he, Edward Houghton, be known forever as the man who, blowing in the wind of advice from a government do-gooder, oversaw the ruin of a once flourishing business? If he hated being a pottery owner, he loathed the thought of being a failed pottery owner even more. His father would look down on him and enjoy it too much. *It is not in your nature to be one of life's successes, Edward, as it is not in mine to waste time on mediocrity.*

'Such changes would make life easier for your workers, too,' Mr Wharburton continued, 'and that is not an inconsiderable benefit of any changes you might make. You know, I assume, the toil and dangers involved in producing these pots of yours?'

'No. You will not imply that fault lies with me and the running of the factory. The manufacturing process is as it is and even my father cannot be held responsible for the use of lead and other contaminants.'

'Indeed that is true but perhaps you can limit your workers' exposure to them.'

Edward felt his patience and tolerance fraying towards the edge of losing his temper.

'I hardly think that I am in a position to employ twice as many people in order to ensure that each only takes half the consequences of the dipping shed.'

'I understand, and I am not suggesting that; you have a business to run, after all. But it is your responsibility to provide the safest conditions you can for the people who work for you. Their health is of paramount importance.'

'And what of their responsibilities? I already provide them with employment, am I to be expected to take on the role of a nursemaid as well? Do you want me to wipe their noses for them and check that they are not too infested with lice? Because I will not. I have seen for myself that they make no effort to take care of themselves in their daily lives and do not see why I should spend my money on improving their lot when all they do is spend the wages I pay them on drink and dissolution.'

'They are your responsibility within the factory gates,' Mr Wharburton said gently, 'but you cannot dictate how they conduct themselves at all other times. I know that it will seem as if it is ingratitude if they slowly kill themselves with gin but it is their choice and they have the right to exercise it; something that is denied them by the nature of the trade they are employed in.'

Edward felt his blood cooling a little. Perhaps he was taking all this a little too personally. He thought it was because he was caught in the unhappy state of not knowing where he stood in his own mind. He was no longer sure he even knew what his own mind was. It was being too clouded by the words and opinions of others. There were those of the man sitting in front of him who was using all the arguments at his disposal as cleverly as one of his old law professors, and then there were those of his father that he could only hear in his head – but they were none the less real for that. And some of them had been coming out of his mouth as if they were his own. However, even if he could discard the influence of these two old men, he was still left with the conflicting conversations he had had with their shadows – Crossly in The Potter's Wheel, and Emily Smallthorne at his home. Each held differing views of the nature of the men and women in his employ and he was at a loss to know which was the most accurate. He had witnessed their drunken licentiousness at first hand but maybe, deep down, they did have a thirst to improve themselves and seek education as a way to a better life.

'Tell me what you are thinking, Mr Houghton?'

Edward stood up and paced around the room.

'It is very difficult to know the truth of the matter.'

'That you even have doubts marks you out as a man of character. I do not expect you to simply agree to everything I say – if you did then I would be suspicious that you would only be doing so to placate me with no thoughts as to the consequences of what you had committed yourself to. Words are too easy, lad, the actions needed to follow them through are the real test.'

'But all I have heard from you are words and I am the one expected to take the actions. Actions that may well severely compromise my livelihood which will, in turn, affect my future. I need to have a secure income if I am to go back to London and resume my studies. Which I intend to do at the first possible opportunity.'

'If you do that you will be leaving Crossly in charge. Your father ruled the pottery with a rod of iron and his foreman is a man from the same mould. He will resist change with every fibre of his being.'

'That I cannot help.'

'Think on. You have the opportunity to change the lives of your workers for once and all.'

'I will not stay here to do so. My mind is made up.'

'But they depend on you asserting your authority. There is no one else who can do it in your stead – even if you had the best foreman in the world and we both know that is not the case.'

Edward stopped his pacing, wheeled around, and slammed his fist down on the desk in one unbroken movement. Dust rose in the air.

'You will not tell me how to live my life. I am answerable to none but myself in this matter.'

'I wish for your own peace of mind that were true, Edward. However I see that in your heart that you do not believe it or you would not be so distressed.'

Edward slumped down in his chair. He had to fight hard to stop himself from raising his hands to his face and exhibiting his despair and frustration. Was he destined to spend the whole of his life being bullied and told what to do by those who seemed determined to always place him in the wrong?

Mr Wharburton crossed and uncrossed his legs in the silence. Edward felt that he was expecting an apology but he would not give one. They were on his premises and it was by his leave that this meeting was taking place at all. He said he would listen and he had. He had never said that he would agree to destroy his own life for the betterment of others. That was asking too much of a sacrifice from any man. He looked up to see Mr Wharburton regarding him with concern.

'You have to take over the management of your factory. It is the only way to both fulfil your aim of increasing the profits, and mine of improving the conditions of your workers. It is the attitudes that prevail in your factory that must change and you know as well as I do that only you as the owner can ensure that such a thing happens. It comes down in essence to the way people are treated: are they respected as fellow human beings or regarded as beasts of labour not dissimilar to a horse pulling a carriage or a mule turning a grinding wheel in a flourmill?'

That is because they are *animals.* Crossly's words came back to Edward. He had not wanted to believe it at the time but he had seen little since to challenge such a view. A belief in the fundamental goodness of human nature was the best that he could place on the other side of the balance. It may well be enough for Emily Smallthorne and, apparently, for Mr Wharburton, but it fell far short of the evidence that his lawyer's mind required. He rubbed at his gritty eyes. He was tired and he wanted this meeting to be concluded as soon as possible.

'Even if I for one moment assume the position of agreeing with you – and I am by no means saying that I do – I confess that I am no expert in the pottery business and would be at a loss to know how to go about achieving such a thing.'

'And that is where I come in. My experience is at your disposal and I will take testimony from your workers to see what further light can be shed on the directions you could take. Rest assured, once we decide on the appropriate course of action, you will be able to implement it in stages and need have no fear of bankrupting your father's legacy. You have my word that healthy and happy workers who do not constantly labour under the yoke of fear are productive workers and will want to do all they can to ensure that your pottery remains competitive and profitable. Everyone's fortunes can only improve.'

Edward tapped his fingernails on the desktop. How easy it was to stand on the outside and point the finger. He knew that well enough because it was the endless debates about the rights and wrongs of things that he so enjoyed about the law. He had not ever expected to be in the position of having to get off the fence and choose sides. He stood up.

'Mr Wharburton, you have given me much to digest but I feel that so far it is a meal without much substance. I believe that perhaps if we were to visit the factory now then that might go some way to rectifying that.'

'And I know that it will.'

'But I want your commentary only. I have had my fill of lecture.'

'If that is what you feel I have been doing then I am truly sorry, lad. Passion and concern are all I intended to convey to you, not judgements.' He reached over and retrieved his hat from the corner of the desk. 'Come, you lead the way. Perhaps we can talk some more when we have finished the inspection. Over a drink preferably. I invariably find that a sherry helps the process of information absorption enormously.'

He was grinning and Edward could not help but smile back. A glass in front of the fire at Houghton Manor was a capital idea. In fact, it was such a good one that it came into his head that they should do that very thing straightaway.

'You have the whole day at your disposal, I trust, Mr Wharburton?'

'I do, lad, I do.'

'Then I have a new plan. Come back with me for luncheon now and then we can conduct the inspection of the factory without the accompaniment of the nag of empty bellies.' Some food and drink might serve to make him somewhat quieter in his mind, too.

The commissioner slapped him on the back in acquiescence before letting Edward lead the way down the stairs to the waiting gig.

The game pie and salad lay heavily in Edward's stomach as he and Mr Wharburton walked down the street to Houghton's pot-bank. He had driven back from the Manor and into town as slowly as his horse would allow but now the moment could be put off no longer. Ahead of them, a flush-faced man rushed out of the entrance to the factory courtyard. He looked in the direction of the river and then up and down the street, his gaze seemingly unfocussed and his mind, undecided. Finally, he noticed the two men walking towards him and he waved his arms.

'You mun hurry! For the sake of everything your father ever done here, hurry!' Then he vanished back under the archway.

Edward looked at Mr Wharburton in puzzlement and then increased his stride. A loaded coal cart rattled past them on its way up from the canal as they turned into the entrance to the factory courtyard.

The place was in uproar.

CHAPTER SEVENTEEN

Stephen stopped speaking. Vivien saw that his eyes were moving rapidly from side to side under his lids. His cheeks were covered in a sheen of sweat and wisps of hair were sticking to his forehead. He was a man experiencing acute distress – or fear. Or both. She picked up his wrist gently and felt his pulse – it was racing. But he was still in his hypnotic state – just.

'I want you to relax, Stephen. Take a

202

moment to breathe deeply.'

She saw his chest rise and fall.

'I want you to count backwards from seven in your head. On each number, you will feel your limbs getting heavier as you feel the tension draining out of your muscles.... Count, Stephen. I want you to begin counting now.'

Gradually his jaw lost its set look but his breathing was still shallower than she would've liked. Beads of sweat had now sprung up on his upper lip. Whatever he was experiencing was affecting him deeply; she knew that although he could hear her and had done his best to comply with her instructions, the film was still playing vividly in his head. Edward hadn't left him.

'Okay, Stephen, I know something is happening that's upsetting you but it's important that you stay with Edward for just a little while longer. Just remember that I am with you and you are safe.'

She allowed the room to be bathed in silence for a moment. She was rewarded for her patience as she saw Stephen's diaphragm take over and his breathing become even once more.

'Can you tell me what is happening now, Stephen? You are in the courtyard...'

He didn't respond. Vivien had no idea whether it was his rational mind or his subconscious that was resisting. It would make a difference. She had to choose her next question carefully to appeal to whichever was uppermost.

'Okay, Stephen, leave that for now. Let me ask you something a little easier. Tell me about the man with Edward. Stay with me here in this room and describe Mr Wharburton to me.'

She hoped that this sort of halfway-house of immersion in Edward's story would help him to move on with the narrative. It was crucial that he did. They were so close to something; maybe uncovering some patterns in Stephen's childhood.

She tried again.

'Is Mr Wharburton your father, Stephen?'

He laughed and she was relieved to get a reaction from him at last.

'Far from it. My dad was nothing like that, more jokey – perpetually the pub landlord. This Wharburton character has a way about him that's sort of wise and gentle. He looks kind but it's more than that; it's as if he understands.'

'Does he remind you of anyone?'

'Yes, as a matter of fact. He's a little like you.'

This really was significant. She didn't think he was confusing fantasy with reality but somehow incorporating one into the other. It begged the question, of course, that when he was living in the everyday real world, how much of him had adopted facets of Edward's life? But the fact remained that two women from Stephen's conscious existence had made the transition into his sub-conscious world. Were they, as she suspected, representative of his own psyche? The conflict he appeared to be wrestling with between guilt and destructive behaviour, and salvation: his wife Hélène, and his therapist.

'Stephen,' her voice was gentle and reassuring, 'I want to take you fully back there again and for you to tell me what happened to Edward. I need to know what takes place next. It is very important... You are standing beside Mr Wharburton at the entrance to the pottery and the place is in an uproar. And...'

Suddenly, Stephen's hands flew to his shirt collar and he started tugging at it. He was panting shallowly and gasping for breath at the same time. A series of coughs racked his body and he began to go into a spasm. Vivien leapt out of her chair and checked that he wasn't in danger of swallowing his tongue. Then she placed her fingers on the artery in his neck and felt his pulse. His heartbeat was rapid but regular. Her touch seemed to calm him and his body stopped twitching. She left her hand on his neck for a moment so that he could feel her presence and then moved away and walked across to the window. Her hand shook as she opened it to let in some air; she hadn't expected such a violent reaction. She returned to his side and picked up his wrist once more. Against all odds, he was still in a trance.

Vivien stood beside the couch and rapidly considered her options. If she brought him back now, there would be a chance that his sub-conscious might latch onto whatever experience it was that had provoked his physical responses. She was pretty sure that it must've been the fire that he'd spoken about in their first hypnosis session together and, if that was the case, would a part of him be trapped in that panic forever, unable to move on?

Her mind was made up. It was a risk but she had to encourage him to explore Edward's situation further and arrive at some sort of resolution. Her attempt at getting Stephen to be present in this world, whilst commenting on Mr Wharburton in the other, had been successful; she would try it again. But first she had to get him back to a state of deep relaxation.

'Come back to me, Stephen. Come back to this room. You are lying on the couch and you are safe. I am here and nothing can harm you.'

She laid his arm down gently and returned to her seat.

'I want you to let go of whatever is in your

head. Just let your thoughts drift away ... you are sitting under a tree in the summer sunshine ... the air is cool in the shade and the breeze washes over you and takes all your worries and anxieties away with it ... you can hear the birds singing and smell lavender. The scent is soothing and you breathe it in deeply.'

'Edward is dead now.'

His voice was strangely vibrant and nothing like his own – or Edward's. He sounded detached; more remote. He had been in a state of aggravated anxiety before but now he seemed better than fine. She had witnessed this rapid transition with patients once or twice before and knew that if she attempted to bring him out of his trance now, he would be unlikely ever to access such a moment of calm clarity again; the state he needed to be in to reveal the root of his trauma.

'If you are no longer Edward, then who are you?'

'No one. And everyone.'

'Where are you?'

'In the space between lives.'

There was no hesitation in his answers.

'Have you been there before?'

'Many times.'

'Describe it for me.'

'It isn't a place, more a state of being.'

'How do you feel?'

'Like I'm floating. There is nothing to hold me down and everything is quiet and peaceful. I'm sort of all energy. There's a bright light and, as I float towards it, I feel like my essence is renewed and it's wonderful.'

'Is anything else happening, Stephen?'

'A white spark is approaching me. It gets closer and I can see a shape. It's a small boy. He wants to share something with me.'

Vivien became aware that she was holding her breath. She had never heard anything like this in all her years of psychiatric practice – hadn't come across it in her reading, either. She observed Stephen for a moment – he seemed utterly relaxed – and took the opportunity to try and make sense of what could be happening to him. He had said that he was "no one and everyone". It was an answer that could just as easily describe the boundary between his rational mind and his subconscious: the ego and the shadow, in Jungian terms. And now this child. Was he meeting himself, his past; about to confront his deeply buried trauma at last?

Vivien felt a frisson of professional excitement. Her gentle probing had led him this far and now he was ready to take the next step. But first she needed Stephen to recognise the child as his younger self in order that he could work out what the vision represented.

'Can you describe the boy to me, Stephen?

Please make it as detailed as you can; it's very important that we can both see him clearly.'

'He is about two or three years old and very happy. He has brown hair and flushed cheeks. He is looking at me with wide eyes and they are brown, too. He is wearing a duffle coat and something strange on his feet. Frog Wellingtons, I think. Now he is kissing me on the cheek. He whispers something and then begins to sing: *"I'm dreaming..."*.'

Vivien clasped her hands together until her knuckles turned white.

'What's his name? Tell me his name.'

'He says it's Jimmy.'

Vivien gasped. 'That's enough, Stephen. When I click my fingers I want you to come out of the trance, now.'

Stephen snapped his eyes open. He took one or two deep breaths and looked around the room. When he spoke, it was as if he was talking to himself.

'That was weird,' his voice was thin and nervous. 'Seriously freaky. One moment I'm sitting with this old guy and then all hell breaks loose. Then it's like I'm dreaming – but I'm already in a dream. And my throat's sore. Why is my throat sore?' He finally turned to Vivien and seemed to register her presence for the first time. 'What the hell is going on?'

'That's exactly what I'd like to know. Who

put you up to this?'

Stephen didn't appear to have heard her. He rubbed his hands several times over his face and then shook his head violently as if to dislodge his thoughts.

'I asked you a question, Stephen. Who put you up to this? Because I know someone did.'

'What do you mean, up to what?'

Vivien stood up and began pacing.

'How could you possibly know what my son was wearing on the day he died? Who have you been talking to?'

'No one.' He pinched the bridge of his nose for a few seconds. When she caught him looking at her again, his eyes were un-focused. 'Look, I don't get this at all. I did everything you asked me and now you're acting like I've done something wrong. Why are you so angry with me?'

'Angry? I'm furious. You've been playing a game with me all along, haven't you? You've set out to mock psychiatry and my methods right from the beginning. This has all been an elaborate joke to you, hasn't it? Your chance to prove your theory that everything we have been doing over the past few weeks has been hogwash.'

Stephen looked as though he had been slapped. 'That's not true. I was sceptical at the beginning, I admit it, but everything I told you really happened. I swear.'

Stephen was leaning forward in his earnestness but she still didn't believe him.

'So the little boy spoke to you, did he? What did he say? Or are you just going to make that up as well?'

'I told you, I've not made up any of this. Why would I? What would be the point? So, I can't now remember every detail of what went on but that doesn't make me a liar. Maybe he didn't say anything at all. I don't know. I'm confused. I can't think straight anymore.'

'Get your story straight, you mean.'

Vivien turned her back on him to stare out of the window. She watched the cars on the street below until she thought she could speak a little more calmly.

'I think you should leave now. I'll let you know whether I decide to continue with your treatment or pass you over to one of my colleagues.'

Stephen said nothing. She supposed that there wasn't very much he could say; she had effectively severed all communication between them. After a long and painful silence, she heard the door close.

Vivien rested her forehead on the glass as she tried to regain control of herself. She was shaking and had to breathe deeply to overcome the feeling of nausea that was settling in her stomach. Her disgust at Stephen had turned into disgust at herself. She had never behaved so unprofessionally; it was unforgivable to take her own emotions out on a patient. She didn't know what came over her. Yes, she did. Horror at what he had said, and confusion as to why he had said it. And that had tapped into her undischarged anger. It was an uncomfortable – and humbling – experience to be analysing herself but she had to do it. Had to try to understand what had just taken place in this office.

Stephen was lying, she was sure of it. But a conscious lie, or an unconscious one? A fantastic story or a fantasy? *You are blessed with intelligence, Vivien; use it.* Her mother's response when she'd been moaning about not being able to marshal any arguments to take the opposing position on the debating team. Okay, what if she imagined for one moment that it was true. All of it. Edward and the fire and Dmitri ... no ... not Dmitri ... she couldn't go that far. But if Stephen had been recounting reality as he saw it, what could that possibly mean?

She had to start behaving like a scientist and establish some parameters. And the first step was to find out more about Edward Houghton's life – and death – if nothing else, it would help her to get back to seeing the case rationally once more. She would ring Seb and take him up on his offer to drive her to the Stoke museum. She could no longer think of any good reasons not to.

CHAPTER EIGHTEEN

Vivien was just about to pick up the telephone when Jean popped her head around the door and told her that Jim McFraser wanted a quick word. She sighed; they were anything but that with him. She set off down the corridor, her chest tight with apprehension. What was so urgent that it couldn't wait? Had he seen Stephen Daunt coming out of her office? One look at his face would've been enough to know that things weren't exactly going well between doctor and patient. Even though they'd both agreed that any request for a further supervisory session would come from her, what if he wanted a progress check? Her thoughts were in such a mess than she felt sure she would inadvertently reveal that she was now inappropriately emotionally involved in this case. To confess such a thing would be humiliating.

He looked up when she walked into his office, and indicated for her to sit. His bulk was almost dwarfed by the piles of files on the desk in front of him. He made a face and pretended to sweep them onto the floor with his arm.

'Departmental reviews,' he said, 'the bane of my life. It could be yours too if you play your cards right.'

His open-mouthed smile exposed his rather oversize incisors. Vivien found herself thinking it remarkable that Seb hadn't nicknamed him "Dracula". She knew that her mind was focussing on such trivialities to stop thinking about why he wanted to see her. *'Just imagine them in their underwear, honey,'* her mum had said when she'd been so nervous about making a speech at school she thought she'd throw up, *'it's one of life's great levellers.'* Her imagination couldn't go that far with Jim McFraser.

'I know you haven't had the time to get an outline of your paper to me yet, Vivien,' he continued, 'but I've been doing a little thinking. Although I still maintain that what's required is something with your usual academic rigour, I wondered if we might consider pushing the boundaries a little with this one. It's in both our interests for people to be talking about your contribution for some time to come and there's nothing better for achieving that end than to treat a room of psychiatrists to more questions than answers, is there? Keeps them on their toes. How are yours these days, by the way?'

Vivien wondered if she had missed something.

'Are you on top of things?'

'Fairly ... absolutely. Completely.'

She crossed her legs and looked back at Jim McFraser with a confident smile that she hoped would deflect from her initial hesitation.

'Good, oh. Because – far be it from me to interfere and I don't want you to do anything you feel uncomfortable with – but maybe you could...'

He stood up and walked across to the window. Vivien realised with a flutter in her stomach that he was as nervous as she was. What on earth was he about to propose?

'...I mean, you are in a unique position having returned back to work so quickly after your ... your ... personal tragedy ... that it could furnish the perfect opportunity to explore the boundaries between personal and professional therapy.'

These last words came out in a rush and Vivien felt herself holding her breath as if he had just used up all the air in the room. Her smile became fixed as it came to her that he might not only have seen Stephen Daunt leaving, he might also have overheard her outburst at him. She knew she'd raised her voice and the walls were thin. Was he really interested in the paper or was he giving her a chance to be the first to bring up her behaviour? Was that why he'd asked her how she was coping?

She laced her fingers together in her lap.

She didn't know what to say. Whichever way she went could be professional suicide. If he had heard but she didn't allude to it then he could think that she was spectacularly lacking in self-awareness but, on the other hand, if he knew nothing about what had taken place and she confessed to her unprofessionalism unnecessarily, then she would almost certainly be disqualifying herself from the coveted role of symposium keynote speaker. Luckily, she remembered just in time that if there was a gap in a conversation, Jim McFraser would be sure to jump in and fill it. She didn't have long to wait.

'It seems to me that the timing is perfect, seeing as you took on a new case on your first day back. I think you could do something remarkable in charting his progress therapeutically, and your own in recovering your equilibrium–' he held his hands out towards her, '– not that I'm inferring in any way that you were unbalanced, except of course that it would be perfectly understandable if you were.' He took a folded handkerchief from his jacket top pocket and dabbed at his upper lip. 'Oh dear, this is so awkward. It was a stupid idea, I can see it now. I'm so sorry, Vivien, if I've offended you.'

Vivien felt herself relax a little. He had no idea how badly she'd behaved with Stephen Daunt. Her relief blunted the outrage she might otherwise have felt at his suggestion; he was right, it was a remarkably insensitive one to make – even for him – but her gratitude that the embarrassment was on his side and not hers made her feel inclined to put him out of his misery.

'It's a novel approach, Jim, I'll grant you that.'

He strode back across the room and sat behind his desk once more.

'So you're not dismissing it out of hand?'

'You know I don't work like that.'

But she did, though. There was far too much about the Stephen Daunt case that she refused to consider; after their session just now she was only just beginning to realise quite how much.

Jim McFraser appeared to have recovered his composure and was getting back into his stride. 'You need not reveal yourself in any way, of course. The paradigm I'm proposing is merely to use your personal experiences as an anonymous case study to set up in opposition to, and contrast with, that of this teacher, Daunt. A sort of Jungian analysis of the four functions of the psyche: rational experience versus irrational perception. You said he was prickly when you first met. Maybe there's an element of projection, too; his powerful emotional responses breaking through his consciousness and becoming externalised. But there, I'm teaching you to suck eggs...'

He couldn't have got it more wrong; the projection had all been coming from her. It was grounding to be reminded of it though; perhaps her reaction to Stephen Daunt's sick and twisted sense of humour – or malice – had been totally involuntary on her part. It made her feel a little better about herself.

Jim McFraser rubbed his hands together as he warmed to his theme. 'And maybe that same phenomenon was at work when he put himself in the position of being suspected of attempting to drown a boy-'

'Jim. I really think you're going too far here.'

'Surely he must've told you the full background to the police investigation?'

He was right; she should've found out the facts by now.

'I know that he was a bystander to a near-accident whilst on a school trip.'

'I'm afraid that's only a fraction of the story, Vivien. He was alone on the deck with that youngster when he ended up overboard. The boy's account was confused so no one but Daunt knows what really happened, and he isn't saying. So the big question is: did he fall or was he pushed? If the former then why the persistent erratic behaviour from which one can only deduce heavy-duty guilt? An accident is an accident, after all.'

Vivien felt herself go cold. She had delayed probing Stephen about the incident in favour of exploring the appearance of Edward but, that aside, even on the little information she'd been given, she'd neglected to suspect Stephen Daunt of deliberating attempting to drown the boy. Why? He'd told her about his nightmares. She should have considered the possibility of them being a fantasised re-telling of what had actually taken place.

She was aware that she was starting to tremble with the enormity of where all this new knowledge was leading her. She tried to calm her breathing. Jim McFraser was studying her intently. What could she say that would make him drop his ludicrous idea but not raise any suspicions about how she felt about the case? She licked her dry lips.

'Jim. I think there's something in what you're saying about comparing the internal and external manifestations of deep-seated trauma,' she said as if she was seriously weighing up the pros and cons, 'but it might be best to go with concluded case studies. There are too many imponderables with anything live for me to draw any real conclusions. I could take a similar approach to the one you're suggesting and look at the extent to which differing responses are a result of inherent personality traits. Perhaps inject that element of controversy you want by slanting it towards the debate on gene therapy and whether the fascination with that new Holy Grail means the death of traditional psychiatry.'

Jim McFraser beamed at her and tweaked his bowtie. 'Brilliant idea, Vivien, just brilliant. I knew I could rely on you to concretise my initial thoughts. You have my full support to off-load any of your patients for the time being onto some of the others while you work on this.'

'Not Stephen Daunt. I want to keep him.'

Although she'd threatened Stephen with it out of anger, she'd never intended passing him on to another colleague. The complexities of Stephen Daunt's mind – whether conscious or subconscious – were so tightly bound up with her thoughts and feelings now that he was hers alone to deal with. Jim McFraser's stumbling over their interdependency, although inadvertent, had a disturbingly prophetic air about it. She shivered.

The next morning, Vivien was getting ready for her trip up to Stoke with Seb. Jerry had come in late last night from the hospital. He had climbed into bed and they had lain back to back without touching or talking – as was usual these days – until she had felt him drift off to sleep. Over morning coffee had been the first opportunity she'd had to tell him about her plans for the weekend. He'd listened in silence and then followed her up to the bedroom.

'Just when did you decide this, Viv?'

'I only phoned Seb yesterday. He'd offered a while back but there's been a few developments recently and I decided to take him up on it. He'll be here around eleven.' She pulled a cardigan off the wardrobe shelf 'I didn't have time to check the weather forecast so I'd better be prepared for all eventualities.'

'Well I certainly wasn't for this one.'

'What do you mean?'

'My wife going away for the weekend with another man.'

Vivien looked at Jerry's reflection in the mirror to see if he was smiling. He wasn't. She felt a flicker of irritation.

'Don't be ridiculous, this is Seb we're talking about. He's a friend and a colleague and I need him to do this for me. You know I couldn't possibly drive myself.'

'No. I suppose not. Sorry.'

'It's only overnight. We could go out for dinner when I get back if you like.'

'Maybe. Perhaps I'll do some work instead.'

Was every olive branch she offered going to be thrown back at her?

'You're working too hard, Jerry.' She opened her underwear drawer and put what she needed into her bag. 'Why don't you

221

just relax?'

'I could say the same to you. You're so on edge these days.'

Vivien stopped what she was doing and sat on the bed, suddenly overwhelmed by a bleak vision of endless weekends where they both went off their separate ways. She sighed and tried once more to reduce the gap between them.

'Let's not make a big deal of this; the simple fact is that I have a patient who has issues I'm nowhere near getting to grips with and this trip might help resolve them. I'm sorry I wasn't able to give you more notice but the timing's critical because I found out yesterday that he might even be responsible for trying to kill a boy.'

'An accident you mean?'

She stiffened. 'Why did you say that?'

'Because ... because ... I thought that was why you told me.'

Vivien stared at him. She knew only too well how his mind worked. She could feel a hard knot of anger forming in her stomach. The connection Jerry was making was un-forgivable.

'You think I'm going on a wild goose chase because of what happened to Dmitri, don't you?'

The fact that he was close to the truth – but for all the wrong reasons – only made it worse.

'Viv, look at it from my point of view; it's a natural assumption to make.'

'No it's not.' She looked at him and saw him flinch as if he had been scorched. 'There's nothing remotely natural about thinking your wife is obsessed with accidents.'

'I didn't say that.'

God, he was so self-righteous. She'd once thought it stoic but now it just seemed priggish. She was tired of feeling that she was the only one so raw and bleeding all the time that every thought or word – said or unsaid – made the wound even deeper. The pain of her isolation made her want to be vicious.

'So what is it then?...' A mocking tone oozed into her voice. 'Oh, I've got it... you think I'm trying to make up for my guilt about what happened to our son, don't you?'

'Viv, please don't do this to yourself.'

'I'm not doing anything.'

'Yes, you are. And it's not very pleasant to watch.'

His studied reasonableness felt unassailable.

'I might have known that you'd see yourself as a bystander. Come on, you always accuse me of not wanting to talk about it. I've heard you telling Sandra and Anne that you feel I'm cutting you out. Well, I'm not now. I'm talking now. So, tell me, you think

I feel guilty about the accident don't you?'

It was as if she couldn't stop herself the words just kept coming.

'Now you've finally brought it up: yes. Yes, I do.'

She regarded him with something so close to hatred burning through the back of her eyeballs that it frightened her.

'Are you sure it's not a projection of your guilt over what happened?'

The hard edge to her voice made Jerry break eye contact and look away.

He sighed. 'Don't play the psychiatrist with me, Viv. Not now.'

They were like mismatched cats circling before a scrap.

'I'm not playing at anything.'

'I'm not one of your patients.'

She drew on every drop of spite in her deep, untapped well. 'Well maybe you should be. Seeing someone about it, I mean. You're obviously carrying around a lot of unresolved issues.'

'There you go again. Can't you just talk to me like a human being for once instead of some sort of neurotic headcase?'

'So it's all coming out now: you're the real doctor and I'm only the shrink.'

'Stop twisting everything I say. You want to pick a fight with me, fine, go ahead, but do it for the right reasons at least.'

'Like what?'

'Like the fact that we never have sex anymore. It's as though I'm now married to some sort of bloody ice maiden. You always make sure you're in bed before me and I know you're only pretending to be asleep half the time. And then, if by some miracle, you deign to notice my presence and I – heaven forbid – try to give you a hug, you just roll over and give me the cold shoulder treatment.' He ran his hand tiredly over his brow. 'Please, Viv, it's just not fair for you to keep going on punishing me.' His voice dropped. 'It wasn't my fault.'

'It was!'

They had got to it at last. The moment she had been dreadfully holding back from since the minute he had come to her in the hospital corridor and callously announced the fate of their little boy. She had been waiting for this for so long.

'It was your fault!' She was screaming now. Her voice jagged with the vitriol of repressed fury. 'You forgot you had that fucking meeting and if you hadn't then our son would still be alive…'

'Don't go there, Vivien.' He was speaking so softly that she could barely hear him above the sound of the blood pounding in her ears.

'…because I didn't have the time to strap him into the car seat properly and if I had of done…'

225

Jerry looked down at the floor and then up at her. 'What happened to our son was simply an accident. There isn't always a reason or pattern behind everything and you've got to stop looking for one; you're only torturing yourself.' He glanced towards the window. 'And me. The only way I can say it is that I feel as though I've lost the better part of me. Dmitri lit up my life. You giving me the gift of a son was everything to me and always will be. Please don't let's spoil our precious memories of him like this.' His voice broke. 'The truth is that if either of us feels that we should have done something different on that day then ... then ... we're just going to have to learn to live with it.'

That was all the confirmation of her guilt Vivien needed. She pushed herself off the bed, took two strides across the room and slapped Jerry's face, hard. Her palm stung; the tingling the focus of all her feeling. She was surprised to notice that she wasn't even crying.

Jerry didn't even put his hand up to his cheek. 'I want you to listen carefully to me, Vivien. Nothing we can do or say can change what happened but if we carry on behaving like this towards each other then we will destroy whatever we've got left. We got married because we loved each other; we had a child together because we loved each other. And if that love can't get us through

226

this, then I don't know for the life of me what can.'

He gave her a long searching look and then turned and walked out of the bedroom.

CHAPTER NINETEEN

Another blue motorway sign loomed. Vivien had grown tired of trying to work out how far they'd come and how many more miles to go. She didn't even know if she wanted to get there quickly or not.

Seb had picked her up outside the house. She hadn't invited him in. Jerry had been on the phone in the hall and she didn't want to subject Seb to the icy anger between them. Besides, she hadn't wanted her friend to have that much insight into what was going on in her private life.

She sat huddled in the passenger seat and watched a stream of cars flash by. Seb was a surprisingly careful driver. She wondered if he was always like that or if he was being ultra-cautious so as not to scare her. Not that she could feel anything right now. Jerry's prognosis for their future together – the slow degradation of their love – had numbed her. She couldn't put him through that. Poor Jerry had suffered more than enough already and he deserved so much better. He was a good, kind man. "You giving me the gift of a son was everything to me..." Nothing else he had said, or could ever say, could possibly give her such an uncomfortable mixture of pride and pain. He was a man born to be a father and she could never give him any more children; she was almost certainly too old to have any realistic chance of conceiving with IVF again – even if she could handle the emotional consequences of success or failure. *True love is loving someone enough to let them go.* The words cut but gave her some sort of comfort. Jerry had been right; she couldn't do anything to change what had happened but maybe she could do something to make amends and give him a chance of some sort of happiness to heal the pain.

Seb took one hand off the steering wheel to switch the radio on. He was probably getting fed up with the silence. She hadn't spoken one word to him since he'd thrown her bag in the boot and they'd headed off. She had nothing to say. Nothing that would make any sense anyway. The journey was beginning to feel like some sort of combination of flight and pilgrimage but she couldn't tell Seb that. Even ignoring the fact that she had no intention of telling him about Jerry, he would want to know what was so special about going to collect a little background detail on a patient. If indeed

Edward was a patient. If he was real at all.

'I'm going to pull off to get something to eat.'

His voice made her start.

'Won't hold us up much, we've plenty of time to get there for your meeting at the museum.'

She nodded and gave him a thin little smile.

When they got to the services, Vivien stayed in the car. She wasn't hungry and she hadn't the energy to move anyway. Seb offered to bring her back a sandwich but she declined. She watched his handsome profile as he walked across the car park and thought how good he was to put up with her in her current mood. He was just letting her be, and she appreciated that more than anything. Everybody else including Jerry – maybe especially Jerry – had expectations of her and she knew that, right now, they were ones that she couldn't fulfil.

Back on the motorway again, Vivien found herself haunted once more by Stephen's words. How could it be possible that he'd known so much about the events of that terrible day? What Dmitri was wearing. He couldn't have guessed it, could he? It was winter and a lot of children wore duffle coats. Frog wellingtons, too – all the kids in Dmitri's nursery had a pair. But what about the fact of him knowing the secret family name of Jimmy? And the clincher: the song *I'm Dreaming of a White Christmas?* No one. NO ONE knew that had been playing at the moment just before the crash. She hadn't even told Jerry because she'd known that was the sort of detail that would break his heart. If she hadn't told anyone then there was only one other person who could have told Stephen that. But that was ridiculous...

She gripped the car door handle, suddenly needing the security of something to hold on to. Seb rested his hand lightly on her knee before flipping the indicator to turn. They were here. The pottery museum. Maybe now some of her questions would be answered. Maybe not. She was shaking as she got out of the car.

The place was not what she expected. When she'd arranged the appointment with the curator, he'd told her that it was a wonderful co-incidence that her enquiry was about the Houghton pottery because the museum was on the very site. She'd expected a collection of old brick buildings and maybe a shed or two but what was before her was a spanking new glass-fronted building with halogen spotlights in the windows shining down on a series of minimalist display cases. She couldn't help feeling a little disappointed. The Houghton family presence was long gone. Maybe Edward's never had been here.

Seb walked through the automatic glass doors ahead of her. An old-fashioned turnstile led to the museum proper. Above it was a rusty and pock-marked sign that had probably come from the original pottery: *No strangers allowed on these premises.* A stand of books on pottery through the ages, and shelves of souvenir key rings, tea towels and boxed plates were strategically placed between the entrance and the ticket counter. A panoramic photo in grainy black and white had been blown up to cover the whole of one wall. Vivien felt a flutter of disquiet in the pit of her stomach. It showed a skyline saturated in a fog of smoke; the dark and menacing outlines of bottle ovens and belching chimneys towering over the roofs. In the top left-hand corner, the blurred image of a winged devil – ghostly and barely discernable in the thick smog – brandished daggers like fistfuls of icicles in each hand. A caption was written underneath: *The Devil in the Potteries.*

'Striking isn't it?'

The voice seemed to come out of nowhere and set Vivien's heart beating wildly.

'Takes everyone that way first time off.' A woman's head had popped up from behind a display of novelty teapots. 'Story is that a local preacher had a bee in his bonnet about everyone drinking so much. Called drunkenness "the devil in the potteries" but this photographer, William Blake, thought all the working people's problems really came from the exploitative nature of the pottery industry so he came up with this. Makes a dramatic statement don't you think?' She shuddered theatrically. 'Not that I'd want it on my wall at home. Too gloomy and spooky by half.'

Vivien smiled weakly. If she had to come up with one word to describe the image, she'd call it terrifying.

'We're here to see the curator. Mr Timmons, isn't it?'

'It is indeed. But he's not here, I'm afraid.'

'But I've an appointment.' Vivien was aware that there was an edge to her voice that was dangerously close to desperation.

'He got called away. His wife's gone into labour. The poor duck wasn't due for another week or so and it fair took her by surprise. Him too. You Dr Blake?'

'Yes.'

'He left a message on your answer machine. Happen you didn't get it. Shame you've had a wasted journey. But he said that he'd found some things he thinks you'll be interested in and he'll photocopy them and pop them in the post when he gets back. Look, seeing as you're here now, why don't I give you a tour? We're not busy and I can call one of the girls to mind the desk in case we get a rush on.'

Vivien looked at Seb and received a shrug

in return.

'Thank you,' she said, 'we'd like that. But it's not the museum itself I'm so interested in, more the Houghton factory and the family history.'

'Factory's all gone now, I'm afraid. There was a big fire way back and the business went into decline and never really recovered. Whole thing was demolished. But the outline's still here if you know where to look. Clues in the height of the buildings around and sort of like footprints in the yard. Here, I'll show you if you like. Hang on a tick.'

She scurried away and disappeared through a door behind the counter. When she re-emerged, she had a young pasty-faced woman in tow.

'Tracy here'll do the honours. Come on, I'll give you a potted history of the pottery.'

She laughed and, despite the whirl of thoughts and feelings churning around inside her, Vivien smiled back. The woman's enthusiasm was infectious.

She led them back outside. The sun was warm on Vivien's back and she had trouble reconciling the demonic image on the wall in the museum with the blue sky, and the peaceful surroundings of the courtyard. Three cars were parked side by side – including Seb's – but other than that, the space was empty.

'You see here?' The woman had walked

over to where one of the long walls kinked slightly. Seb and Vivien dutifully followed. 'This is where the Slip House was. It would have been full of large tanks of liquid clay that would've spilt out and made the floor very slippery.'

Stephen's story of Edward visiting it with his friends sprang instantly into Vivien's head. She could almost smell the claggy dampness.

'I suppose this was quite a place in its heyday,' Seb was saying, 'lots of people worked here did they?'

'Hundreds at its height. On various jobs from making the clay itself right through to packing the finished products. They'd have done that over there. The Packing Shed would've been full of crates and straw; with horses and carts outside waiting to be loaded. You'd think it was one of the safest places to work – knowing what we now know about some of the lethal chemicals used in most of the processes – but there were always sparks flying out of the chimneys. One of those landing in the straw and ... whoosh! The whole place goes up.'

'Is that what happened? In the fire, I mean?'

'No one knows for sure but it's a pretty safe bet.'

Vivien muttered a 'yes' under her breath.

'Notice that the rest of the courtyard is

cobbled but that bit there's flagstones. That's so as the pots didn't get banged about and broken on their way out. See the trammels in the stone? They've been worn away from years and years of iron-rimmed wheels running over them. The carts were enormously heavy by the time they were fully loaded.'

'Houghton's did a lot of business then?'

It was just as well that Seb was showing an interest; the sorts of questions Vivien wanted to ask would have sounded crazy – that's always assuming she could've put them into words.

'Tons and tons. The whole town was full of potteries – Stoke is six towns really linked by the canals and then the railways – but Houghton's was one of the most successful. Not the biggest firm, mind, but they churned out the wares consistently. Until the fire, that is.'

The fire. It all came back to the one thing that Vivien wanted to know most about. Would there be any record of Edward being present when it happened? She doubted it; when she'd first spoken to Mr Timmons on the phone he'd said that the pottery owner was Matthew, not Edward. But standing here – maybe even on the very spot where Stephen had said that Edward had witnessed Crossly thrashing the boy – it was impossible to believe that it had all been a figment of his imagination.

'The bottle ovens were over there.' The woman pointed to the far corner of the courtyard. 'They were called hovels. It's a shame they pulled them down but they were probably in such a bad state of repair. There's plenty around here been restored if you fancy taking a look at one.'

'Where did they live?'

'The workers? In terraced houses mainly. Slums really. The poor ducks had a hard time of it. But the records show they still managed to enjoy themselves right enough. You remember that photo on the wall?'

How could Vivien forget it?

'There was something in what that preacher said about drunkenness. The workers would spend all their weekend letting their hair down.'

'I can relate to that.' Seb turned and winked at Vivien but she looked away before he could see how uncomfortable this whole visit was making her.

'Each pottery sort of had a favourite amongst the local pubs. Houghton's workers used to go to The Potters Wheel. It's not here any longer – a block of flats sits there now – but it was only down the high street a little ways and I expect it was just a question of them falling in there of a Friday night and tumbling out again on Monday morning.'

Vivien began to feel a little sick.

'There was a pump here. For the workers to wash themselves and probably to douse their heads after a too-heavy weekend session.'

Or after a fire. Vivien felt her vision blurring. She saw the smoke from the kilns being displaced by the smoke from the fire. Heard the sounds of the pottery shards cracking in the inferno and the flints exploding. Felt the heat emanating from the brickwork. All around her, women and children were crying as the men covered themselves with wet towels and rushed into the Moulding Room to tackle the blaze. Edward was standing looking up at the third floor of the burning building; staring at the young boy's face in the window; his shoulders bowed by the hostile stares of the workers, and the weight of his responsibility.

She must've made an involuntary groan because Seb turned to her.

'You alright, Vivien?'

'Fine,' she managed to mutter.

'It's pretty impressive, eh?' he continued, 'Amazing how the past can come to life when you've got a good guide to show you.'

But Vivien hadn't needed the woman to tell her how everything had been. She knew. She knew and she could see it all exactly as Stephen had. And Stephen had seen it through Edward's eyes. The realisation was blinding: Stephen had been telling the truth. But if he had then that meant ... that meant...

The last clear thing she saw was Seb's anxious face. Her breathing turned shallow and she felt her legs go weak. She couldn't stop herself as she collapsed to the ground.

CHAPTER TWENTY

Vivien leant back on the pillows. The hotel bed was surprisingly comfortable and she felt much better. She remembered vaguely how she had got here but it had felt like sleep-walking. Seb had helped her into the car and told her that she had fainted and needed to rest. The drive to the hotel had been a short one and she'd been registered and taken to her room in double-quick time. Then she'd slept.

She opened her eyes properly. The curtains were drawn and the bedside lamp was glowing softly. Seb was sitting in an armchair watching her. She felt ridiculously self-conscious and wanted to pull her skirt down over her knees.

'How long have I been here?'

Her mouth was sticky and her tongue felt thick.

'Hello, Sleeping Beauty.' Seb's voice was

kind and concerned. 'And I didn't even have to kiss you. Or turn into a frog.'

Good old Seb. He could always diffuse a potentially awkward situation with a joke. She began to relax again. He looked at his watch.

'It's just after eight. You got about four hours solid sleep, I'd say. And boy, you must've needed it.'

'I've not been sleeping too well lately.'

'Well, I'd never have guessed! I'm a doctor remember, Vivien, I know the signs; saw them the first day you came back to work.'

'It's not surprising.'

'No, it's not. But something tells me that you're not looking after yourself very well. What happened to "physician heal thyself"? You can't do others much good if you don't take care of your own needs too.'

Vivien had never known him to be so sweet. He wasn't lecturing her, just expressing a friend's concern. She gave an apologetic shrug.

'When did you last eat, Dr Blake?'

'Yesterday morning I think.'

'No mystery to the fainting fit, then. Tell me what you fancy and I'll ring room service and get them to whistle you something up.'

'In a bit. I couldn't face anything quite yet. A drink of water would be nice though.'

Seb went over to the mini-bar and pulled out a baby-sized bottle of mineral water.

'The price they charge for these. You should take one of those comfy pillows home in compensation. Clean out the bathroom complimentaries, at least.'

Vivien took the water from him and drank gratefully. She immediately felt her system coming more alive. Her elbow hurt where she must have banged it when she collapsed and she would have a tremendous bruise on her hip in a day or so but, apart from that, she was physically alright. What was in her head though was a different matter altogether. She looked around the room to steady her whirling thoughts. Her bag was on the floor just outside the bathroom door. She would have to take out her clothes for tomorrow and hang them up before the creases became too entrenched. But that would have to wait. Just having an excuse to lie still and do nothing was such a novelty; if she was at home now she'd be rushing around trying to fill her empty time with trivial activities.

The room was comforting too, in its own way. Anonymous. Functional. Furnished for purpose and no more. When she was younger, she'd dreamed of a life like that, stripped to the bone with no baggage and no distractions. But then she grew up. It was impossible to be so focused, so determined to shake off everything that drew her away from the core person she was inside. She wondered if that was the same for everyone, or if that was just her. She looked at the reflection of the back of Seb's head in the mirror. He was focused. He was determined. He had succeeded in becoming a bestselling author against all the odds. But he was unhappy in love; always looking for the perfect partner, the ultimate conquest. And she was happy in love ... had been ... was. Perhaps the human condition boiled down to never having it all and always wanting what was lacking.

Like Jerry. He wanted to be a father more than anything in the world. She thought that, deep down, he wanted that more than he wanted her. She allowed herself to think back once more to their awful row. Had it only been this morning? It felt as though it had happened years ago. The worst of it hadn't been that he'd as good as blamed her for what happened to Dmitri; after all, that was what she had wanted, what she had pushed and pushed for so that she could finally unleash a reaction against the dreadful truth. No, the worst thing was the thought that she was preventing him from ever having the chance to be complete again. Because he never could be with her. But if he was free ... to find someone else to give him what he needed... It would be agony to lose him but at least she wouldn't be holding him back.

Except how could she ever broach the subject: *Darling, I'm thinking of giving you a divorce so you can start again with someone new?* And even if she did manage to find a better way to say it, Jerry loved her too much to let her make such a sacrifice. However, if she made it so that he thought she no longer cared about him, no longer wanted them to have a future together; if she pushed him away by doing something that he would find impossible to forgive?

An idea came to her that was shocking in its simplicity: she would have an affair with Seb. He had always been trying to get her into bed and, given her joking about his reputation, Jerry would know that it was something that she'd entered into willingly. Rumour wouldn't be enough – they were probably the subject of idle gossip already – but it wouldn't have to amount to much between them and it almost certainly wouldn't cause any complications as far as working together went. She would merely be taking him up on his standing offer. Once Jerry had overcome his hurt at what he would almost certainly construe as her punishing him for his jibe about her being an ice maiden, he would be able to start a new life. Be a father again. And she would have the solace of knowing that she had committed at least one truly selfless act in her life.

She took another sip of the water and

wondered if she'd banged her head on the cobbles when she'd collapsed. It was unlike her to be so scheming. Or perhaps she had become unhinged by grief. She knew that wasn't just a turn of phrase; she'd seen the results in her consulting room many times. If she was losing her grip on reality, as this outrageous plan seemed to demonstrate, then it appeared that she didn't have very far to go. But she had to test out just how far. She cleared her throat.

'I have to talk to someone, Seb, and I want it to be you. Will you promise just to listen and not psychoanalyse me? I don't think I could cope with that right now.'

'I can assure you that whenever I am in a hotel bedroom with a beautiful woman I never, ever, resort to cheap mind-games to get them to talk – or anything else for that matter. Fire away, I'm all ears.'

Vivien stared at the bottle she was holding.

'It's this recent case of mine.'

'I thought as much.'

She threw him a warning look. 'Seb...'

'Sorry.' He pretended to button his lip.

'Things are going on that I just don't understand. And it's not just all that stuff about Edward and the fire at Houghton's either; even though that is baffling enough.' She took a deep breath. 'In the last session, the patient – oh, this is stupid. Stephen, his

243

name's Stephen. Stephen told me that Edward was dead and that his spirit – or soul, or something – was floating in a place full of bright light. And then ... and then ... a little boy appeared. Seb, he described my son right down to the clothes he was wearing on the day he died and the song on the radio he was singing. I know this sounds hysterical and is probably just wish-fulfilment on my part but he came to him. Dmitri was there. It was as if he was in the room with us.'

'Now who's doing the psychoanalysing? Give yourself a break, Vivien, and stop trying to force yourself to find internal explanations for everything. Sometimes things happen so far outside our experience that there is no point trying to rationalise them. Why don't you go over what happened again and this time tell me every detail? Things might become a little clearer in the re-telling.'

Vivien did as he asked.

'Do you want me to tell you what I think?' Seb said when she had finished.

'Yes.' Vivien's voice was as small as a child's.

'I've been doing a lot of reading on comparative religion for my next book and I reckon that what Stephen was describing was the Bardo plane.'

'The what? I've never heard of it.'

'Well you wouldn't, would you? You're not a Buddhist and neither are you a bestselling author in search of a dynamic angle with which to wow his editor. So, there you remain, in a state of less than blissful ignorance.'

'Seb, Stop it. I'm not really up to you teasing me about this. I'm confused about what's going on, and I'm scared of what it all might mean.'

'I'm sorry. I know you are. Look, I'm no expert but from what I can gather it's not an actual place, more a state of existence.'

'Okay, I suppose that sort of makes sense given Stephen's elaborate fantasy about Edward.'

'If it is a fantasy.'

'It's based on fact, granted, but it can't be anything else. So, is this Stephen's way of bringing the fantasy to an end?'

'Vivien, you're not listening to me at all, are you? Like you didn't really listen to Stephen. He told you that Edward's spirit was floating. So that's what the Bardo plane is: a state of existence between two lives on earth.'

'That's rubbish. There's no such thing.'

'How do you know there isn't?'

'How do you know there is?'

'We can keep this up all night if you like. Vivien, I could shake you sometimes you're so stubborn in needing sound evidence for everything.'

'Not always.'

'Yes, always.'

'Not as a child I didn't.'

'Aha, eureka.' Seb grinned with delight as if he'd just been handed the key to the hotel penthouse suite. 'Allow me to jump into that open door with both feet. I have a question for you...'

Vivien regarded him warily. 'Go on...'

'Did you believe in Heaven as a child – as an actual place, I mean?'

She could see where he was going with this a mile off. 'Of course I did. It was a construct taught to us to explain the unexplainable: death.'

'But what if it wasn't? What if it was the truth and it really did exist complete with fluffy clouds and angels playing harps?'

'Now you're being stupid.'

'No, I'm not. I'm just being literal. It is perfectly possible that it is both a construct – a metaphor if you will – and a celestial Happy Days Retirement Home for souls no longer grounded by their cumbersome bodies.'

Vivien snorted. 'So we're talking about a heaven then with saffron robes instead of wings?'

'I knew I could get you to use your imagination if I kept at it. But you haven't got it quite right. The Bardo plane is more like a spiritual railway station at rush hour. They hang around a bit and then when the first empty vehicle comes along, they jump in and travel on into their next allotted life.'

'As a scientist you can't believe that reincarnation exists?'

'I don't believe or disbelieve, Vivien. But there is a lot of literature out there and thousands of years of established religion behind it. Take my advice for a moment and stop worrying about whether something is true in the narrow confines in which you define that word, and just suspend judgement. I'm sure that part of your distress recently is because you are trying to deal with two conflicting belief systems – the rational and the irrational: your head and your heart, if you will.'

Seb broke off and attempted to stick his fist in his mouth.

'Now I've gone and done it,' he said past his knuckles. 'Sorry.' He removed his hand and laid it in his lap once more. 'That bit of doctoring sort of slipped out. I'll refrain in future; if you want me to go on, that is?'

'Please, Seb.'

She didn't give any credence to what he was saying but she did have to admit that there was something stimulating in being challenged this way. It was as if she had been waiting for someone to press a button to release her in order to see the world in a different way. It made her feel more alive than she had for a long time.

'Okay. You know of course that reincarnation is loosely about the transference of life? Apparently, according to Tibetan tradition, what happens is that after someone dies and before their next birth they experience a variety of phenomena peculiar to this stage in the process. Straight after the physical death, the experiences are clear and tangible and presumably can be recalled and described if someone were to ask them.'

Vivien shivered, her scepticism lessening hold as she remembered back to Stephen's description of Edward.

'But later, this state of blissful grace ... don't you think it's amazing how I can't seem to explain this without placing it within Judeo-Christian constructs? But I digress ... so, after the joy of release comes the regrets. I think it's probably what we in our simplistic ignorance would call "karma" when the essence is haunted by hallucinations arising from the impulses of all their previous actions. Awareness of their inner drives, I suppose in clinical language. Now, for some, the very act of dwelling on their past behaviours can impel them into a less than desirable rebirth but for the spiritually enlightened, their time on the Bardo plane can offer great insights and liberation. Be transcendental. Self-knowledge leading to self-determination? Not sure. But we certainly can't dismiss it out of hand.'

Vivien sat and regarded him for a while.

'So you think this Bardo plane exists.'

'I'm not saying it does, and I'm not saying it doesn't. But the concept of what it represents certainly – with or without the reincarnation – the idea of spiritual awareness and awakening leading to a deeper and more profound experience of life.'

Vivien was amazed to realise that she had lost all desire to take issue with him. In fact, his open-minded approach was both encouraging and inspiring. And if she could just make herself take one more small step then the answer she had been seeking could be there right in front of her.

'Seb, would it shock you to know that I'm almost tempted to believe Stephen's whole story?'

'Only that it's taken you so long to admit the possibility that he might be telling the truth.'

'I didn't have the full picture before now but, with what you've told me, I think I might be able to begin to piece it all together logically. If I accept that there is a possibility that reincarnation does occur, then Edward could indeed be Stephen and visa versa. Then, building on that, if this Bardo plane exists as a place of transference between lives, then Edward would have gone there after his death and encountered all the other life-forces, spirits, whatever, also waiting for the next stage. And that means that if Stephen and Edward are the same person, then Stephen could have met Dmitri.'

It didn't sound so fanciful. And it was a relief to be able to put into words the explanation for why she had over-reacted so badly to what Stephen had said at the end of their last session. She had been so desperate for it to be true but could find no way to make sense of it all. But now she could. Seb had gifted her the belief that Dmitri still existed somewhere other than in her heart, and that he was trying to communicate with her through Stephen. It changed everything.

Not quite everything. It made no difference to her relationship with Jerry. But then again, perhaps it did. Perhaps it made her crazy idea of sleeping with Seb in order to give Jerry a way out of their marriage something that she could actually go through with. Because she wouldn't have to pretend her feelings of love and gratitude towards Seb. They were genuine. Love. She hadn't used that word about anyone other than Jerry for so long, she felt she had to test it out to see what it meant: friendship; admiration; deep concern for another person's welfare; compassion; a shared sense of together in – and against – the world; a curiosity to get to know them deeper...Yes. She felt all of that towards Seb.

She smiled across at him. 'I don't know about you but I think a drink's in order. I'll buy you one for being such a patient teacher and you can buy me one for ... for ... letting you be.'

They both laughed at how neatly she had summed up the dynamics of their relationship. Seb levered himself out of the depths of his armchair and walked over to the minibar.

'Not one of those,' Vivien said, 'a decent bottle of red from the bar perhaps. A Rioja if they've got one.'

'Your wish is my command m'lady.'

Vivien reached across to the bedside table and picked up her keycard. 'Take this with you and let yourself back in. I'm going to take a quick shower. What with one thing and another, I feel as though I've been put through the wringer today.'

'That's the ticket; use up those complimentaries. Take your time. I'm going to get them to make us a couple of sandwiches while I'm down there. Wine on a stomach as empty as yours is never a good idea. A spectacular waste of a good Rioja, in fact. Cheese okay?'

'Anything. Suddenly I could eat a horse.'

'I'll see what I can do...'

Vivien watched him walk out with a spring in his step. Once again she weighed up the likelihood of offering herself to him. His

Pavlovian response to wine, women, and hotel rooms would remove the necessity for any schoolgirl shyness or embarrassing misunderstandings; the timing and circumstances were right. She was cosily wrapped in a fluffy bathrobe when Seb came back into the room. He had borrowed a tray and had assembled a feast of crisps, sandwiches, wine, and a small bowl of grapes.

'You are the archetypal hunter-gatherer.' Vivien laughed. 'I'm sure that now I've said that you'll tell me that you were a caveman in your last life.'

'Now who's teasing? Glad to see you smiling again though. You had me worried for a while back there.'

'You weren't the only one. I thought I was about to lose every perspective I ever had.'

She waited until Seb had poured the wine and handed her a glass. 'Just one sip and then I'll eat something, I promise.'

She allowed the full-bodied wine to glide over her tongue. It tasted good.

'Vivien, can I ask you something?'

'Of course.'

'Just this one thing and then I'll drop the subject – for good if you like.' He looked a little sheepish. 'Do you think there's a chance, even a remote one that you...'

Vivien found that she was holding her breath.

'Might have unconsciously put some of

those thoughts in Stephen's head; made the connections for him?'

That was not what she had been expecting at all. She shook her head slowly. 'Why would I want to do that?'

'Because you loved and miss your son so very much.'

The tears started to roll down Vivien's cheeks before she could stop them.

'I'm sorry. I didn't mean to upset you.' Seb walked over and took the glass from her hand. He placed it on the bedside table and sat down next to her. 'I wouldn't hurt you for the world, you know that. But I do have a little experience of what it's like to yearn for someone who's out of reach. Someone who you feel you're very close to but can never quite hold.' He was stroking her wrist now. 'Vivien ... I...'

The broken sweetness in his voice was too much. She threw up her hands to her face as she lost control. She sobbed. Huge sobs that shuddered through her and felt as though they would never stop.

Seb put his arms around her and pulled her to him. His body was warm against hers and she felt herself melting into him. She'd missed the consolation of physical contact more than she'd thought possible. The simple act of one person holding another to share and lighten their pain.

She rested her head against his shoulder

until she felt that the worst of it had passed and she could pull back and look up at him. She could read concern in his face ... and understanding. That was what she had been longing for these past, hard, months. Someone to understand without judgement. She didn't think it was too much to ask and it was Seb who had given it to her. The indebtedness she felt towards him was enough to wipe away any remaining doubts. She leant forward and kissed him on the mouth. His lips were soft and opened slightly at her touch. To her surprise, Seb broke contact almost immediately.

'My, Dr Blake,' he said, 'this is a day for firsts.' The look in his eyes was soft but there was a seriousness about his expression that made Vivien feel a little like she had just kissed a favourite uncle inappropriately. 'I know I'm going to hate myself in the morning for saying this but, we can't. Not that I don't want to, Vivien, desperately. But you're upset and I'd be frightened that afterwards you might think I'd taken advantage of you. And you're the only woman I've ever cared about what she thought of me. After; before; during; at all times.'

Seb stood up and brushed a stray strand of her hair away from her forehead. 'If we are ever in a similar situation again and you still want me...'

He caressed the top of her head as if

reassuring himself that she was real, before walking out of the room and closing the door gently behind him.

CHAPTER TWENTY-ONE

Back in her office on Monday morning, Vivien was fidgety: "ants in her pants" her mother would've said. It was shaping up to be one of those warm June days when anyone confined indoors would dream of sitting on the beach, or in a park with an ice cream. She looked at the pile of case notes on her desk then sighed and slipped her shoes back on. She had to do something to release her tension. There was no point in trying to concentrate on her paper for the symposium; she'd take these files back to records herself. Jean had enough to do and getting out of the office – even if it was just down to the next floor – would be good for her.

She scooped the manila folders into her arms and walked out of the room. Jean was at her desk speaking to someone on the telephone and made a "thank you" face at Vivien as she passed. Vivien was jolted by a voice coming from around the corridor corner. It was Seb. She felt a flush of schoolgirl embarrassment and, if she was honest, humiliation. How could she have nearly used him like that? It wasn't what you did to a friend. And the situation had led him to exposing himself about his feelings towards her. He'd all but said he loved her. She couldn't face him now for both reasons. She quelled the stab of panic that was threatening to root her to the spot and ducked through the open door of the office in front of her; she'd rather have to explain herself to the surprised inhabitant than to Seb. But there was no need; the office was empty. Vivien waited until she heard Seb pass by and then nipped out and hurried down the corridor.

She spent the next few hours on mindless activities. The clock seemed to take forever to tick around to 12.30 and her appointment with Stephen Daunt. She'd phoned him the minute she'd got into the office. It had been a difficult call but she'd managed to persuade him to ask his headmaster to release him at short notice.

But finally the time arrived and he was sitting in front of her, wrapped in hostility.

'Stephen, thank you for coming and giving me a chance to explain.'

'Couldn't resist it. It's not every day a shrink is willing to admit that she's more freaked out than you are.'

Vivien fiddled with her wedding ring. 'I

wouldn't put it quite like that but, as I said on the phone, I do owe you an apology for my behaviour at the end of our last session. I'm afraid you took me completely by surprise and I over-reacted. I really am very sorry. At least you now know that psychiatrists are only human.'

'I guess so.' He grimaced. 'Seems we are more or less in the same boat.'

'I want you to know that up until that moment I think we were making great progress in getting to the root of your problems but now I truly believe that we – the both of us – have had a major breakthrough.'

'I suppose you could say that you losing it like that was quite an eye-opener.'

Vivien felt the heat of her blush on her cheeks but refused to dip her head in shame. She had behaved unprofessionally and this man deserved to know the reasons why. Besides, she had an obligation to him as a patient. She had promised to help him get his life back together and she would. The fact that he might well hold the key for her doing that for herself was purely incidental. Or so she wanted to believe. His needs had to come first.

'Stephen. I want to be frank with you. Do you remember that picture you saw on my desk the first time you came here? I told you that my son had died but I didn't tell you that it was in a car accident less than six months ago. It's been...'

She sought for the right word to sum up her personal hell but couldn't find it.

'...hard. And then when you started describing him in such detail, well, it threw me.'

'What? What are you talking about? I imagined a little boy, that's all.'

'No, Stephen. You saw my son. It couldn't possibly have been anyone else.'

'Jesus.' He bent forward and rested his elbows on his knees. Vivien could see his hands shaking. 'I thought I was making all this up and now you tell me that at least one of the people in my head was real?'

'I thought you knew that already and were playing some sort of sick joke on me.'

Stephen snapped upright and glared at her. His eyes were hard sparks of anger. 'Why the hell would I do that? What a bloody disgusting thing to think about me. You must have me pegged as a right bastard.' His voice filled the room. 'Look, I have no idea how I knew all that stuff but I did.'

His face relaxed a little as he looked away from her and down at the floor.

'I'm sorry if what I said upset you. And I'm truly sorry about your little boy.'

Vivien gulped back the threatening tears. Having made herself so vulnerable, she now had to rein in her emotions and get back some clinical detachment; it was the only way either of them were going to get through this.

'I believe you, Stephen. I suspect a part of me believed you then or I wouldn't have felt the shock of it so much. But it was more than just shock, it was the thought that maybe everything – and I mean everything – that you have been experiencing under hypnosis was based solidly in fact.'

Stephen folded his arms and hugged himself.

'You ... said ... that ... it was my sub-conscious trying to tell me something.' He began to rock back and forth in his chair. 'But now you're saying that all of that – the fire included,' his voice broke, '–actually happened?'

'I don't know for certain but I think it's time we seriously considered the possibility.'

She waited for a while for him to come to terms with the idea; it had taken her long enough. When she saw the line of his shoulders sag slightly, she carried on.

'Reincarnation, Stephen. What do you know about it?'

Stephen barked out a laugh and unfolded his arms. He seemed to be on slightly safer ground now he'd been given a question he could answer.

'Only that it's something monks dressed in saffron robes believe. It all seems a little way-out to me. I've a logical brain, remember, maths teacher and all that. I thought you had, too. Don't tell me that you're now going over to the other side?'

'There are no sides in this. No positions. It's a question of forming a hypothesis based on the facts. And I can only call it as I see it. The base fact is that you are telling the truth; I have spent my entire professional life studying and listening to people and I'm convinced that you are not deliberately lying to me. Fact two: a fantasy, a product of the sub-conscious, can only be constructed from what the patient already knows. You told me that you had never come across Edward Houghton and the potteries before but I've done some checking and everything I've been able to verify has been so accurate that it can't be put down to educated guesswork. And you certainly had no way of knowing what you did about my son. Fact three...'

'Okay, okay, don't go on. Now you're really spooking me. Do you mean to say that I am ... was ... Edward?'

'At this point in time there doesn't seem to be any other logical explanation.'

'And that after he died – I died – oh, bloody hell this is all so difficult for me to get my head around. After Edward died, he went to a sort of a limbo spirit land where there's no such thing as time and so was there at the same moment as your son? It's too fantastic.'

'The Bardo plane. It's called the Bardo plane. And you're right, it is a little like limbo where the essence of a person released by physical death goes to await rebirth.'

Stephen leant forward and rested his elbows on his knees once more. He dropped his head into his hands. His fingers clutched at his hair as if he was trying to hold on to reality. Vivien almost wanted to reach out and comfort him.

'I don't want this to be happening to me. I want you to make it go away. I've got problems enough of my own without having someone else's inside my head.'

'I believe they are connected, Stephen. They are all part of the same thing and it explains why whatever it is that is causing your current internal conflict is so deep-seated. I thought it was your subconscious hiding it from you but now I need to consider that it is your rational mind that is the culprit – mine too – for not being able to take all this at face value. Does that make sense?'

'Sort of. But, God, I wish it didn't.'

'Do you trust me, Stephen?'

'I ... I suppose so. I haven't always liked what you've said but you've played straight with me all along.'

'Then I want you to agree to what I'm

261

going to suggest.'

'I've a pretty good idea of what you're going to say.'

'I want to hypnotise you again. To take you back to the Bardo plane and see if we can access any more memories; find out what happened to Edward.'

She almost had to bite her lip to stop from saying: *and Dmitri, too.*

'You and I have started a journey, Stephen, one that follows your own life – or lives' – journey and we have to see it through to the end.'

Stephen stared at her for a long while. She could see fear and doubt and conflict in his eyes. But, ultimately, resignation. He bent down and unlaced his shoes.

'You'd better do your worst then.'

Vivien felt an overwhelming gratitude for the man's faith in her. She would do everything in her power to ensure that it wasn't misplaced.

She wasn't surprised that it took a lot longer than it had before to get Stephen into a trancelike state. The poor man must have so many thoughts whirling in his head. But finally he was able to let go and was relaxed enough for her to begin.

'Who are you, Stephen?'

Vivien felt a stab of surprise at her first question. In the past, she'd always asked "where are you?" Now, it was "who?"

'Clarence Harvey, mam.'

He spoke with a strong American accent. Vivien looked up from her notepad and scrutinised his features for any change in his appearance. There weren't any. She didn't know why she had thought there would be. Except she had been expecting Edward – perhaps in some sort of transition phase – and the strange voice had thrown her. She wanted to intervene and ask Stephen what had happened to Edward but knew that if she wanted to find out his next step of the journey on the Bardo plane then she had to be patient. It was not one of her natural attributes but psychiatry demanded it of her. She would just have to endure her frustration.

'How old are you Clarence?'

'Twenty-five, mam.'

At least that tied them all together: Clarence, Edward, and Stephen were all the same age. She had to try to find out what else they had in common. Childhood was a good place to start. She knew about Stephen's and had elicited a little of Edward's. Perhaps Clarence's would parallel one – or both–of those.

'Can you remember being a little boy, Clarence? Can you tell me about it?'

'Clear as day. We lived on a farm with hogs and hens. Would still be there now if it weren't for me signing up and all.'

'Signing up for what, Clarence?'

'War, mam. We all of us wrote our names on the paper as soon as we could. There was some only able to make their mark but I'd been learning my lettering. Not that I'd ever paid much attention to schooling but I could write my name. The army taught me the rest.'

'So you enlisted.'

'Sure did. Some men came to the town square and gave us a rallying talk. Sounded a darn sight more exciting than roping hogs so we left with them. Them early days, I thought tramping was the only thing we were ever going to do but that sure changed.'

Vivien tried to dredge up her American history. Edward had been alive around 1840. Clarence could be talking about the Civil War or the American-Spanish War, or conceivably one of the two World Wars.

'Who is the President of the United States, Clarence?'

'That don't mean nothing to me but the Commander in Chief of the Continental Army is George Washington.'

Vivien felt herself floundering. Just when she thought she'd grasped the concept of reincarnation – the patterns that were carried over from one life to the next – Stephen appeared to be recounting a totally different existence. It couldn't be Edward's next life because they were going back in time. Right back to the War of Independence. Was that significant? A clue that Clarence wasn't, in fact, connected to Edward? If so, that meant that the only thing the two personas had in common was Stephen. It came to her that Clarence might be a completely separate incarnation. Was it possible that things had got mixed up on the Bardo plane, sort of a little like wires getting crossed? It would complicate matters but there was no reason to believe that he wasn't still there. With Dmitri.

'Where are you, Clarence? Is there a bright light in front of you pulling you towards it?'

'No, mam.'

Not the Bardo plane, then.

'I'm on Bunker Hill.'

'Who is there with you?'

'Some of my men.'

'No little boys?'

'None that you'd call little exactly, but many are no more than boys right enough.'

Vivien fought hard to keep her disappointment from clouding her judgement. For a moment she had allowed herself to hope that her son was still with Stephen and would somehow find a way to make contact with her. The longing for his presence was physically painful. She folded her arms across her chest and hugged herself; she was getting far too involved. She tried to slow her breathing to match that of Stephen.

When she was sure she could speak again without her voice betraying her emotion, she resumed her questioning.

'Clarence, I wonder if you can let me speak to Stephen for a moment. I need to ask him a question and it's one I know you can't help me with.'

'Sure can, mam.'

'Stephen? Stephen, I want you to tell me if you recognise any of the people around Clarence? It's very important. We are looking for patterns, remember.'

And she was looking for Dmitri.

'There's an old man standing near him.'

Stephen spoke slowly and calmly and seemed to be experiencing no difficulty in shifting between personas. Indeed he hadn't all along; that was why she had been so convinced that it all been a product of his sub-conscious.

'He's some sort of doctor, and he reminds me of you.'

Vivien's stomach knotted. This was the second time that she had turned up. When she'd been working along the lines of the fantasy theory, it had seemed quite natural that she would be present in the guise of Mr Wharburton, the government commissioner in the potteries, but now? Was he just making a loose connection between people in the medical profession or was this pointing to her having experienced some past lives, too? She couldn't even begin to articulate how difficult she found that.

'Okay, Stephen, thank you. Just take two or three deep breaths and, when you're ready, take yourself back to Clarence's world.'

This was not how she'd thought this session would go at all. But although she could guide Stephen with her questions, she couldn't force him to go somewhere or be someone he was not. She would have to leave trying to access the Bardo plane again for another time.

'Feel what it is like to be him and tell me his story.'

CHAPTER TWENTY-TWO

The dawn crept over the horizon heralding another clear warm day. A day ill-designed for the carnage that lay before him. Clarence's habitual frown deepened as he looked down at the man who had been like a surrogate father to him. He tried not to wince at the sight but it was difficult to reconcile the prematurely aged man with that of the farmhand he'd idolised and followed everywhere. Gone were the full cheeks and the glittering smile; in their place, a mask of pain. Clarence remembered when he'd been about ten and gone with him into the barn and they'd come across old Jeb sleeping on a pile of straw. Abraham had dragged down his cheeks with his fingers and begun to drool in imitation; he had been at least twenty (old enough to a small boy) but the idea that he'd ever look so ancient had made Clarence roar with laughter. It had taken a handful of seconds for it to come true.

Clarence tore his gaze away and tried to compose himself. He could not afford to give vent to his feelings, some of the men under his command might interpret it as weakness and a bad example was worse than no example at all. Luckily the last of them had left to trudge up the hill some time before disaster had struck. It hadn't been lucky for Abraham, of course. He had been in exactly the wrong place at the wrong time. Two minutes before he had been standing in waist-high grass, calling across to Clarence about the gut-rot he'd had after last night's supper and now, here he was, lying on the scarred earth, his gripes forgotten in the agony of everything else.

Two, three deep breaths and Clarence turned his attention to the figure of the medic who was fussily rearranging his inadequate instruments in his bag. He caught Clarence's eyes and shook his head slowly. It was an unnecessary gesture.

Clarence had no medical training but even he knew that a man whose legs had been blown off could not survive.

'Do what you can for him, Corporal Harvey,' the medic said. 'A sip of water perhaps or a few comforting words. They are the only things that could possibly make any difference to him now.'

Clarence lifted off his tricorn hat and threw it on the ground. Then he pulled the leather strap of his canteen over his head and knelt down. His hands shook as he unscrewed the cap. 'Abraham. Can you hear me, Abraham?'

He removed his neckerchief and dampened it a little before dabbing it on his friend's forehead and cheeks. Then he supported him behind his neck and gently raised his head, holding the canteen to his mouth.

'Take a little. It will make it easier to swallow.'

Abraham looked at him with uncomprehending eyes but his lips opened slightly as the thin trickle of water touched them. Clarence watched as he struggled to swallow. He found himself trying to gulp down the saliva in his mouth in unison. He had to make himself speak. To say something. He owed it to his friend to make his last thoughts on this earth as carefree and peaceful as possible. He could lie with the best of them. He'd had a lot of practice recently;

giving the same spiel about noble causes he'd heard the day he had joined the Massachusetts militia. He'd been back working on the farm by then but the call to defend his birthright, and the desire to follow in Abraham's footsteps and re-enlist, had been too great. But he didn't want to think about that now. He had to find a more pleasant memory. It came to him so strongly that it made him want to cry.

'I was thinking back to when you caught that giant catfish. Remember? You hauled it out and ended up lying on your back then, too. Darn thing nearly bit your hand off, would'a done if I hadn't whacked it with my fishing pole. Sun was shining then too. I was playing hookey from chores and you'd said you'd come with me and we could hear Jeb hollering that we was both wanted but we weren't going back until we'd landed the monster, were we? Reckon there's another even bigger one waiting for us in that creek. I'm sure anxious to get back there with our fishing poles, chewing baccy and watching for him to be stirring the mud up. But it's my turn this time. I ain't having you being the only one able to go about bragging.'

He didn't know how much longer he could keep this up. The world he was creating and the world around them were too heart-breakingly different. He only hoped that his words were soothing Abraham; they were tearing him apart.

'My pa. What's going to happen to my pa?'

Clarence looked up. He had forgotten Samuel Langhorne was there. It wasn't difficult. The boy was half Clarence's size, little thicker than a river aspen. If he turned sideways in the tall grass it was easy for your eyes to skate over him. But he would have time to fill out; he was just sixteen, the same age as Clarence had been when he'd had his first stint as part of a militia. He was twenty-five now and had seen many horrors fighting the Mohawk Indians but he'd never had to watch his father dying before him. No wonder the boy was hopping about from foot to foot and looked like he was caught up in a bad dream. There probably wasn't any way that you could prepare for such a thing but the British cannonball had flown out of nowhere. His father had been standing a yard or so behind and the direct hit had taken his legs off as cleanly as a scythe cutting through dry corn. Clarence forced a hard edge into his voice; someone had to remind the boy that he was a soldier; it was the only way he was going to ever close his eyes again at night.

'He's going to breathe his last before the shadows lengthen so, if you have anything to say to him, you'd better say it now.'

Samuel's mouth moved but no sound came out. He looked as stricken as his father. Clarence felt a twinge of pity for him but this was war. Unforgivable things, and unforgettable sights, happened in war. The boy would just have to get used to it; there was no way back to a quiet life on the farm from here.

He felt a hand weakly clawing at his tunic and bent his head towards Abraham's mouth. He had to stop himself from recoiling as he saw a fringe of bloody spittle froth out from between his friend's lips.

'I ... want ... you...'

His breathing was laboured and the words barely discernable.

'Take ... care ... of ... my ...boy... He's...'

A thin shudder – nothing more – and the life left Abraham Langhorne's body. Clarence watched his eyes film over in death. He got to his feet. The worst moment of his war, so far, was over. There was nothing he could do but get on with his duty and leave it behind.

'You'd better come with me. We're ordered to move further up and onto Breed's Hill. We must get to where we can defend from higher ground.'

He picked up his musket and started to walk away. Samuel didn't move. His gaze was still riveted on his father's bloody and shattered corpse. The medic, who had removed himself to a little way off, beckoned Clarence over.

'Go easy on him, Corporal. His mind is clouded with shock. Even those with more battle-weariness on his shoulders than he has would have a hard time swallowing what he has just seen. Death can shutter out reason and sudden death can make a man lost to it completely.'

Clarence stared at him harshly. 'I'm a soldier of the American army, not a schoolteacher.'

He retreated two steps, grabbed Samuel roughly by the arm and tugged him along. He had no choice but to honour the last entreaty of a dying man but how he wished that he hadn't asked it of him. He already had a platoon that it was his duty to command and protect and the extra burden of a grief-stricken boy could not make that task any easier.

It was a hot and slow climb over Bunker Hill. Clarence was forced to pause on numerous occasions to allow Samuel to catch up with him. He daren't just leave him and trust that he'd follow. It wasn't that Samuel was a disobedient boy – he knew the penalties of not following orders as well as any of them – but he was hardly thinking straight right now. The last thing Clarence wanted was to have to institute military discipline on someone who still had his father's blood on his boots.

Clarence ran his hand through the waist-high grass and took a moment to look around him. He was surrounded by a coiling sinuous snake of water sparkling in the sunshine. To his right was the Mystic River; his left, the Charles River and, ahead, Boston Harbour. Below him he could see Charlestown, and beyond, the masts and sails of the British warships. It was the perfect vantage point; once they'd completed the redoubt on the shoulder known as Breed's Hill, they'd be able to defend the whole of the Charlestown Peninsula.

He felt a trickle of sweat rolling down his spine. Surely it was the heat that was affecting him and not the thought of the battle ahead? He was beginning to regret choosing deer leather for his hunting frock – most of the other soldiers wore homespun or linen. But he had felt his six years of earlier service fighting Indian skirmishes had warranted something that made him look a campaign veteran; a fierce countenance and solid muscles were commonplace enough and, although won the respect of his men, weren't sufficient to convince his superior officers that he was a man worthy of great command.

He reached for his neckerchief to wipe his brow. Blast it. He had left it on the ground beside Abraham. Along with his canteen. That had been foolish. He would need a drink before the hot and heavy work of digging-in had finished. That damned boy had distracted him. And where was he? Clarence turned around and shielded his eyes as he watched Langhorne trudge in his wake through the grass. The young private better have his pick and shovel with him or he would send him back down to fetch them.

The work on the redoubt itself had finished by the time Clarence reached the northern escarpment of Breed's Hill. It was an imposing structure and a miracle that it had been built so quickly. Eight rods square, it had six foot earth walls. There was a post and rail fence in front of it stretching down the entire east side of the hill to the Mystic River, padded thickly for cover with long grass mown from the meadows behind. He found his platoon snatching a rare moment of repose. Some of the soldiers were stretched out on their bedrolls, their faces turned towards the sun; others were whittling with their bayonets or making running repairs to their uniforms. As one, the men stood as Clarence arrived amongst them.

'The time for rest is over,' he said in a loud and commanding voice. He could see the weariness in the eyes looking back at him but battles were not won by giving in to tiredness. 'It's fallen to us to stop the British advance. We're to throw up another earthwork down aways from this one, as the first line of defence. And it's to be as high as we can make it. If the redcoats are able to break through then they'll be set to reinforce their besieged troops and Boston will be lost. We cannot ... we will not ... let that happen.'

He could see some of the older men in his command wondering why he was pushing them so hard when they were already almost at the limit of their endurance but he also knew that every one of them trusted him not to let them go into battle unprepared. He watched the farmers and blacksmiths and woodsmen who had once worked the land for food, pick up their tools and make their way down the slope.

It took hours under the hot sun before the earth wall was even up to waist height. Clarence walked up and down the length of the parapet with words of encouragement and jokes to try and ease the desperation on the men's faces. He could see the redcoats massing like a spreading stain on the shoreline of Moulton's Point and knew he was in full view of the British gunners but that didn't deter him. It was up to him to set an example of bravery and show that discipline in the ranks amounted to no more than the personal discipline of every single one of them. He watched as two boats rowed away from one of the warships and across the harbour.

'You have to dig deep,' he told the men in front of him, 'but they have a long trek to reach us. Across the water, and up the hill. And the sun sure ain't kind to those wearing heavy overcoats and carrying knapsacks. They will scarce have enough energy to reload their flintlocks when they reach us.'

But he knew from the faces that looked up at him that they were in no better condition; they had little food or water and were exhausted from lack of sleep.

'Just a few feet more. Until you can stand and lay the barrel of your Brown Bess on the earth with only the top of your tricorn to be seen. Then, even if they are lucky enough to get a shot off, the lead will only whistle above your head and there is plenty enough sky for them to aim at.'

He stopped his pacing. Below him, in a trench no deeper than his knees, was Samuel Langhorne. Clarence jumped down beside him. He bent forward so that the men on either side couldn't catch his words.

'And you will lose your head as sure as your father lost his legs if you don't work that pick harder.'

He knew they were harsh words but if the boy didn't put his back into it some more then he would be felled by the first volley. Samuel looked at him. Grief was etched on his features but there was also fierce determination. He swung the pick high above his head and thudded it into the ground. There was a metallic clang and Samuel's hands flew away from the shaft as if he had been stung.

'I hit a stone,' he said, shaking his wrists, 'there are so many in the ground here.'

'Tell the excuses to the redcoats when they are filling their priming pans.'

The man on the other side of Samuel threw a glance at Clarence. He had spoken too loudly in his frustration with the boy. He needed him to be scared – it was only fear for their lives that kept them safe in the end – but he didn't want those who already felt it to tip over the edge into incapacity. Or running away; he had seen too many militia men sink to that already.

He reached for the discarded pick. Resting the shaft against his thighs, he stripped off his hat and hunting frock, then spat on his hands.

'Go back to the redoubt. Find the officer in charge and tell him I sent you. He'll put you to good use.'

'But my place is here.'

Clarence thought about putting him on a charge for refusing an order but decided against it. What had the medic said? *He was in shock.* Maybe he just didn't understand. He was only a boy after all.

'If this spot ends up being a weak point then you'll put the whole line in danger.

Maybe the whole of the American army, too. Do you want Boston to be lost just because you weren't able to dig fast enough?'

'I want to stay here and I want to fight. I'm my father's only living kin and it's beholden on me to uphold the family good name. I'd defy you not to want to do the same. I signed up for battle and I won't stand aside and watch others take all the glory.'

Clarence was torn between wanting to lash out at the boy, or pull him to him. Even though he had seen the horror of his father's death, he still didn't comprehend the realities of battle; didn't realise that before the morning was over, he would most likely lose an eye or an arm: or his life. It was a fate that they all must face but it should be faced with knowledge; with understanding. It wasn't right that someone so innocent should be mown down, like the grass around him, in ignorance. He felt his heart clench as he realised that the greater part of him wished that he was untainted too. Life had been so simple at sixteen.

From out in the bay, the sound of the British fleet's ordinance started up again. Clarence could see palls of grey smoke rising up to form little clouds; the only ones in the sky. There was a soft plosive thud as one of the twenty-four pound cannonballs buried itself in the slope ahead of them. It was a fair way off but it wouldn't be long before they found their range. There was no time left for arguments.

'Don't just stand there gawking. If you're staying, grab that shovel. And dig as though your life depended on it because before the sun is much higher, it surely will.'

Clarence had the uncomfortable feeling in the pit of his stomach that he had just made a bad decision. But Samuel wanted to stay and fight when so many others would have taken his orders and scurried away happily with them. He didn't have so many men in the line that he could spare one with a fighting spirit such as his. Maybe the boy's earnest foolishness would keep him safe; he had a platoon to command and wouldn't have the time to. He lifted up the pick and stuck the point deep into the ground at his feet. What a damn awful way to be spending his birthday.

Vivien looked at her watch. The hour was almost up. She felt her frustration keenly; she wanted – needed – to get Stephen to work through this quickly so that they could get back to Edward – and maybe Dmitri – again. The only way to speed things up was to get him to come back again tomorrow.

'Stephen. I want you to start counting backwards from five. Nice and slowly. When you reach *one* your eyes will open and you will feel relaxed and refreshed.'

It took him a moment to comply then he stretched his arms and leapt off the couch.

'Well, who'd have thought it?' He seemed almost pleased with himself. 'It's quite fun, this past lives lark. Maybe not fun, exactly. I don't know why I couldn't have been a millionaire on a yacht in the Bahamas instead of a hay-seed soldier; I'd have looked great in a dinner jacket.'

Vivien knew that his garrulous humour was his way of defending himself from the reality of what had just experienced. Predictably, as soon as he stopped speaking, his face collapsed back into betraying his fright and confusion.

'How much longer is this going to go on? I don't think I can take much more of it.'

'I don't know, Stephen. But we are making progress. We are getting deeper to the heart of what is going on with you.'

'But why does it all have to be about death?'

'I know it's not going to make you feel much better but, ultimately, most of our issues about life come down to our difficulties accepting the concept of mortality.' She was acutely aware that she was echoing her own transparent need. 'And, in your case, they are compounded by your regression into your past lives. It is inevitable that they will focus on death because that is what happened to them.'

'Sometimes...' his voice was barely more than a whisper, '...I think that my own death would be preferable to this...'

Vivien tried not to show her alarm. 'That is never a way out, Stephen. I understand why you feel that way at the moment but it is just where you are in the process. We are revealing too much for you to comprehend at the moment. So please just try to believe that it will get better. We will resolve this. And you're not alone. I will be with you every step of the way. I want you to make an appointment with Jean to come back tomorrow. Tell her that I said she should clear my diary if necessary. It is vital that we find out what happens to Clarence as soon as possible.'

'If you say so, but I can't see my headmaster liking it much.'

'I'll give him a call now and stress the urgency.'

'I don't know if I can get through the night.'

Vivien got up and walked over to her computer. She found Stephen's details and ordered up a prescription.

'I want you to go to the pharmacy on your way out. I'm only giving you two pills and I want you to take both of them. They are excellent in dealing with acute states of anxiety. You won't have nightmares, I promise you.'

Stephen stared at her with sagging shoulders. Vivien briskly walked across the room and opened the door; prolonging their time together wasn't going to make it any easier for him to fully reenter the real world. As he had to. She allowed herself a brief pat on his arm as he passed by.

Vivien picked up the telephone to make the promised call to his headmaster. She wondered if the time was right for her to try to confirm Jim McFraser's hints about the boating incident. She still didn't know if Stephen had intentionally tried to drown that boy. The more she got to know about the state of his mind, the more she thought that it could be true. But she wouldn't. In some absurd way, it would feel disloyal to Stephen to go behind his back. She had to wait until he was ready to tell her himself.

CHAPTER TWENTY-THREE

Vivien settled down to write up her case notes. Jean popped her head around the office door to tell her that she had managed to fit Stephen Daunt in. Lunchtime tomorrow. Vivien was pleased to hear it was so early; another few hours less to wait. She picked up her pen. But before she could begin, there was a perfunctory knock on the door and Jim McFraser breezed in with a smile almost as wide and bright as his bow tie.

'Do you ever get the feeling that things were just meant to be?'

Vivien had been so lost in her thoughts about Stephen's case that she thought for one disorientating moment and he was talking about Dmitri.

'I've just had the most extraordinary morning,' he continued, 'full of synchronicity so great that even Jung would be tempted to put it down to co-incidence.'

She had never seen him looking so pleased with himself. He was even rubbing his hands together like a bookmaker who'd just accepted the odds of the century.

'The British Psychological Society is holding a reception tonight for some visiting professors from America. It was to be at their place but there's been some cock-up over a scheduled overhaul of their computing systems. Anyway, to cut a long story short, they'll have their tech boys swarming over their offices all evening and they're scouting around looking for another suitable venue. I've said we'll host it for them. Short notice, I know, but you don't have to do anything but be there.'

'They're not expecting me to be, surely, not if I wasn't on the original guest list?'

'But there's the beauty of it. I volunteered our services because a little bird told me that this little do is to be more than a social get together. It's a sort of a powwow for the bigwigs in advance of the symposium you're presenting your paper to.'

Vivien felt a stab of guilt: the paper had gone completely out of her mind.

'Sorry, Jim. I'll get my outline on your desk by the end of the week.'

'No, no, you misunderstand me. My sources in the know have whispered to me that your name has been put forward to be included on the shortlist for an outstanding achievement award to be presented later in the year. It'll be great kudos for University College Hospital and the department in particular. For you too, of course,' he added.

Vivien felt a flutter of excitement. It would indeed be an honour to be on the shortlist, and if she were to actually win then she would almost certainly have first option on Dr McFraser's position when he retired...

'So you can see why you just have to be there,' he was saying, 'once you've dazzled them with your brains, beauty and charm, it'll be all but a forgone conclusion. They'll be rounding them up at their various hotels and bringing them here. Nine thirty. Jean and the other secretaries are up in the conference room now getting everything organised. You'll just about have time to go home and dig out your glad-rags – I know how important your armour is to you ladies. See if you can get that husband of yours to come along. You'll want him by your side for such a big moment. Not a word to anyone about the shortlist though. It's supposed to be all behind closed doors. But you can tell Jerry, of course, he will be so proud.'

Vivien heard herself muttering a jumble of inconsequential words of surprise and thanks as Jim McFraser exited her office shouting instructions to some unfortunate minion about catering.

Vivien spent a full fifteen minutes in front of her wardrobe back in Hampstead deciding what dress to wear. It was vital that she make the right impression. In the end she picked the first one she'd held up against her and rooted around for the matching shoes. She'd fling everything she needed into a bag and change back at the office. She'd already phoned for a cab. She was feeling panicked enough as it was without worrying about whether she had left herself enough time. Her hair would just have to do.

She was walking back down the stairs when she heard the key in the front door. Jerry. What was he doing home in the middle of the afternoon? When he came in he looked equally startled to see her.

'Viv. What's with the bag, you're not going away again are you?'

'No, no, nothing like that. I found out a couple of hours ago that Jim McFraser has rashly agreed for the department to host a reception tonight and it seems – that in his eyes at least – I'm to be the guest of honour. My name is on a shortlist apparently for some award or other; he was a bit sketchy on the details. I'm just going back to the office now to see if I can find out anything more so I don't look like a complete idiot in front of everyone.'

'That would never happen. And it's great news about the award – whatever it is. Congratulations, I know you would've worked hard for it.'

'Thanks. I'd assumed you were working late as usual or I would've phoned and invited you.'

She felt a little guilty at the blatantness of the lie. She and Jerry had arrived at an awkward – but workable – truce since she'd returned from Stoke but neither of them had actively encouraged spending time in each other's company.

'Normally I would be of course but we also had a little bit of drama this morning. I was called for an interview at the Royal Free Hospital. They've asked me to sit on the Government's review body for paediatric medicine. The previous incumbent had a heart attack and they need the place filled immediately. It's a great honour and a once in a lifetime opportunity.'

'That's wonderful, Jerry.' She was genuinely pleased. Maybe a new job would give him back the zest for life that she so obviously could not. 'I know how much something like this means to you. Look, I'm sorry, and I know the timing's lousy but we'll have to postpone talking about it properly until later. My taxi should be here at any minute.'

'Can't you send it away and order another one? We really have things to discuss.'

'I've barely enough time as it is.'

'I'd offer to run you in but I have to get my passport over to them.'

'The job's in another country?'

The way things were between them, she no longer knew whether such a massive change would be an unwelcome prospect or not.

'No, but there will be some overseas travel involved and they need the number for their records. That's why I popped back.'

A car horn honked outside.

'There's my taxi. I have to go.'

'Viv. Look, if I can, I'll come down to your reception tonight. I'd like to be there for you anyway and it'll give us a chance to talk about this. I'm not going to accept the job unless you agree.'

'Why? It sounds like just the sort of thing

you've always wanted to do.'

'It is but there's a catch... It's only a short-term posting – three months maximum – but it starts straight away. And it's in Newcastle.'

'Ah ...'

The taxi honked once more. Vivien was glad that there was no time for an adequate response. She wouldn't know what to say anyway.

'I'll see you later then,' she said as she opened the front door.

'If I can, Viv. I said: if I can. I can't make any promises with the way things are at the moment.'

He could have been echoing her thoughts exactly.

Back in her office, Jean twittered around her. The reception was due to start in about half an hour and Vivien had already wasted valuable minutes watching a fleet of black cabs draw up outside the building and deposit a gaggle of grey-haired professors and eager bright young things at the Gower Street entrance.

Her stomach felt uncomfortably hollow. She should have eaten something. But at least the front of her dress was nice and flat. It was the green and blue silk creation she'd bought last month that had cost more than her mother would ever believe possible for something so simple. But it was beautifully cut. And she did look good in it, in a classic rather than a showy way, and the fitted waist really complimented her figure.

She finished applying her mascara in front of the mirror and turned to seek Jean's approval.

'So, will I do?'

'Dr Blake, you look fab.' Jean squinted sideways at her for a moment. 'But you're not wearing those earrings are you? They don't really go.'

Vivien sighed. She didn't always trust her secretary's taste but knew that she would never hear the end of it if she insisted on wearing the pearls.

'Didn't you bring any others?' Jean insisted.

Vivien walked across to the coffee table. In her bag amongst the make-up and perfume was a pair of diamond drop earrings. She'd thought them a bit flashy for the occasion but had brought them anyway. She held them up for inspection.

'Perfect. Here, let me.'

Jean waited until Vivien had removed the offending pearls and then fumbled to thread the alternatives through the holes in Vivien's pierced ears.

'God, you're more nervous than I am,' Vivien said as Jean dropped one of the butterfly fastenings on the floor. 'Anyone would think this was a big occasion.'

'Well, isn't it?' Jean secured the earrings at last. 'With the prize in the offing. We're all so proud of you, Dr Blake.'

'How did you know about that? I thought it was supposed to be a closely-guarded secret.'

'Dr Nicholls told me.'

Seb. That man could gossip for Britain.

'I thought he was leaving today for another book-signing tour.'

'Not until next month now. It seems his publisher has got wind of some television psychiatrist about to do the same sort of thing and is waiting for him to fall flat on his face first. Or so Dr Nicholls says.'

He would. Seb's ego was not one to take having a rival in the field and he would, no doubt, be doing his best to spread a few professional rumours to discredit the other man's work. All's fair in love and the bestseller lists; Vivien could hear him now.

'Will he be here tonight?' She felt a flutter in her stomach as she asked. Anxiety or anticipation? It was impossible to tell.

'Try keeping him away. You know what he's like, free booze and food and wall-to-wall attention...' Jean stepped back and eyed Vivien critically, 'but with you looking like that, I doubt he'll even get a look in.'

Vivien smiled and walked back over to the mirror. Jean had been right. The earrings were perfect. Not remotely party-girl as she had thought but more a touch of elegance. Maybe it was time she ditched insecurity-induced understatements like the pearls; now was a time to shine if ever there was one.

She sat down and buckled up her high-heeled sandals.

'I only hope I can walk in these.'

'All you have to do is get down the corridor to the conference room in one piece. Once you're there you won't have to move; the men will all be falling over themselves to go to the bar for you.'

An image of doddery professors tripping over their Hush Puppies made Vivien laugh. She would enjoy tonight. She would. She'd stop worrying about how to handle any awkwardness with Seb and just take the situation as it came. And that went for what she'd say to Jerry about his news, too. That was if he turned up. The only thing she did know was that the day had thrown up so many surprises that she had no reason to believe they would stop just because evening had fallen.

CHAPTER TWENTY-FOUR

The conference room was half-full when she walked in. She felt a stab of childhood self-consciousness as the conversation died a little and everyone seemed to turn and stare at her. She thought for one awful moment that her bra strap was showing or something. It was Seb who saved her from blushing gauchely.

'Vivien. You look the belle of the ball. Allow me.'

He was wearing a glamorously inappropriate white tuxedo and he held his arm out to her in the manner of a gallant southern gentleman straight out of *Gone With The Wind*. Vivien swallowed her embarrassment at seeing him again; if he could ride this out so casually then so could she. Neither of them need mention what happened when they were last together.

She placed her hand on his forearm and Seb escorted her over to a quiet corner and then left her side to go and get them both a drink. Vivien looked around. Someone (not Jean, she suspected) had done wonders with the room. The boring institutional tables were covered in crisp white tablecloths and vases of flamboyant flowers broke up the formality. Young men and women – Vivien recognised one of her former students – dressed in black trousers and white shirts, were circling around carrying trays of canapés. A large pile of blood-orange jacketed books were stacked on one of the tables underneath the window.

'Sorry, they're fresh out of mint julep,' Seb said as he returned with a glass of chilled white wine for them both.

'How could you?' Vivien nodded towards the books. 'Isn't that flagrant display of self-publicity a bit much, even for you?'

'If I don't blow my own trumpet then who will?'

'Not the first kid on the block anymore then, Seb?'

'Far from it. They're all crawling out of the woodwork on the back of my success.' He looked serious for a moment. 'Truth is, Vivien, I don't know that I can hack it much longer. It's all beginning to feel a little empty somehow.' He took a sip of his drink. 'And it's all your fault.'

'Mine? What did I do?'

'You know very well. You fired me up again,' he looked at her over the rim of his glass, 'and I know the feeling's mutual.'

'Seb ... I ... about what happened...'

He raised his eyebrows. 'Come on, you know me, I've forgotten about that already.'

She should've been grateful to him for closing the door on that episode so effectively but, absurdly, she wasn't. And it wasn't just her vanity that was piqued. His reaction seemed to confirm how badly she was misreading people these days. She thought he'd come as close as he dared to telling her that he loved her – could she possibly have got it wrong? It wasn't the sort of thing that she would've imagined. Unless she wanted to... She shook her head to rid herself of the thought.

'No, much as I hate to admit it, I'm the victim of professional jealousy.'

Vivien couldn't make the mental leap and she looked at him for a moment as she tried to get the image of them alone in the bedroom in Stoke out of her mind.

'Explain?'

'Oooh.' His hand flew to his cheek like a falsely modest beauty queen at her crowning. 'Are we going to talk about me? It's my favourite subject.'

'Seb, I'm serious. Why did you say you were jealous?'

A second's pause.

'Apart from the obvious, you mean?'

He had such an uncomfortable knack of doing this; making her feel that she was safe with him then giving her just enough rope with which to hang herself. She bought herself some time by taking a drawn-out sip of wine. The glass reminded her of the pressure of his lips on hers.

'Come on, Vivien, use your imagination.'

She was. A little too much. A flush crept up her neck. She knew by the gleam in his eye that Seb had noticed.

'Okay, I'll come clean. That case of yours has got the old juices flowing again. I was a practising psychiatrist for years and, the truth is, I miss it. Writing's all very well and lucrative but – and I never thought I'd say this – I want to get back inside some messed-up poor bugger's head again for real. It was fun.'

Vivien controlled her breath so that it wouldn't sound too much like the sigh of relief it was.

'I don't remember you ever saying that at the time.'

'Well, maybe not. But the grass is greener and all that.'

'Why don't to speak to Dr McFraser. He'll take you back – even though you're such a pain in his butt.'

'No point. I happened to get a sneak preview of his staffing forecasts when I accidentally opened and read the budget folder on his desk.'

'Oh, Seb.'

'There are no vacancies at the moment. So all my hopes for the future rest on you. It could be said by someone more poetic than me that my entire happiness lies in your hands.'

'What do you mean?'

She was feeling edgy again; they were skating too close to the un-discussable and with every pass, it became more likely that they would fall into the depths and never be able to regain solid ground again.

'Quite simply that tomorrow is another day. You win this award and in the fullness of time Fat Man McFraser is pensioned off to the waiting room of lost souls. You slip effortlessly and elegantly into his place and, hey presto, a Seb-shaped vacancy miraculously appears.'

Vivien wondered if it would be such a good idea now to even consider the possibility of becoming the head of department. To be Seb Nicholls' boss as well as his ... his ... friend. Besides, she didn't need his expectations added to those of Jim McFraser's – and her own. The prospect of failure weighed heavily on her shoulders.

'Best not to count your chickens, Seb. My name's not even on the shortlist yet.'

'Oh, but it is. I just happened to get a glimpse of that top-secret document too. Ate it afterwards, of course.'

Vivien laughed and felt her shoulders drop as all the tension of the day fell away. Seb beamed at her and she knew that he saw this as some sort of personal victory. And it was:

she doubted if she'd ever have had the courage to come back to work at all if it hadn't been for Seb's discreet but persistent encouragement.

'So how's it going with the mystery man – or should I say *men?*'

Vivien twirled the stem of her wine glass in her fingers. It took so little to feel as if he was by her side instead of being a sparring partner. Simply an interest in her and her work. Something that she felt she hadn't had from Jerry in a very long time. She shrugged off a pang of disloyalty. It was unfair to compare them; Seb was the easiest person in the world to talk to – when he wasn't teasing her or playing some elaborate game of his own – and he had a knack of pulling the truth out of her. About her work, at least.

'I'm scared, Seb,' she said softly, 'I'm scared that I may not be able to resolve this one. Just when I thought I was beginning to grasp what you told me about the Bardo plane, in our session this morning another past life popped up. I have no idea what is going on.'

'Nonsense. You're the best practitioner I know – apart from yours truly of course – and if anyone can work this out, you can.'

Vivien felt a glow of pride. That was praise indeed. Seb was not known for issuing professional compliments and he really was a very good psychiatrist. He was gifted with the most open-minded approach of anyone she had ever met. Okay, it bordered on the amoral sometimes – particularly in his personal life – but she thought she'd probably forfeited the right to make judgements like that anymore; her actions in Stoke had hardly been those of someone deserving a place on the moral high ground.

'And there's more,' she found herself saying, 'I'm frightened that I'm in danger of losing sight of my patient's needs in all this. The only thing I can seem to think about is the possibility of getting in touch with Dmitri again through him.'

'Don't be so hard on yourself, Vivien. You're only human. You can't shut up all your feelings in a little box and throw away the key.'

She looked up at him sharply. 'Is that what you think I do?'

'Sometimes. Much of the time, in fact.'

'And is there anything so very wrong in that? It's a healthy approach in a psychiatrist.'

'But not in a woman.'

'And what would you know about it?'

She was aware that she had raised her voice and a number of the people around them had turned to look at her. She was getting to the stage of being beyond caring. Was it the wine or the fact that Seb was in danger of overstepping the line that he had just made such a heavy point of establishing?

'Very little, I grant you. But I know you are in pain and confused. You have to admit that our little trip together was evidence of that if nothing else. So...'

'What?'

'Are you going to tell me what's going on with you or do I have to go through the twenty questions routine?'

She sighed. Maybe he was right and it was time she unburdened herself a little. God knows, she couldn't talk to Jerry about anything without it threatening to turn into a row.

'You will have heard it a million times before; my sub-conscious is hardly original and it's the usual, I'm afraid. I'm finding it hard to forgive myself ... let go ... move on ... accept there is hope for the future,' her voice broke a little, 'and learn to live with loss.'

Seb laid his hand gently on her forearm and stroked away the goose-pimples.

'It's only natural and a key stage in grieving. You need to work through all this so that you can heal.'

'But I'm at all not sure that I want to. That I'm ready to yet.'

'You are or you wouldn't have been open to the experience of Dmitri appearing on the

Bardo plane. You wouldn't even have been open to the concept that it might exist; witness how resistant you were at the beginning. Your willingness to challenge your beliefs in certainty proves that you are ready, Vivien, but you have to stop trying to protect yourself from the pain of the process. It's the only way you can start to live like a whole person again.'

Seb grasped the corner of his top pocket handkerchief, pulled it out and handed it to her.

'Can't have my very own Scarlett O'Hara with smudged mascara, can I? It's all about image you know and someone might well think I've been a beastly cad to you and that really would be the final nail in my career coffin.'

Vivien dabbed her tears away discreetly. Seb had a way of anticipating her every need and doing just the right thing at the right time. She was only beginning to appreciate just how precious a friendship such as his, really was. She had been foolish to try to risk turning it into something else – whatever the reason. She finished her glass of wine and held it out for a refill. When he returned a minute or to later, she was composed again.

'So,' he said as he handed her wine to her, 'what are you going to do when you've finished this case? Write it up and get it published? Because I tell you, I'd kill for a juicy little mystery like this one.'

'Funnily enough, Jim McFraser already suggested something similar. He wanted me to use Stephen as the focus for my symposium paper. But I'm not going to, of course.'

'Why ever not? Lights and bushels, Vivien, lights and bushels.'

'For a start I'm nowhere near resolving what's at the root of his trauma, and besides...'

'What? Spit it out.'

'I think I'm too personally involved.'

'Nothing wrong in that; is there any way to get involved other than personally?'

He was grinning at her and, for the first time that evening, she felt able to smile back in complicity. She no longer had the energy to go on pretending that there was nothing between them. Repression didn't make things go away; she should know that by now.

'Jerry's had a job offer.' Now why did she tell him that? What had that to do with anything? 'In Newcastle.'

'Good.'

'Seb!'

'Vivien, I know what you're going to think of me for saying this but I'm going to say it anyway. This is your moment and he's holding you back.'

'What right have you go to say that? You know nothing about my relationship with Jerry. In fact, he's very supportive of my work.'

'I don't mean that. Have you told him about Dmitri and the Bardo plane?'

'No, not yet.'

'I wonder why. Could it be because you know he wouldn't approve of you exploring the possibility of the unexplainable? He's a surgeon grounded in corporeal reality, remember.'

She could almost taste her resentment at the way Seb was able to put his finger so sharply on her deepest thoughts and fears and pull them so cleanly out into the open. She took a large gulp of her wine.

'What makes you such an expert on me all of a sudden? One near miss together in Stoke and you think you know everything about me?' Oh God, she'd said it.

'Far from it. I think I'm only just beginning to glimpse the real Vivien underneath the cool and clinical exterior. And I think you are, too. You probably don't want to hear this right now but what you need is the opposite of safe and secure support; your soul is crying out for someone to push and challenge you.'

'Someone like you, you mean.' She couldn't look at him.

'Now we've stopped flirting around the

edges: yes.'

Vivien barked out a sarcastic laugh. 'You don't challenge, you provoke. It's all a flippant game to you.'

'I just try and enjoy life and take what it has to offer – trust you to think that is flippant. All you do is build up barriers to protect yourself from hurt and it's about time that you realised that you can't do that. Life – shit – happens and you really should get used to that concept.'

Vivien shot him a glance. His jaw was set and there were knives in his eyes that she'd never seen before. A part of her felt a spiteful thrill that she had got to Mr Perfect at last.

'I know I'm far from being the ideal candidate for the most rounded person of the year award,' he said as if he could read her mind, 'but at least I put myself out there and take risks. You wouldn't know one if it was staring you in the face. You nearly took a risk with me in Stoke and now you want to deny it and behave as if it never happened.'

'You were the one who said you'd already forgotten.'

'Only to see what you'd say.'

'That's childish.'

'And so is toying with someone's genuine affections. That's just using people.'

'You're a fine one to talk.' She felt as though she were a tiger waiting to spring.

'You just look at what you want and take it.'

'And what's so very wrong with that? At least it's honest. You don't know what it is you do want. Or rather, I think you do but you're not prepared to face the consequences of following any desire through to its logical conclusion. I'd rather be a thief than a coward any day.'

'You think I want you, don't you?'

The muscles in her clenched jaw were aching with the effort of keeping her voice under control.

'I don't think, Vivien, I know. And Jerry knows he's lost you and that's why he wants to go away to Newcastle.'

She felt as though he were invading all her secret places. 'I never said he was going. In fact, he won't accept the job unless I agree.' Now she was the one sounding childish.

'And will you?'

She couldn't answer. It wasn't just anger at Seb's temerity that was blocking the words. The thought that maybe Jerry might be thinking of engineering the end of their marriage in the same way as she had was ... was ... what? Frightening? Humiliating? Salutatory? Welcome? She had no idea what she felt. Damn it! She started to shake and gripped her wine glass so tightly that she thought at any moment she might explode blood-coated splinters all over the room. Seb had pushed her into demonstrating how out of touch she was with own needs, yet again.

'I don't want to hurt you, Vivien, really I don't.' Seb had bent his head close to hers and was whispering in her ear almost like a lover. 'But unless you come to terms with your true nature then you can never be happy. With yourself ... with Jerry...' he started to walk past her as if he had suddenly spotted someone else to talk to, 'or with me.'

CHAPTER TWENTY-FIVE

Left alone, Vivien helped herself to another glass of wine. Who cared if she got drunk? She certainly didn't. Seb had done his best to destroy her equilibrium and she might as well finish the job off. The only alternative was to leave – she'd done her bit and put in an appearance – but what if Jerry turned up and she wasn't here? He might think that she'd set him up in some way; particularly if someone told him that she'd been seen talking to Seb all evening. God, she was getting paranoid. Damn and blast Seb.

She looked across the room and caught a flash of Jim McFraser's striped bowtie. So she wasn't a risk taker, eh? She'd show the arrogant, self-opinionated jerk that he was way off beam with that little piece of spurious analysis from the back pages of his very own self-help book.

Vivien swayed a little as she crossed the room. She put it down to her lack of practice in walking in high heels and arrived to stand confidently at Jim McFraser's side. He laid his hand briefly across her shoulder in greeting as he introduced her to the man he'd been talking to. He was elderly, wearing a regulation-ageing-psychiatrist tweed jacket and had fuzzy sideburns, a large nose, and hair coming out of his ears.

'Ah, the elusive Dr Blake,' he said in an American accent that made her think of her father, 'I've been wanting to have a word with you all evening. Dr McFraser tells me that the excellent reputation your department has is all down to you.'

'He's too kind. I'm sorry but do you mind if I take him away for a while? I just need a quick word; I'll bring him straight back.'

Without waiting for an answer, Vivien steered Jim McFraser over to an empty space at the edge of the room.

'It's about my paper for the symposium. I've been having second thoughts.'

'Don't tell me you're going to pull out?' There was something akin to panic in his voice. 'Because that would look very bad indeed for all of us; they'll never be able to find a replacement of your calibre at such short notice.'

'Calm down, Jim. You'll send your blood pressure through the roof. The fact is that I've changed my mind and I'd like to go back to something like your original idea.'

'Capital, Vivien, capital. So you've come to some conclusions about the functions of the psyche and projection?'

'No. Well, actually, yes. But not in the way you mean.' She'd show Seb. She'd go the whole hog and to hell with the consequences. How dare he say that she wasn't a risk taker? 'I want to explore the evaluation and perception of experience through the re-emergence of past lives and posit the theory that regression therapies can, in fact, both expose and support the existence of reincarnation.'

A wave of excitement washed through her. Maybe this is what Seb meant about living life on the edge. It certainly did feel thrilling. Jim McFraser was looking sideways at her.

'I know I said I wanted you to push the boundaries a little but I didn't mean for you to go right off the map. Ground-breaking ideas are one thing but there's only a thin line before you step over into becoming a laughing stock and I fear you will be with this one. You'd be risking the reputation of this department – and, I'm sure I needn't add, your future in it – if you even make reference to something as outlandish and unscientific as reincarnation. I'm intrigued though, what on earth made you dream that approach up?'

'Some unanswered questions. A bit of lateral thinking. Exposure to new ideas and, finally, the gathering of empirical evidence to back up my hypothesis.'

'What do you mean, evidence? I thought you were using case studies; there can't possibly be any emanating from here. No recently closed ones anyway; if there had of been, I'd have hauled the practitioner in and insist they join the first-year students for a refresher in the rudiments of basic psychiatry.'

'It's not a closed case, it's live. And you haven't seen the notes because I haven't shown them to you.'

Jim McFraser ran his palm over his jaw. 'Forgive me, Vivien, perhaps I've had a little too much sauce but you're not making any sense.'

'Stephen Daunt regresses to his past lives under hypnosis.'

She thought Jim McFraser's eyebrows were going to shoot right off his face.

'The school teacher? He's having you on. You can't possibly be telling me that you believe such nonsense? I thought you were just taking a misguided leaf out of Dr Nicholl's book and going for shock value in proposing that topic for your paper.'

'It is shocking, I'll admit, but it's not any the less true for that.'

Vivien no longer knew what she was saying and why. At first she had been goaded into it by Seb's dig at her but Jim's out-of-hand dismissal of everything she'd managed to piece together fuelled her determination to push on.

'Don't you see? What I'm saying isn't so very different to the Jungian theory of the collective unconscious, except it is focussing down on an individual level. Jung's ideas were dismissed as crackpot by many too at the time but now we accept them as workable and useful paradigms in the understanding of the human condition.'

She was aware that someone had arrived and was standing by her side. She turned. It was Jerry. She felt a flood of embarrassed guilt as she remembered the content of her earlier spat with Seb but covered it by reaching up on tiptoe and kissing him on the cheek.

'She giving you a hard time, Jim?'

'Good to see you, Jerry. I should say so. Once she gets the bit between her teeth of an idea then there's no stopping her. But you already know that. Look, sorry, got to go; I can see Dr Nicholls has buttonholed Professor Tierney and if I don't step in there p.d.q. then I'll have a hell of a job ever getting this department taken seriously again. And with that in mind, come and see me first thing in the morning, Vivien. Damn, no, I'll be at a conference in Manchester for the next few days. Better make it as soon as I get back. Check with Jean. And please don't go committing professional suicide in my absence. Catch up with you later, Jerry...'

For a big man, he spirited himself away surprisingly quickly. Vivien wasn't sure if it was an air of disbelief or disillusionment that he left behind. There wasn't any more that she'd intended to say to him but she did wish he'd stayed around a little longer; she didn't know if this was the right time to be on her own with her husband. Her blood was up and she was self-aware enough to know that the edges between discussion and argument were in danger of being blurred by all the wine she had been drinking. Jerry seemed pleased to see her though.

'I must say, Viv, it's so good to hear you sounding just like your old self again. You always could run rings around Jim Mc-Fraser. What have you got him floored on this time? You must've really got him going for him to admit that there is such a thing as professional suicide.'

Would she tell him? Could she? Had she really meant any of it anyway? She began to feel deflated as exhilaration drained away to leave a residue of sticky doubt.

'Why don't we get ourselves a drink?' Jerry said. 'I could certainly do with one. I've been at the hospital all this time ironing out last minute issues about the proposed secondment.'

Vivien looked at him properly for the first time. He was still wearing the suit she'd seen him in earlier this afternoon – it was a looking a little rumpled by now – and his face was tired and drawn. She felt a pang of concern for him. It would do her good to remember that she wasn't the only one who sometimes felt she carried the weight of the world on her shoulders. They found one of the students circulating with a tray of wine and got themselves both a glass. Vivien was just deciding how to relieve Jerry's burden a little by taking the initiative to open up a conversation about Newcastle, when Seb came up to join them.

'Jerry. What a very pleasant surprise. Vivien wasn't at all sure that you would make it.'

Vivien felt herself stiffen as if to parry a blow. What was he playing at? She hadn't said that at all. She shot him a look that would've stopped an elephant in its tracks but Seb just smiled serenely back and waved his hand airily.

'Well, as some sort of co-host of this shindig, I see it as my bounden duty to bring you up to speed with all the gossip you've missed.'

He looked around the room and then leaned conspiratorially towards Jerry.

'See that dried up old stick over there – the one with the stunned mullet expression and B.O? The lovely Jean told me that he's having an affair with one of his students.' He tapped the side of his nose in masculine solidarity. 'Psychiatrists are disreputable coves on the quiet. Must be all that intellectual probing going on that makes them want to venture a little deeper.'

'Seb!'

'What's the matter, Vivien? Surely you don't think your husband believes that we men of the mind are above all that hanky-panky nonsense? I'm sure you've filled him in on one or two of my own indiscretions over the years.'

'Funnily enough, no. We usually have better things to talk about than you.'

She tried to keep her voice as light as his but she wasn't as adept at the game as he was and knew if they carried on with this conversation that she would give something away. Quite what, she didn't know but to display anything but indifference to Seb at this moment would be dangerous. Her empty smile froze on her face. Oh God, she was so slow on the uptake: no wonder he could play her like a fiddle. That was exactly what he wanted her to do. He was attempting to set her up to take a risk. With him. Or Jerry. Or both. Well, she wouldn't. It wasn't cowardice in her eyes to walk away when you know that your opponent is so much more skilled at wielding weapons than you.

'I think I'd better circulate a bit; I promised Jim. I won't be long.'

She turned her back on them and walked away before either one could object or threaten to accompany her. It felt like a mini victory of sorts. She was feeling hemmed in by both their agendas. In a flash of uncomfortable clarity, she realised that she'd been subject to men cornering her into situations all her life. First her father, then Jerry, and now Seb. Oh, they dressed it up by saying that it was for her own good or they had her own best interests at heart but really it was their interests that were uppermost in their minds. The only time she'd truly felt free to be herself had been as a mother. And that had lasted such a desperately short time. She felt her self-righteous indignation begin to tip over into self-pity and she made a conscious effort to pull her shoulders back and smile confidently at the group of people in front of her. Seb had been right in one thing at least: she had to learn to listen to her own needs and, right now, they were to wow as many people as she could in the room and get herself the front-runner for the award.

For the next half an hour, Vivien worked the room and managed to submerge herself in a debate about whether neuro-linguistic programming was the only treatment worth considering in patients with acute depression, and an altogether gentler encounter with someone who had read some of her old case studies and wanted her to pay a visit to his drug-treatment centre in Austin.

Her ego boosted and the rough edges of her prickly apprehension smoothed off, she threaded her way back to where she'd left Jerry and Seb. As she got closer, she could see that her husband's face was a mask of suppressed emotion. He had the tell-tale lines around his mouth of a set jaw and his broad forehead was furrowed. He was less tolerant than her of Seb's flippant attitudes and Vivien felt a twinge of remorse. It had been unfair of her to skip off and leave him to Seb when he was at his *I'm an eccentric psychiatrist* best – or worst. She'd rescue him and perhaps they could smooth over their recent difficulties over a glass or two of good malt whisky back at home. Then maybe, just maybe, she'd show him just how much she'd miss him if he went away.

'Well, that's my duty done for the night; would you like to go?' she said as she arrived at Jerry's side.

'I wouldn't mind a little more wine if it's

alright by you.'

Was it her imagination or was there a frosty edge to his voice? In fact, the whole atmosphere seemed more than a little chilly.

'You can quaff this stuff if you like but I'm off to get a decent drink,' Seb announced, 'I happen to know that Fat Man McFraser has a couple of good bottles secreted for the favoured few somewhere. Every time he disappears he seems to come back with a glass of something that doesn't look remotely like this palette-numbing Chardonnay. Maybe I'll go and find the lovely Jean to help me sniff it out. Two noses are always better than one.'

Was her earlier paranoia coming back or did Seb seem indecently eager to leave? Not that she didn't want him to, the mood he was in he seemed intent on making trouble. And she'd had more than enough of his games for one night. Seb smiled easily at them both and then made a point of walking around Jerry to pass by Vivien. 'You'll thank me for this one day,' he whispered. And then he left.

Vivien felt the familiar knot of anxiety settling in the pit of her stomach. Just what did he mean by that? If Jerry noticed the exchange, he gave no sign. The mellow composure she'd been bathed in vanished as she scrabbled around for something to say. Seb's words had been ominous to say the

316

least; she only hoped that they were a product of alcohol and his heightened sense of drama, and that they meant nothing.

Jerry got in first. 'I've just been having a very illuminating conversation with Dr Nicholls,' he said, 'about you.'

She felt her legs grow a little weak. Surely he couldn't have said something about Stoke? Even Seb wouldn't stoop that low.

'I thought that coming back to work would help you to turn a corner in coping with our loss.' His voice was frighteningly cold and crisp. 'I didn't realise that it would be an opportunity for you to dabble in the occult.'

'Jerry.' Vivien's voice was louder than she'd intended and she cringed a little as one or two faces turned her way. 'I don't know what you're talking about.'

'Oh, yes you do. Telling everyone you've encountered our son. How could you?'

She felt unbalanced as if the floor was rising up to meet her. 'Seb is the only one I've spoken to.' She was careful to ennunciate every word slowly and carefully so that she wouldn't sound as reeling as she felt. 'And he should never have told you. It's a breach of confidentiality as far as my patient is concerned.'

Not to mention a breach of her confidence.

'Your patient wasn't even mentioned. I

commented on the fact that you seemed much more at ease with yourself and he said that you'd had some sort of intervention that has helped you come to terms with things. I thought he meant that you'd been receiving hypnotherapy or something but when I probed him on it, he told me that you think you've seen Dmitri.'

'Not seen him, no.' Vivien could feel the threat of tears pricking her eyes. 'It's complicated. My patient said something and at first I though he was playing a sick joke on me but then he told me details about the accident that only Dmitri and I could possibly know. Jerry, I hadn't even told you. So how would you explain that?'

'A vivid imagination comes to mind.'

'Don't patronise me.' Her mounting anger made her voice harsh. 'Don't you think I haven't gone over and over this in my head looking for every other alternative explanation? But there is none. I knew you wouldn't believe me and that's why I didn't tell you. I didn't believe it myself but Seb convinced me.' How could they be having this conversation here and now?

'Why does that not surprise me? You obviously take an awful lot more notice of him than you do of me.'

'Don't be stupid.'

'Me? You're the one who seems to have abandoned all rationality. You really must get a grip on yourself. You seem to think I'm not suffering too, but life goes on. I miss Dmitri every day but at least I've not descended to holding some sort of séance and imagining him wafting around in a wreath of ectoplasm.'

Vivien could hardly keep her shock in check. Jerry was being deliberately vicious and belittling her profession in the process. He knew very well that she wouldn't have been doing any such thing; both of them had always said how much they deplored so-called mediums who prayed on the desperate vulnerability of the bereaved. And that was before they had lost their son; didn't he even comprehend how much more angry such a charade would make her now? She looked up at him. The gap was so wide between them that she didn't even know how to go about breaching it.

Jerry refused to make eye contact with her and reached over to put his glass on a nearby table.

'Do you know what hurts me most of all?' His voice was lost and lonely. 'That you would choose to share this with your colleague and not me. You should have told me.'

'I didn't know how to. It's not the sort of thing you bring up at the breakfast table and I rarely see you at any other time these days.'

'So it's all my fault then?'

'Don't twist my words.' She sighed and

laid her hand on his arm. 'I don't want us to get into another fight, Jerry. Please just accept that I didn't know what to say about it but that I was going to tell you–'

'But not tonight.'

'No, not tonight.'

'Then how? By some well-crafted email where you could hide behind your perfect placement of facts?'

Vivien felt all the energy drain from her body. She wanted to do nothing more than curl up in a ball in the corner and go to sleep. She couldn't cope with this on top of everything else.

'I'm sorry, Jerry. Truly I am. And I know how much it must have hurt you to hear it from Seb first.'

'I don't think you do, Viv. You're always so self-contained in your grief and I feel shut out. I'm not blaming you but that's just the way you are.'

'We just work through things differently, that's all.'

'But, if there's to be any future for us, we have to learn to work through this together.'

'Give me a little time, Jerry. I just don't know if I can right now.'

'Time is something we haven't got, I have to tell them whether I am going to accept the job in Newcastle tomorrow morning. And now all this.' He shrugged in a gesture of hopelessness. 'Look, why don't we go home and see if we can discuss where we go from here like normal people without you getting all defensive on me?'

So it was all her fault again? Vivien wanted to scream with exasperation. Every time she thought they were beginning to appreciate each other's point of view, he seemed to want to put her in the wrong.

'I'm not sure there is any decision to make. You said you'd go if I agreed and I do. I think you should. Perhaps some time apart will do us good; we seem incapable of doing anything but damage each other when we're together right now.'

'So that's it, then?'

'Can you see any other way of making things even remotely workable? Because I can't.'

She didn't know she was going to say that until she had. Did she mean it or was it just her sense of failure speaking? But the words were now out there between them and there was no taking them back. The best she could do was to try to soften things for him.

'It's only for three months after all. Maybe I will feel differently about things when you get back but, for now, I need to be on my own.'

'That can be arranged. I'll pack a few things and stay with Sandra until I'm due to leave.'

'Now you're being silly.'

'No, I'm not, Viv. I'm trying to be practical and grown-up about this because one of us has to be.'

Vivien felt her resolve hardening. If this was how he wanted to play it, then she would too. But she wouldn't close down all hope of a reconciliation.

'You'll come round and say goodbye before you go?'

'Of course. And we'll stay in touch the whole time I'm away. I'm not leaving you, Viv, only leaving the situation.'

He bent down and gave her a kiss on the lips and then walked out of the room without looking back.

CHAPTER TWENTY-SIX

The British fleet had ceased their bombardment and it was now so quiet that Clarence could hear the breeze from the water rustling through the grass. The cannon had been firing for a full hour, the thud of the iron balls hitting the ground getting closer and closer as the Naval gunners had corrected, and eventually found, their range. But now the ominous explosions had stopped and the silence was the most welcoming thing he had heard in a long time. The best of it was that there were no wails of pain and anguish arising from his men. He glanced either side down the line. All of them were as covered in dirt as ground-hogs and had sweat-streaked faces but none appeared to be injured. He was relieved beyond measure to find that the earthwork had done its job.

Clarence stood on the little rampart he had fashioned for himself in the bottom of the trench and peered over the wall. The slope of the hill stretched out before him. It was immediately apparent why the cannons had fallen silent: the redcoats were advancing. Thin streaks of colour against the meadow green. The soldier in him marvelled that their lines were so straight; it was discipline that did that. He knew that if he were to order his men to take similar action, they would be snaking all over the place. Once, just once, he'd like to have the time to drill them properly. But there would be no opportunity for that now. He felt a frisson of fearful anticipation.

The sound of pounding feet behind him made him step down off the rampart and turn around. A breathless runner scooted up and stood awaiting permission to speak. His hat was rammed down on his head and slug-trails of sweat made his face look as though it was melting.

'Well?'

'Order, sir. From Colonel Prescott himself. There's to be no fire until you're sure of a killing shot.'

So the battle tactics were beginning. He wondered if all the rest of the orders would be up to him to issue. The thought weighed down on shoulders. It was his duty to make sure that his men put up a decent fight but the Colonel was right to be concerned about ammunition. Each of them only had twenty-four cartridges and from what he'd seen of the strength marching relentlessly towards them he knew that even if every single one of them resulted in a direct hit, it would probably not be enough. The knowledge sent an aspen quiver through his body.

'Go down to the end of the line and repeat that order. I'll ensure it is passed on from this end.'

The soldier stumbled off down the ditch, his hand attempting to press his flapping leather orders' pouch against his side. Somehow in his hurry to deliver this one, he had forgotten to pick up his flintlock. Clarence only hoped that he would be able to make it back to the redoubt before the action started.

Once he had walked a hundred yards or so in either direction and made sure that his men understood what they were required to do and could relay the order to the others in the line, Clarence returned to his position on the rampart. He saw several heads bob up as some of the other soldiers did the same. The redcoats were making slow but inexorable progress. He wondered what was going through their minds – if anything – as they picked their way over the low stone walls that fringed the lower reaches of the slope and fought their way through the tangles of long grass. He hoped they were dispirited and demoralised, but he doubted it. The only advantage his soldiers had was the cover of the earthwork and the fact that they'd had an hour to recuperate from their exertions. They certainly didn't have numbers on their side.

He retreated to the far side of the ditch.

'Stand easy, men,' he instructed, 'and check your firearms. And take your time about it; they've got a lot of hill left to climb yet.' He hoped he sounded more relaxed about the inevitable onslaught than he felt.

Clarence set the example by pulling a rag out of his ammunition pouch and running it along the length of his Brown Bess musket. It had a long, sleek muzzle and was as beautiful a piece of engineering as he'd ever held in his hands. It was lighter than his old hunting gun and the stock was shaped to fit snugly against his shoulder. This was just as well as the firearm, although elegant, was as inaccurate as any other musket and any undue recoil in the conditions of battle would make it even more so. Clarence pinched the rag between his thumb and fingers and paid particular attention to cleaning the area around the flint, and the striking surface. If there was a layer of dirt or a lump of grit lodged on either when he pulled the trigger then the powder in the firing pan wouldn't ignite.

The comfort of conducting a familiar routine made him feel almost peaceful. His hands moved automatically and freed his mind to think of other things. He could smell the freshly turned soil and the sweet scent of the grass as it dried in the sun. Somewhere on the hill behind him, a cricket chirruped and received an answer. If he closed his eyes to the wall of earth in front of him, he could almost imagine that he was sitting at home on the farm preparing for a deer hunt...

The bag of bread and boiled maize that his mother had prepared was at his feet and he was clutching his father's second-best musket – the one he had given him on his fourteenth birthday. The dawn air was chill and clear and he could hear the birds heralding the new day. His legs felt stiff from the sacking tied around them for protection from the rough and thorny scrub. He filled his powder horn and his stomach flipped at the thought that today might be his chance to bag the honour of making the first kill. His father was striding out of the house and whistling for the dogs. All of them – even the animals – were trying to curb their excitement. He wanted nothing more at that moment than to smoke a pipe to settle his nerves but knew that their quarry would be able to pick up the scent on the softest breeze...

He was prevented from drifting further into a daydream of pleasant memories by the anxious voices of a group of soldiers gathered a few yards away.

'I ain't never seen so many.'

'Must be thousands.'

'You know why they wear them red coats, don't you? So the blood don't show.'

'What would it matter if you saw your own? It would be too late by then anyway.'

'But not if you saw the blood of the man next to you. Plenty of time left to run because it would mean that it was your turn to bite the lead next.'

Clarence laid his firearm down, stood up and walked over to them.

'Don't worry about them; you have enough of your own dealings to attend to. Get those muskets so clean I wouldn't be ashamed to take them home to meet my mother.'

One of the pale-faced soldiers was Samuel. Clarence waited until the others had recommenced inspecting their firearms and pulled him away out of earshot.

'I want you to take up a position between

Perry and Holbrook. They're the most experienced soldiers I have and will see you right. Keep your mind clear and do like them and you'll do okay.'

'I'll be doing what I have to for my father.'

Clarence wanted to shake him.

'You'll be fighting to keep yourself so you don't end up like him is what you'll be doing. Hasn't anyone ever told you that there are no heroes in battle; only those who are corpses now and those that'll be corpses next?'

Samuel gave him a sick little smile and pulled the ramrod from out of its cradle under the musket barrel. His hands were shaking. Clarence wondered what use he would be when the redcoats were finally upon them; he had heart and the determination to prove himself but would that be enough? Samuel began fumbling to slip the ramrod into the barrel. Clarence snatched it from him.

'Not yet. Have you checked no dirt from the earthwork got in there first?'

Samuel shook his head.

'You tamp down now and if you've jammed a bit of earth down then, when the time comes to fire, you'll blow your head off. Tip the musket upside down – keep the end of the barrel clear of the ground – and bang it with your hand gently to make sure there's nothing in there. Then see if the ramrod has a smooth passage. If not, for God's sake don't use it. Stick to the bayonet.'

He left him to it.

Clarence walked amongst his men and gave similar advice and instructions to the greenhorns – of which there were far too many – and encouraged the veterans to protect themselves from untimely and potentially dangerous explosions by keeping an eye on the youngsters. Everyone was showing his fear in one way or another: an inability to stand still; white lips and pinched nostrils; retching up the last drink of water; one or two even had tears running down their faces.

He returned to his rampart and his next peek over the top of the earthwork had his own nerves fluttering. He could clearly see the white bandoliers crisscrossed over the redcoat's chests and the black cockades on their hats as the advancing line drew close enough to break up into a series of individuals. The sun glinted off their fixed bayonets. This endless waiting would soon be over. He didn't know whether he wanted it to be or not.

'Load your muskets,' he ordered.

Up and down the line, the men followed the lead of the soldier next to him as the order filtered down. First they began rooting in their ammunition pouches and then each pulled out a paper cartridge and ripped it open with his teeth. Clarence did the same. A waft of pungent saltpetre filled his nostrils. He tipped a small quantity of the gunpowder into the musket's firing pan. The rest he poured in the muzzle and stuffed the cartridge paper in behind as a wad. A few tamps with the ramrod and he rolled the musket ball down.

'What are we waiting for?' he heard, 'much longer and we might as well give them devils a gift of the hill. They'll be on us to take it soon enough.'

Clarence glanced over the earthwork once more and then back down the line.

'No one is to cock their flintlocks until they can see the whites of their eyes.' His voice was steely with authority. 'They are still 200 yards off and no one can aim and kill a man at that distance. Break into three ranks. When you are at the earthwork, fire when I give the order, then retreat and reload. There are to be continuous volleys.'

There was a flurry of activity as the men organised themselves. The ditch they had expended so much of their energy on digging was wide enough for the men standing up at the wall to aim and fire without his companions behind being unduly blinded by smoke or the flash from the gunpowder. But there wasn't a lot of room for them to move around and change over. Clarence was sure that when the time came, many of them would get in each other's way.

However, the order had been given and there was little he could do about it now. If it was the redoubt he was defending then he would have the luxury of having some soldiers kneeling ready to fire through the grass-stuffed post and rail fence but here they had no option but to fire one at a time and step back to reload before their turn came to fire again. One break, one delay in the chain of shots and each man's position would be weakened. He looked into the faces of the two soldiers he had assigned to cover him. They looked no better or worse than the rest; he hoped they were amongst the more accomplished at reloading.

The minutes stretched into lifetimes as he watched the redcoats loom ever closer. He could hear the distant purr of snare drums floating up from the beach. He shielded his eyes against the sun and tore his eyes away from the mesmerising sight of the advancing lines, and down to the water's edge. More and more boats were landing; there wasn't a patch of water between the British fleet and the land, not rippled by oars. Was there to be no end of them? Just how many soldiers could those ships hold? And what if there were more of them rowing their way up the Mystic River with the intention of out-flanking them? He knew that Colonel Prescott had positioned a line of defences strung out from the redoubt in case such an eventuality but that wouldn't help his men; they were in front of all that.

He cast his gaze back to the slowly moving lines dominating more and more of the slope; he could see the detailing on their lapels and epaulets now. Not much longer to wait. They would be within range soon. He could hear the relentless pounding of their footsteps and the swish of the grass, above his own rasping breath. One hundred and fifty yards ... one hundred ... only another thirty to go...

CHAPTER TWENTY-SEVEN

Clarence's body convulsed with shock as there was a flash and roar of musket fire from the top of the earthwork to his right. He immediately felt his bowels threaten to turn to water. Someone had let his nerves get the better of him and loosed a round off early. He glared at the culprit through the telltale smoke that surrounded him. It was Samuel. Goddamn it! He knew that he should have listened to his instinct and insisted that the boy take his place behind the lines in the redoubt.

'Quit firing!' Clarence yelled. 'Hold your fire!'

But it was too late. Too many others had seen the flash for themselves and automatically pulled on their triggers. Clarence continued to shout pointlessly as a cloak of grey gunpowder smoke enveloped the ditch and the air was split by an uneven series of musket roars. There was nothing he could do to stop them; the men who had already fired had retreated to reload and their places taken by others equally anxious to get the battle underway.

Clarence refused to be similarly infected himself and watched as a number of the redcoats in front of him stumbled and fell. Even though they were technically still out of range for anything but a lucky shot, the British line was being broken. Clarence began to hope that they might escape being punished for their indiscipline. But his optimism was short-lived as he saw a wave of British soldiers run up from the ranks behind and slip into the places of their fallen comrades. The lines were complete once more. And still advancing.

His vision was full of nothing but the red of uniforms, the brown of muskets, and the gleam of bayonets. He squeezed on his trigger and his gun fired. He was momentarily deafened by the blast and his shoulder felt bruised as he absorbed the recoil. He sucked the acrid smoke into his lungs and began to cough. He stepped back from the earthen wall to reload and heard, above the roar of the muskets firing all around him, the boom of the big guns as a renewed cannonade from the warships in the harbour started up. The first of the missiles flew clear over their heads and thudded into the ground far behind them – their trajectory set deliberately to miss their own troops – but he could feel the sense of fear inside the ditch increasing. The men were becoming distracted too, some pausing in the act of reloading to look back over their shoulders to see where the cannonballs had landed.

But the thunder of the distant guns seemed to produce an opposite reaction in the British soldiers as the advancing line pulled itself tighter together and picked up speed. They were also getting quicker at renewing their ranks when any of the shots from behind the earthwork found their mark.

Clarence continued staring at them for a moment after firing off yet another round. He was beginning to believe the rumours he'd heard about the British having their hearts removed when they joined the army and having them replaced by pendulum clocks. They were behaving like automatons. He could see their faces through the smoke and they were expressionless. They hadn't even given way to nerves and returned any fire. How he wished his men had been disciplined enough to save their ammunition.

He took a few paces back and then ran his fingers through his cartridge pouch. He counted. Eighteen. He only had eighteen shots left and he'd waited until they had been in range and hadn't fired off as many as the others. He tried to do a quick calculation: a well trained soldier could make two or three discharges a minute; they had started firing how long ago? Four minutes. Six maximum. Each soldier took his turn at the earthwork every third shot. That meant ... he gave up. They had as many cartridges left as they had left. Fretting about it wasn't going to magic any more out of thin air.

'Tell them to retreat. Get them to the redoubt!'

It was the medic. Clarence hadn't expected him to be in the firing line; he had thought he would be cowering somewhere waiting for the worst to be over.

'Get out my way; I have a battle to fight.'

The man stood his ground. Clarence tried to push past but he grabbed his arm.

'They need time to get their wits about them. Pull them back. Most of them don't know if it's today or yesterday and wouldn't know the breech of a British musket if it was stuck between their eyes.'

'If you don't unhand me I'll shove mine so far down your throat that you'll think you're a Thanksgiving turkey on a spit. Your job is to patch up those that are too far gone to fight; mine is to see all the others mow down as many of the redcoats as they can. I won't put any more than I can help into your sorry hands.'

'Don't be a mule and listen. We are too outnumbered. Pull back and give them time. They are next to useless to you as they are now.'

'They'll be more useless dead which is what they will be if I don't get down the line and keep them reloading. You want to do something instead of standing there like a clutch of wet Sundays? Then steady the hands of those who are shaking too much to prime their pans. If you don't step lively and help out then you'll soon be so deep in body parts that you won't know which bit's come off which man.'

'I joined the militia to save men's lives, not assist in taking them.'

'You joined to follow orders. Same as we all did.'

'But how can you when you know them to be foolhardy?'

'I don't know nothing of the sort. General Prescott is depending on me to hold this line to the best of my ability and that I'm gonna do if it takes the last breath in my body.'

He finally managed to snatch his arm away from the medic's claw-like grasp. The man's fingers were almost rigid with fear. Clarence felt a shiver of pity; being a medic was one of the worst jobs in the army, all he could do was to stand and watch men turning into patients before his eyes.

'If you want to go back to the redoubt, you'd better go. It'll not be long now.'

'It's not my skin I'm concerned with saving. I just know blind terror when I see it and you've too many green boys who ain't gonna be able to think straight unless they have a step back to marshal their wits.'

'You want to give them a better chance? Get up to General Prescott and ask him to send reinforcements. I'm the senior officer in the line here and that's an order I'm issuing. My men – boys or not – are every inch drilled and know what they have to do. They'll do you, and me, and the American people, proud. Don't worry about none of us down here and go. Go!'

Clarence gave him a shove and hefted up his musket. He wished he felt as confident as his words had sounded. His fingers fumbled and he dropped the musket ball in his attempt to reload. He bent and picked it up. When he looked up once more he could see the top of the redcoats' hats bobbing just above the rim of the earthwork. They were on them already. Because of the goddam medic, he hadn't even had time to shout the order to fix bayonets. He ran up and down and directed his men to do so immediately and to be prepared to engage in hand-to-hand fighting. The outline of soldiers disfigured the skyline as the first of the British reared up and leapt on top of the wall. Some were immediately felled by close range musket fire but many more were able to plunge their bayonets downwards into the faces and chests of the increasingly disorganised defence.

Clarence's ears were full of screams and shouts and blood-chilling wails pierced by the intermittent roar of musket fire. The smoke was so thick that he could hardly make out which were his men, and which the enemy. Another wave of redcoats breached the earthwork as he struggled to fix his own bayonet, and rally his men to stand firm at the same time. He could smell gunpowder and blood. It was beginning to resemble the deer hunt of his imagination. They were trapped with nowhere to go but to retreat up the hill behind them and into the certain path of a volley of musket fire from the redcoats perched on top of the earthwork. The bodies of some of his men who had tried to flee were already sprawled on the grassy slope. Suddenly there was an enormous flash of gunpowder as someone forgot the routine and cocked his flintlock before he'd finished reloading. The muzzle of the musket exploded and sent slivers of red-hot metal, shards of bone, and gobs of flesh in every direction.

Clarence ran up and down the back of the line and exhorted his men to defend their positions at all costs. He flicked a quick glance up to the redoubt. Why hadn't Colonel Prescott sent any reinforcements? He must be able to see that they were being overrun. He could order the small artillery to fire, at least. Even if a few of their own soldiers were hit, it would be worth it to disintegrate the British attack.

Through the smoke up ahead, Clarence saw the insubstantial figure of a soldier desperately trying to steady himself enough to get his ramrod down the muzzle of his musket. Didn't he know that it was already too late for that? He wouldn't even have time to raise it before they would be upon him. It was Samuel. Why hadn't the soft-brained jackass done as he'd been told and stayed under the watchful eyes of Perry and Holbrook? He was too vulnerable standing where he was with his back to the earth-work. He was about to scream at him to be a goddam soldier for once when a redcoat loomed out of the smoke and stepped into his path. He raised his pistol and Clarence thought that he was about to experience the cold taste of lead but then the soldier turned, as slowly as the figure striking the hours on his hometown church clock, and shot Samuel clean through the neck.

It had taken a day. No more than a day for him to break his promise to Abraham: *Take care of my boy.*

An all-consuming rage swept over Clarence and he roared out his frustration and anger in one long howl. How dare Abraham ask the impossible of him in a time of war? How dare the British with their red coats and sharp bayonets stand on American soil and slaughter the sons of farmers with barely a break in stride? And how dare they turn him into what he knew he had become: a murderer by neglect?

Clarence howled once more and threw himself into the melee. The first British soldier, he cracked on the skull with the butt of his musket. The second, he kicked in the groin and finished off with a chop on the back of the neck. By the time the third approached him he had his bayonet in his hand and, wielding it like a knife, he slashed at the soldier's throat until his stock became as red as his coat. His muscles sang with an impulsive energy that he'd never felt before and he struck out at whoever was around him with the self-disregard of a madman. Two British soldiers were ahead of him. He could take them both; he would show them that they couldn't do this to him, to his men, to his country, to Abraham's boy...

But the yell that he was intending to make

turned into a whistle of breath. He felt a pressure in his chest as if someone was sitting on it. He looked down. A rosette, a perfect parody of the ones on the redcoats' hats, was spreading out from the centre of his hunting tunic and turning the brown deer leather, black. He didn't understand. It had just begun to dawn on him that he didn't really need to when his knees weakened, his legs buckled, and he fell.

Vivien's apprehension writhed like snakes in her stomach. Everything depended on how she handled the next few moments.

'Stephen. Listen to me. I want you to take Clarence a little further forward in time. You can do that because he has already lived his life and is just waiting for what unfolds next. I want you to concentrate on what happens after he leaves the battlefield. Let his spirit rise to meet you and take him with you to the next stage.'

She was straining forward on her chair and was aware that her breathing had become as shallow as Stephen's.

'Leave the distress of death behind, Stephen, and move on.'

He gave no sign that he had heard her. Was she pushing him too hard and too fast? Was there something else that she didn't yet know about that he had to experience before he could access the Bardo plane? Before she could find out if Dmitri was still there waiting for her?

'What are you feeling, Stephen?'

'As if there is nothing holding me down anymore and I am floating.'

'Is the light there yet, Stephen? Can you see it? Is there anyone else there with you? Concentrate, Stephen. Concentrate hard. Is there anyone else with you?'

Stephen's eyes moved rapidly under his closed lids and he was licking his lips as if preparing to speak. Vivien clenched her fists until her fingers cramped. This could be it. This could be the moment. She'd be ready for it this time. She knew what to expect. She'd ask the right questions. She'd find out exactly what it was her son wanted to say to her.

A piercing sound broke in on them. Vivien let out an answering yelp of anguish. The fire alarm. The bloody fire alarm. Not now. Not now. She was so close.

'Stephen, stay there for a moment longer ... hold on to it... Tell me where you are and what you can see ... describe it to me ... my voice is the only thing you can hear, nothing else...'

Stephen's eyes snapped open and he shot an unfocused look at her.

'Christ, what the hell is happening? What's that noise? Is it the cannons? Why don't they stop? My ears are going to burst. They are too close. Tell them to pull back! Order them to cease firing!'

Vivien stood bolt upright. She couldn't believe what she had just done. Risked this man's sanity by breaking all the rules about hypnosis being a patient-centred experience, and potentially risked his life by keeping him in a place of danger for moments longer than was necessary. She injected a confident authority into her voice that she didn't feel.

'It's okay, Stephen. It's just the fire alarm. Put your shoes on quickly and come with me.'

'But the fire was the other one. It was Edward... I am Clarence...'

'No. You are Stephen Daunt and you are with me in University College Hospital. But we have to leave now. Come on. We'll walk calmly together out of here and down the corridor and I'll make sure you are safe.'

It was a little late to offer him that reassurance. The man was totally disorientated and may, for all she knew, be deeply traumatised by being ripped out of his past life at precisely the wrong moment. She couldn't say that things felt any different for her.

The foyer on the ground floor was full of people. The noise of chatter rose up to meet them as they walked down the last of the stairs. Vivien was aware that Stephen could be experiencing a high level of claustrophobia after being in his trance-like state, so she moved aside to allow him to walk between her and the wall and be protected from the bodies pressing all around them.

At the bottom of the staircase they turned towards the closest fire exit at the side of the building. Vivien reached out to take Stephen's arm and lead him outside. But he was no longer there. She scanned the faces around her, a flood of panic making her feel sick. She saw him being herded towards the large door at the front. She would try and find him again once they were at the assembly point. Go somewhere quiet and take him through a guided meditation to relax him. She had to make good what her lack of professionalism might have done. The fire alarm going off like it did wasn't her fault but she had been pushing him too hard before that had even happened. And then when it did ... when it did... How could she have ignored the instruction to evacuate her office immediately?

But she knew. Dmitri. Her son. She would do anything for the chance to feel his presence again; to have someone speak his words to her. Where was he now?

'Wait for me, Dmitri,' she said under her breath, 'I promise that mummy will come and see you again as soon as she can. Just wait for me, darling. Wait for me. Please...'

CHAPTER TWENTY-EIGHT

Vivien stood and watched as Jerry put the last few things in his suitcase. He'd spent the last couple of nights at his sister's and even in that short time apart they had been transformed into polite strangers. She looked out of the bedroom window. It was going to be a beautiful June morning. The sun was already lifting out the various greens of the trees. It was far too nice a day for such a sad moment as this.

'Do you have everything?' she asked.

'I think so. Nothing I can't do without anyway. It won't be for long, Viv, remember that. And you can always fly up for the weekend when I'm settled.'

'They've fixed you up with somewhere to stay have they?'

'I've got an apartment. It'll be far more comfortable than staying in a hotel. They keep it for visiting expert witnesses appearing in front of the commission but because of the short notice of my appointment, I've got it. I'll give you the telephone number when I get there.'

Vivien nodded. She wished the taxi would come to take him to the airport. It was excruciating to be here like this with him with nothing to say. Predictably, neither of them had mentioned what had happened at the reception; their complicity in avoiding the subject only proved that she had been right to tell him to go. She wondered if Seb's words about thanking him had been prophetic. She certainly wasn't angry at him anymore for telling Jerry about Stephen and Dmitri. It seemed that his intervention had merely forced them to reach the crossroads a little earlier than they might otherwise have done.

A car honked outside. The taxi at last. Vivien picked up Jerry's suit bag and walked behind him down the stairs. At the door they hugged long and hard. When she pulled away, she saw that Jerry's eyes were moist.

'Three months. That's all,' she said. 'Ring me to let me know that you've arrived safely. If I'm not here, just leave a message. I've got a busy day ahead and don't know what time I'll leave the office.'

'Try not to work too hard, Viv. Give yourself a break. I think you're in the early stages of exhaustion.'

She tried hard not to bristle. He was saying it out of concern, not criticism, and would it really hurt her so much to make a concession and allow him to believe his version of the truth? She thought that Seb would probably say that it would be a sign of strength, not weakness. And it really wasn't too much to ask. She owed Jerry an awful lot more than a fond farewell. She tipped her head to one side as she always had when she'd been listening to her father's misplaced advice.

'Maybe I did go back to work a little soon and work too hard to make up for lost time. But I'm fine, honestly.'

He gave her a kind smile and she was glad that she'd made the effort.

'You'd better go,' she said. 'The traffic's heavy this time of day and you don't want to miss your flight.'

A kiss, and she watched his broad back walking down the path. She stood in the doorway and gave a small wave as the taxi pulled away.

A few hours later, Vivien was in her office wrestling with just how much of the Stephen Daunt case she was going to reveal in her symposium paper. Jerry and Jim McFraser's reactions had made her realise that she had been foolish to think she could go down the whole past lives route but she did want to see if she could weave in some of the dilemmas to traditional psychiatry her new thinking had thrown up.

There was a knock on the door and Jean bustled in.

'Package for you, Dr Blake. Looks interesting. Stoke postmark.'

Vivien smiled across the desk at her. 'Have you taken it down to the x-ray department to see what's in it yet?' She was determined to carry on as usual and leave her personal problems at home; if she let on what a terrible start to the morning she'd had, Jean would only try to swamp her with clumsy sympathy.

'Don't be like that. You know getting anything across my desk other than boring reports brightens my dull little life.'

'I'll tell you what; if you promise to bring me a cup when you next make coffee, I'll let you stay and watch me open it.'

Jean beamed. 'It's a deal. Go on then, don't keep me in suspenders.'

Vivien took the envelope from her and tore off the flap. She would be lying if she said that she didn't feel some excitement. This must be the material the curator had promised to send her. She tipped the contents onto the desk.

'It's from the Stoke Pottery Museum,' she said, 'some background research I asked for.'

'Is that it?' Jean looked disappointed. 'I was expecting a gold-edged invitation to go somewhere exciting at least.'

'You live in a fantasy world, Jean,' Vivien laughed. 'Since when have I ever received one of those? I'm a psychiatrist remember, not a media celebrity.'

'Sebastian Nicolls gets them all the time.'

'Well, he would, wouldn't he? Now that he seems to think he's become one. Now scat and let me sort through this.'

'Don't forget your paper, Dr Blake.'

'I know, I know...'

'I need time to get the copies made and run it past Dr McFraser well in advance.'

'I promise I'll have it done in time. And you owe me a coffee, don't forget. Anytime now would be nice.'

'You're a hard woman to do business with; give me ten minutes and I'll be back.'

'That'll be perfect. And hold any calls for the moment will you?' Vivien added as Jean closed the door behind her.

Vivien kicked her shoes off and walked around to the other side of her desk. She picked up the slim sheaf of papers she'd released from the envelope and took them over to the coffee table. She made herself comfortable in one of the low chairs and spread the bounty out before her.

On top was a handwritten note from the curator apologising for not being there to meet her when she'd visited and saying that he hoped she would find the enclosed of some interest. She remembered the reason he had missed her appointment with a pang and thought that she must make a point of congratulating him and his wife when she next contacted him. It would be painful but it was the decent thing to do.

She picked up the first of the documents. It was a photocopy of a newspaper article. The original must have been blurred with age because it was difficult to decipher in some places but the gist was clear enough. The curator had written: *Staffordshire Advertiser. June 1840. Page 1* on the top in looping handwriting. Vivien got up and turned on the overhead light and then settled back down to read.

TRAGIC EVENTS IN LOCAL WELL-KNOWN POTTERY

There was an immense conflagration that broke out in our town on Wednesday last. It took place in Houghton's potbank and it was a miracle that it spread no further.

Eye witness accounts report that the red glow could be seen from the furthest bank of the River Trent and that there was little time to call the engines before the spectacle turned into tragedy. The workers were filling the kilns when...

Vivien knew this much already. She looked up briefly when Jean entered with her coffee. She nodded her thanks and set it aside to pick up the next photocopy. The curator had annotated it: *Staffordshire*

Advertiser. June 1840. Continuation of story on inside pages. Intervening report of the account missing. Vivien hoped that wasn't going to turn out to be the vital information she needed to make sense of Stephen's story.

TRAGIC EVENTS IN LOCAL WELL-KNOWN POTTERY continued

The fire appeared to start in the packing shed and spread with great rapidity to the next door moulding room.

The flames took hold immediately and, despite the workers' valiant attempts to extinguish them with pails of river water, they destroyed everything in their devastating path.

EMINENT BYSTANDER

Both the owner of the pottery and a Government Commissioner, a Mr Wharburton of Whitehall, were on site at the moment of combustion and it is the latter's testimony that forms the greater part of this report.

'I have never seen anything like it in my life', Mr Wharburton recounted later, 'and I sincerely hope I never do so again. It is my opinion that although fires are a natural hazard in an industry engaged in the firing of wares and therefore requiring a vast amount of coal and other combustible ma- erials, if more attention were paid to the construction of these factories and therefore the safety of the workers within them, then this terrible event need never have occurred'.

Vivien could almost hear him saying it. Stephen had described Mr Wharburton as a wise and sincere man; his first reaction would of course have been to draw the public's attention to the possibility that such a thing would be very likely to happen again. Stephen had also said that the government commissioner had reminded him of her. It was a compliment that after her last session with him – and her inability to find him again after they'd all trooped back into the building – she didn't feel she deserved. She turned to the next page and tried to ignore the pricks of guilt.

This extract had to also be from *The Staffordshire Advertiser*. The column was headed 'Obituary' in big black letters. Her hands shook as she read the name underneath. She picked up her coffee and took a sip to wet her mouth. And then it hit her: the significance of the date.

She pushed herself out the chair and lunged for Stephen's case file sitting on the edge of her desk. She opened it to the last page of her notes. Yes, she was right; Clarence had died on his birthday. On the cusp of turning twenty-six. And, according to his obituary, so had Edward. If she had never really held with co-incidences she certainly didn't believe in them now; the facts of this case had thwarted every attempt she'd made to explain things away in such a logical fashion.

Vivien was feeling shaky as she walked over to the filing cabinet and pulled open the first drawer. She fingered her way through the copies of essential medical records they kept on each patient until she reached Stephen's. She didn't even have to pull it out of its folder to read it. There in the top right hand corner was his date of birth. The nineteenth of June. Tomorrow. Stephen Daunt would be twenty-six tomorrow.

She slammed the draw shut and reached for the office door.

'Jean,' she shouted before she'd even got it half open, 'I need you to ring Fairway Manor School for me. It's urgent. Tell them that it's imperative that I speak to Stephen Daunt. I'll try his home number.'

Her fingers were trembling as she picked up the telephone and dialled. It rang twelve times before Jean came into the office. Vivien replaced the handset.

'Well? Have you got him?'

'I spoke to the school secretary. He's not

turned up for work today. Nobody knows where he is but I managed to winkle his wife's number out of them. They didn't want to divulge it to me at first but I told them it was a matter of life and death.'

Jean wasn't far wrong there.

'She's in France with her parents,' she continued, 'it's a long shot but you might want to give it a go.'

Vivien took the piece of paper from her and punched in the number. Jean hovering over her desk was making her even more nervous. 'Do me a favour,' she said as she listened to the drawn out dialling tone, 'leave a note for when Jim McFraser gets back from Manchester alerting him to the fact that something critical has come up in the Stephen Daunt case. I'll fill him in later. And check I've no appointments.'

Jean did as she was asked.

And then a thin voice came onto the other end of the line.

'Oui?'

'Hello, can I speak to Mrs Daunt please?'

'That's me.'

What had he said her name was? Hélène, that was it.

'Hélène, you don't know me but I'm Dr Vivien Blake. Stephen has been coming to see me at University College Hospital for the past two months.'

'Oh yes, hello. He mentioned you.'

That would make things a little easier.

'I need to talk to him urgently and I can't seem to get hold of him.' She heard a sharp intake of breath at the other end. 'Hello, hello, are you alright?'

'Yes.'

The voice was wavering with something; pain? Apprehension?

'I don't know where he is at the moment, I'm afraid. But he did call earlier. He sounded very distressed. He said he was coming over here. I couldn't get much sense out of him and he hasn't turned up yet. I'm very worried about him, Dr Blake.'

She wasn't the only one. Was he going to France to run to Hélène, or to try to put some distance between himself and Clarence's dreadful fate? He had been so confused and disorientated after his hypnosis session yesterday – and the shock of the fire alarm – that she wasn't at all sure that he would know what he was doing. God, how she wished that after she'd lost him in the crowd she'd rung him at home to check that he was alright. She might even have been in time if she'd tried this morning – but she'd been too preoccupied with Jerry leaving for Newcastle. She tried to keep her anxiety out of her voice.

'When he arrives just do everything you can to get him to relax. He's a little over-wrought at the moment so he might need some help in staying calm. I'll catch the next flight over and do what I can to get him into a more rational state of mind.'

'Are you saying Stephen's irrational? He's not dangerous is he? I mean we're out here in the middle of nowhere...'

'Hélène, I have to ask, you're not scared of him are you?'

'Of course not, I just meant that he'll have to hire a car and drive from the airport and if he's not thinking straight, what with being on the wrong side of the road and everything.'

'I thought you might be referring to the reason you went over there in the first place and the incident with the pillow.'

'He told you about that?'

'It came up in the course of his treatment, yes.'

'That was a long time ago now... Dr Blake, I have to go. I'm not feeling too good. I think I need to lie down. When you get to the airport, tell the taxi to drive towards Bellac and take the road to Saint Saveur. My parents' house is down the end of a long track that branches off after the barns. You can always ring if you get lost – I won't be going anywhere in my condition – but it is easy to find once you get to the village.'

'Thank you. Are you sure you're okay?'

'Yes, fine. I'm pregnant, that's all. I'll see you later.'

The phone line went dead.

CHAPTER TWENTY-NINE

Vivien gripped the armrests as she felt the wheels leave the tarmac. Flying had always been her least favourite mode of transport. Except she supposed that had now been overtaken by car travel. She tried to force herself to take deep breaths and relax as the plane soared up and into the first layer of clouds. She'd been lucky that Jean had been able to get her a seat on this flight at all at such short notice. She obviously hadn't had time to go home and pick up any overnight things but she was sure that Hélène would be able to lend her anything she needed.

Vivien felt a touch of distress on the poor woman's behalf at having a stranger arriving on her doorstep in a few hours' time but she'd had no choice. She'd been convinced all along that the key to her understanding – and subsequently resolving – Stephen's problems lay in her being able to identify the patterns in his life. And she had it now. She had the both of them now; layered on top of each other like thin crusts of rock on top of a volcano.

The breakthrough had come when she'd discovered that Hélène was pregnant. She had known all along that Stephen was holding something back from her but had thought that it was information lodged deep in his subconscious, not an ordinary fact of his life. Why hadn't he told her? Had he been afraid to after the revelation of his nightmares about children? Was he frightened that she would read into them and conclude that he wasn't entirely happy about becoming a father? Except it was his impotence in the face of responsibility that his dreams revealed to her, not his desire to have a family. His repression of such a significant development in his life explained his high degree of anxiety when they had first met. So children were the first pattern. The other one centred around the knowledge that Edward and Clarence had both died on their twenty-sixth birthdays. She hadn't had the chance to do any further investigation into reincarnation but her gut instinct told her that if they did, then there was a chance that the person who seemed to carry their lives as part of his own, would too. Unless she could help him to break free.

The plane shuddered in a moment of turbulence and Vivien's stomach clenched. She reached for her handbag under the seat in front of her and pulled it onto her lap. She needed a distraction from the uncomfortable – but illogical – feeling that she might never set her feet on solid ground again. She'd just had time before she'd rushed out of the office to scoop up the rest of the museum curator's documents, intending to confront Stephen with them when she finally managed to catch up with him.

She flicked through the photocopied newspaper article she'd already read and came to, what appeared to be, an extract from a coroner's report. She skimmed the first paragraph which was just a repetition of the circumstances of the fire. But then she saw something that made her throat constrict. The piece of paper shook in her hands. Was this it? Was this the connection she had been seeking?

Vivien willed the plane to go faster. She had a little over six hours to try to save the past from reaching forward into the present but couldn't help the premonition that it wouldn't be nearly enough time.

She was lucky and there was a taxi waiting at the rank outside the terminal building. She got in and handed the address to the driver. The car pulled away violently. Vivien felt queasy as they merged into the stream of traffic. Her apprehension only increased as they reached the outskirts of the town. The driver drove with a recklessness that had sweat rolling down Vivien's spine. She wanted to ask him to slow down as the last houses whizzed by and they plunged into open countryside. Poplar trees lined the road and the evening light flashing through them began to have a hypnotic effect. She felt as if she was back in her office directing a film in which she appeared.

She hoped she was doing the right thing. Hélène had said that Stephen had been *very distressed;* would she be making matters worse by turning up and confronting him with the things he was trying to escape? And she was still worried as to why hadn't he told her that his wife was pregnant? He was very protective of her – that much was evident when she had cropped up in their conversations – but was he also obsessive? Could it be that he feared a rival for her affections? And if he was, would the shock of seeing his wife again propel him into doing something that might put an end to those fears? She shuddered. The boy on the boat. She wished she'd found out about what had happened with the boy on the boat.

She pulled her mobile phone out of her handbag. She'd ring Hélène and check if Stephen had arrived. The voice at the other end was breathy and agitated.

'He's outside. Been here for ages. My father had forbidden him to come in so he drove away but now he's back and he keeps shouting and banging on the door.'

Vivien could hear dull echoing thuds in

the background.

'When he left the first time, my father thought he'd got the message and gone for good so he felt safe leaving me to take mother into the village for a hospital check-up. But I don't feel at all right with me being in here and Stephen out there like he's some unwelcome stranger or something. Are you anywhere near here yet?'

'I think we've just left the town.'

'I do wish there was a way you could get here sooner but it'll still take the best part of an hour.'

'Are you okay?'

'Yes ... no ... I don't know. Look, I'm going out to see him.'

'No! Don't. He's in a very volatile state and might not even recognise you.'

'What do you mean? I'm his wife.'

'But he's not himself. Stay inside, Hélène, until I can be there with you.'

'I ... can't ... I have to,' she let out a scream of anguish, 'have to be with him...'

'Hélène, please, just wait–'

The connection was severed as Vivien's mobile battery died.

The next forty minutes were some of the longest of Vivien's life. Anything could be happening at the house right now and she was powerless to stop it.

The taxi turned right sharply. It had started to rain. She had no idea where she

361

was. The night was beginning to come down in earnest and she could only see the dim shapes of trees through the window. They were driving down a bumpy track. She checked her watch. It was nearly ten o'clock. Only two hours left until Stephen was due to turn twenty-six.

'Nous sommes ici, madam.'

Thank God for that. Vivien leant forward to peer through the windscreen. There was no sign of the house yet. Two lights appeared up ahead. Vivien watched them grow closer and then was momentarily dazzled as they became bright headlights. The vehicle was travelling very fast and seemed to be heading straight for them. Suddenly there was a red flashing light and the blood-chilling wail of a siren. She was overwhelmed by a sense of panic that she was too late. In an involuntary reaction to the nightmare that was screaming towards her, she screwed her eyes shut and clutched on to the back of the driver's seat. She heard the rush of tyres as it sped by.

'Alors. Mon Dieu.'

She opened her eyes again at the sound of the driver's voice and saw him cross himself. She wanted so much to do the same in the hope that the ritual would make everything alright. But in her case, she knew it would only be superstition and would neither change the situation nor give her any courage or comfort about what she was about to face.

The track ended abruptly. A farmhouse sat a long way back down a gravel driveway. There were no lights on. There was the dim outline of a car parked on one side beneath some bushes. The taxi driver stopped and gabbled something to Vivien. He had to repeat it twice more and add hand gestures before she realised that he wanted to leave her here and turn the car. She paid him and got out into the rain. The air was bone-numbingly cold. She pulled the collar of her inappropriately thin jacket tightly around her neck as she watched the taillights of the taxi receding. For a moment she felt frighteningly alone. The thought of being stuck out here in the middle of nowhere made her shivering worse.

She picked her way carefully on the un-familiar path towards the house. In the gravel she could see the parallel lines of fresh tyre tracks. Had that vehicle been taking someone away? Hélène; Stephen; both of them? The thought made her break into a run that set her heart thumping. She stumbled up the step to the front door and banged on it with the heavy iron knocker. The sound echoed hollowly in what she imagined was a stone-flagged passageway. She tried again, louder this time. Still no light flicked on in response. There was no one here.

The rain dripped off the ends of Vivien's

hair as she stood in the shelter of the narrow porch and debated her options. She didn't have many; she could stay here and wait for someone to turn up and relieve her of the agony of not knowing, or she could leave. Except she couldn't. She hadn't taken a card from the taxi driver and, even if she had, her mobile wasn't working. For a few seconds she felt like screaming and kicking her heels with frustration as Dmitri would've done. Why hadn't she thought things through a little better? If she'd hired a car at the airport then at least she could've left under her own steam. She peered out through the rain at the car parked under the bushes. Maybe someone had left it unlocked? That didn't sound as unlikely out here as it would be in central London.

Vivien pulled her jacket over her head and ran out into the rain. As she got closer, she saw that the side windows of the vehicle were steamed-up. This new discovery sent a stab of panic through her. Who the hell would be sitting out there and not in the comfort of the house? It dawned on her that something else could've gone on here, something that didn't involve Stephen or Hélène. Not directly anyway. She had a flash of the terrifying nightmare that'd visited her after she'd read Truman Capote's *In Cold Blood* as a teenager, where a whole family had been murdered in their beds. Living on an isolated farmstead as

364

she did, she'd dreamed nightly of strangers turning up and murdering her and her family in random acts of torture and violence. She should run. If she got to the main road she could maybe hitch a lift or find a house willing to take her in and let her use their phone.

But she couldn't move; fear had rooted her halfway between the porch and the car. Her wet skirt clung to her thighs and her feet were growing numb as she willed her mind to stop thinking the worst. How was she to know that the person – or persons – in the car hadn't been left behind by Hélène expressly to await her arrival and tell her what had been going on? But if so, why didn't they approach her or at least call out and let her know that they were there? And then it came to her: she wasn't able to see who was inside through the rain and the condensation, and they wouldn't be able to see her either. They probably wouldn't even have been able to hear the taxi because he had turned and left way before the start of the driveway.

Whatever, she couldn't stand here all night or she would die of hypothermia. Vivien screwed up what little courage she could muster and walked up to tap on the steamed-up window. A moment's hesitation and then it wound down. It was Stephen. Vivien wanted to gabble her relief that he was safe; that he wasn't a murdering stranger; that she was no longer alone; that she would have sanctuary from the biting rain. But the words died in her throat as he turned his head away to stare straight ahead, his focus fixed on something that she couldn't see. He hadn't even appeared to recognise her. He looked almost maniacal. But at least she wasn't too late.

Vivien slipped on wet leaves as she stumbled around to the passenger side of the car, wrenched the door open, and climbed in.

CHAPTER THIRTY

She reached up and switched on the car's interior light to take a better look at him. His cheekbones were sharp and his jaw set. Gone was the overgrown schoolboy that had first appeared in her office a little over two months ago, and in his place was a worn-out puffy-eyed man who looked as though he hadn't slept in the thirty-six hours since she'd last seen him. She became aware of his hands increasing their grip on the steering wheel. She could feel Stephen's anger so strongly that she wondered if it had just been discharged or was just beginning.

'Stephen, it's Dr Blake. Vivien. I want you to breathe deeply and try to relax.'

'What the hell are you doing here?' His voice was obscenely loud in the confines of the car. 'Haven't you done enough damage already?'

But the real question was: had Stephen done any damage? Now she was safe, the shock of the siren careering towards her came back; he looked hell-bent on self-destruction and may well have felt the need to take someone else with him.

'What happened, Stephen? What's been going on here?'

'Wouldn't you like to know? Always interfering, meddling, making things worse. Hélène's where she is now because of you.'

Vivien felt her breath catch in her chest. What had he done to her? Had she told him of her own imminent arrival and he'd been scared and that she might find out something that he wanted kept secret?

'Where is she, Stephen? Tell me.'

'In the back of that ambulance you must've passed.'

'My God, Stephen, what have you done?'

'Me? Me! It's always bloody me, isn't it? First, I'm accused of pushing a stupid boy overboard when all I tried to do was stop him leaning too far over the rail; then you assume I'm warped and twisted enough to make up stories about your dead son. Now, to fucking top it all, you even think I've attacked my wife.'

He had let go of the steering wheel and his hands were fists of frustration in his lap. Vivien felt her anxiety threaten to make her jump out of the car but she forced herself to put her fears for her own safety to one side and concentrate on the damaged man sitting opposite her. But she couldn't stop her voice from shaking.

'You may not think it, Stephen, but I'm here to help you. I'm on your side.'

'The only side you're on is your own. I know you think you can get to your dead son through me.'

'Dmitri. His name was Dmitri.' She took a deep shuddering breath. 'Is he why you didn't tell me your wife is pregnant?'

Stephen seemed to uncoil suddenly and punched the dashboard. The whole car rocked. Vivien bit back a scream. His voice, when it came, was knife-edged.

'I suppose you don't credit me with many of the finer feelings in life but it seemed a little insensitive to bring it up. I nearly told you when you thought that I'd concocted all that about him appearing to Edward; I wanted to hurt you for thinking that I was such a bastard as to do that but I couldn't. I may be screwed up but I'm not heartless.'

'I know you're not. And I'm truly sorry that the thought even entered my head. It's no excuse, but I was shocked and upset.'

'I bet you were. So maybe you know something of what I'm going through now.'

'I'll try to understand, I promise, but you have to tell me exactly what's been going on since you got here. Is Hélène alright?

'She's in safe hands now, if that's what you mean.'

'Why did you suddenly come out here to see her?'

'Because she's my wife. Because I love her and wanted to be with her and because I don't know how much longer I can cope with everything you're putting me through without her by my side.'

'But she's not by your side now, is she?'

Vivien swallowed the saliva that was pooling in her mouth. She felt sick. What had happened to Hélène? Why she wasn't in the house safe and warm, resting as she should be in her condition?

'No, she's in a bloody state on her way to the hospital.'

A wave of panic washed over Vivien and she felt slug-trails of sweat begin between her shoulder blades and behind her knees. The roof and dashboard of the car pressed in on her. He was sitting too close and she could smell stale beer on his breath. Something like a whimper lodged at the back of her throat. She couldn't speak. Couldn't move. Couldn't think.

'Don't look at me like that. There you go again thinking I'm an axe-murderer or something–'

Her professional training kicked in at last and found her voice for her. 'I don't think anything of the sort.'

'Yes you do and I'm pissed off with you trying to shoulder the blame for what's happened onto me. It's your fault she's where she is. It was your fucking phone call. You frightened her with your *I'm rushing over on a mercy mission* routine and she's gone into early labour.'

The shuddering relief Vivien felt that Hélène had not been the subject of a frenzied attack – he hadn't been too far off the mark with the axe-murderer remark – was swiftly replaced by the fear that her intervention could be responsible for a dangerously premature birth. God, would she ever be able to forgive herself if she had to live with another child's short life on her conscience?

'Everything you've done has messed up my life so far. You're here to help me, Dr Blake? I'd laugh if I had the energy to find anything funny anymore. Have you got any bloody clue what it's like knowing you have two other people inside your head and that the life you are trying to live may have nothing to do with you and who you are, and everything to do with them?'

Vivien shook her head slowly. She couldn't even begin to comprehend what that must feel like. The only thing she did know was that Stephen was running out of time in which to get the upper hand over his fate. She tried to imagine for a moment that she was back in the secure world of her office; that Stephen was just another patient in distress needing her calm reassurance and clinical detachment.

'Stephen, please tell me because I don't understand. Why are you still here? Why didn't you go with Hélène?'

'That's exactly where I should be, isn't it, with my wife? Even you can see that. But not here: we should be back in London with me fussing around while she lies on the sofa with her feet up. She came out here to this cold, damp, soulless house to get away from me, and what she thought I might do to her. I'd begun to win her around over the past couple of weeks to the thought of coming home but then I come out here and fuck it all up. I'd seen her parents drive off and I was sitting here waiting for her to come out to me and she did. I was so happy that she was willing to defy her father's stupid edicts about ignoring me and I'll go away but, when it came down to it, I let her down after all; in a worse way than even he could possibly imagine.'

'What went on between you?'

Vivien's skin prickled: she still only had Stephen's word for it that Hélène had gone into labour at all and that was why the ambulance had taken her away. The thought still wouldn't leave her that he might have done something to affect the impending birth: the man was seething with guilt and remorse.

'She came out of the door with her arms under her belly. She shouted at me to drive her to the hospital. But I couldn't. I just sat here like the useless lump of shit that I am and stared through the windscreen. I couldn't even take my hands off the steering wheel to get out of the car and help her. My wife was screaming at me to do something and I did nothing.'

'What happened then?'

'She went back in the house and must've called the hospital because the next thing I knew, the ambulance had arrived and driven off again and my wife and child were being taken away from me. And I don't know if I'll ever see either of them again.'

Vivien felt a shiver of empathy. She knew the lonely place that Stephen was in only too well. Her son, who she had thought was lost to her forever, had touched her life again briefly but would the circumstances ever be right for her to access him again? She only had what was left of this short night left to find out. And Jerry. What of

Jerry? Had he too been spirited away to what might as well be a foreign country, never to return the loving partner who had once placed all his trust and faith in her? Maybe Stephen and she had even more in common than they thought: both destroyers of their own happiness through guilt. The fear of failure begets failure itself.

'So, in the opinion of such a great psychiatrist as yourself, what sort of man does that make me, Dr Blake? I'm too much of a bloody mess to even look after her when she most needed me. And even after she left, I couldn't bring myself to follow her.'

Vivien could the line of tears on his cheek.

'I should be beside her holding her hand, not sitting here too fucking wrapped up in myself to move. Some sort of father I'll make, huh? Jesus, I always knew I was a selfish bastard but this is right up there with all the rest. You do realise, don't you, that because I wouldn't do anything to jeopardise my cosy existence that I condemned children to an early death in the hell of the pottery?'

'That was Edward.'

'No!' His voice was as ragged as if it had been torn out of him. 'If I am Edward then that was me. And Clarence, too. He refused to look after that young boy properly and just look what happened.'

'They were your past lives, Stephen, and

you could do nothing to change the events that took place in them.'

'Okay then, you want me to focus on the here and now? What about that child I let nearly drown? Me, Stephen Daunt, conscious adult and supposedly responsible teacher.' His voice was beginning to rise on a wave of hysteria.

'Calm down, Stephen. Breathe deeply again. It's over. You're not living it again.'

'It bloody feels like I am. Do you have a clue what it's like to know that you're perfectly prepared to stand there and watch a kid drown rather than act to save him?'

'It was nothing you did on purpose, Stephen. You couldn't help your reaction; it was purely involuntary.'

'Try telling that to the parents.'

Vivien shuddered in her own involuntary reaction.

'Listen to me. It's all part of the same pattern. Your anxiety, the insomnia and violent nightmares, and now your reaction to Hélène going into labour. It's guilt. Guilt for what might have happened and your inability to do anything to prevent it. We can work on that and find ways for you to let go of it.'

'It's not guilt. It's spinelessness. It's being a waste of space. It's letting everyone down. It's knowing that I'm a fucking apology for a man and don't deserve to be taking up space on this earth.'

'We all deserve that, Stephen.'

'I don't. Christ, imagine what it'll be like for a child to have to grow up with a father like me.'

He switched the ignition on. The fan blasted air onto the windscreen. Vivien sat and watched the mist clear upwards and outwards. Stephen seemed to be mesmerised by it too but then he reached out and clicked a switch on the dashboard. The headlights sprang into life and picked out ghostly shadows in the trees.

'Get out, Dr Blake.'

Vivien felt the pit of her stomach fill with ice.

'What are you going to do?'

'I'm going a long, long way away from here.'

'You can't run away from yourself, Stephen.'

'That's just where you're wrong. If there's no self to run away from then I'd say it was mission accomplished, wouldn't you?'

'I want you to switch off the engine, Stephen.'

'Don't be stupid.'

'Then I'm going with you.'

'Have it your own way.'

The car leapt forward and slewed sideways as the tyres spun in the gravel. Vivien stifled a scream and struggled to fasten her seatbelt. The engine roared as Stephen put his foot down. She braced herself as they rocketed through the gateway and the world outside the windows became nothing but a blur.

CHAPTER THIRTY-ONE

The unfamiliar road wound through the countryside. Vivien's whole body was shaking and she was clutching onto the dashboard so hard her fingers had gone numb. Without warning, the hedges on either side disappeared and a gust of wind buffeted the car like a giant hand. Squalls of rain punched the windscreen. They were on some sort of promontory, exposed to the worst the weather had to throw at them. She screamed at Stephen to stop but he was like a madman in his intensity. The road dipped suddenly and followed the line of a flimsy wire fence. A light shone in the distance way off to their right. It disorientated her for a moment as she realised that it was moving. Not towards or away from them but sideways.

The car rocked under the pressure of another violent gust and Vivien understood with a stab of horror that they were on the cliff top she had seen from the airplane just minutes before they landed. The beam she could see sweeping the night was from the lighthouse. Stephen twitched the steering wheel and the car skated on the wet road surface towards the grass verge. The headlights picked out a wooden fence post. Vivien felt the tears on her cheeks. She could almost hear again the rip and tear of metal. *The past is gone: it cannot touch me*, she chanted under her breath. It was what she had taught Stephen but now she had to learn to apply it to herself.

Stephen slewed the car to a stop. The rain was beating down on the roof. Vivien sat and listened to it keep time with the tick of the cooling engine. She finally released her grip on the dashboard and looked across at Stephen. He was sitting slumped forward with his head resting on the steering wheel. He was muttering something that she couldn't catch.

Vivien wanted to get out of the car and throw up. That had been the scariest drive of her life. The second scariest. She had no idea how far away from the town they were and doubted that Stephen did either. But it didn't matter. They had stopped. The interior light was still on and she looked at her watch. It was just gone eleven. She had a scant hour in which to save Stephen from destroying himself. She took some steadying deep breaths, licked her lips, and forced herself to speak.

'Stephen, you once told me that you trusted me. Do you still?'

'How can I when I don't even trust myself?'

His voice was muffled but she could hear the despair in it clearly enough.

'We've been on a long journey together these past few months but it's one we have to complete. One of the reasons that you're feeling so desperate at the moment is that you haven't yet reached a resolution. Closure, Stephen. You need closure.'

'That's just shrink talk.'

She thought that the time was now right for some more self-disclosure. It might help him to move on to the next stage. She didn't really want to say the words because she knew it would be painful; but it was a price worth paying if it meant not failing him. Her hands fluttered like clipped-winged birds in her lap.

'You are about to have a child, Stephen, and you will look back on this moment in your life forever with a sense of glorious hope for the future. I know because I felt that hope every day for three years.'

Her voice cracked slightly. She looked at the night on the other side of the windscreen and forced herself to breath evenly. She tried again.

'A new life is magical and it is an extraordinary privilege to be part of bringing it into this world.'

She turned towards him.

'But the opposite is true also. The loss I felt when Dmitri died was more devastatingly painful that I can ever begin to describe; the words just don't exist. And it never goes away.' Her voice became softer. 'But there does come a point when it can no longer rule your life; define who you are.'

She felt as though she was sitting in a confessional and sharing the secrets of her heart.

'That's closure, Stephen. Not the forgetting of events or the wiping away of the feelings, but the acceptance of them. And acceptance can only begin with understanding.'

'You're telling me that you understand why your son had to die? Because I don't believe you.'

'No. I'll never understand that. But I have begun to understand an awful lot more about life. And about my life and who I am.'

'Then you're way ahead of me. I seem to be living three lives all at the same time and I've no bloody idea what any of it means and where they end and I begin.'

Vivien injected a note of authority into her voice. 'You are Stephen Daunt. And you've always been Stephen Daunt. Son of a publican, logical-thinking maths teacher, husband, soon to be father. You are all those things and more. But there is a part of you that is blocked off – and whilst your rational mind is uppermost, we don't have access to it. What is clear is that something lodged deep in your subconscious is trying to undermine all that you stand for. Only you have the key to unlock it. You have to finish this journey of self-discovery. You have to go back to the night of the fire.'

'No. I won't. You can't make me.'

He sounded like a petulant child. Which was probably exactly how he felt.

'You have to, Stephen. Let me hypnotise you one last time. It is imperative that you experience the rest of Edward's story.'

'What; here? Now?'

'It has to be now. Trust me, Stephen. The timing is crucial.'

He was silent for a long moment.

'I can't see the point. Edward's dead.'

'But you have the whole of your life ahead of you. I'm giving you the opportunity to ensure it is a happy and healthy one.'

She was feeling much more like a psychiatrist again and switched tack to appeal to Stephen's rational mind rather than his emotions.

'The presenting problems that you came to me with – the violent nightmares and erratic behaviour patterns – all sprang from the incident on the boat trip and have been your reactions to it and Hélène's pregnancy.

I can help you to understand why you were so frozen and unable to react that day. Once brought out into the light of examination, you will be able to exorcise it. Knowledge is power, Stephen. You need to understand so that you can take control again.'

But she couldn't control her fear. Her legs were still shaking. Two pinpricks of light caught her attention. Another vehicle was up on this wasteland with them. Her stomach flip-flopped at the thought that they might not be far enough off the road and in the dark...? She wanted to tell Stephen to switch on the headlights but any distraction now might be too much for him to process. How could she possibly know that he wouldn't just automatically press his foot on the accelerator and send them careering forward once more? The cliff edge couldn't be far away. She forced herself to stop focusing on her worst fears and concentrate on what might be going on in the mind of the man sitting beside her. She chewed the inside of her lip and could taste blood before he responded.

'I'm scared to after the last time. It was horrible.'

'The last session was exceptional and it won't happen again. I promise you that I'll get you into your trance-like state nice and slowly and bring you out of it equally gently. It was the alarm going off that shattered the illusion of Clarence's life being separate from yours. Your conscious mind didn't have time to readjust and that partially explains why you've been feeling lost and not like yourself ever since then.'

Stephen raised his head finally and looked at her. A long searching look that she felt went right down to her bones. She was desperate to glance at her watch to see how much time she had left but she didn't want to break eye-contact with him. If she didn't regain his trust now, then it would all be over. There wouldn't be another chance.

He shrugged and punched the release on his seatbelt.

'What have I got to lose?'

Vivien heard the words *only your life* so clearly in her head that she was afraid she'd say them out loud. Instead, she undid her own seatbelt.

'Swap places with me, Stephen. There's more room in the passenger seat and you'll be able to make yourself more comfortable.'

Vivien leant into the wind that tugged at her and threatened to sweep her off her feet as she ran around the front of the car. She felt a shiver of sick remembrance as she battled to pull the driver's door shut and slid behind the steering wheel. She was grateful to have the time to clear her mind of the last time she'd been in this position as Stephen fiddled with his seat until he was leaning back as far as it could go. He looked pathetically vulnerable with his head on the headrest and exposing his throat, and his legs stretched out in front of him. She turned the ignition key and switched on the parking lights. The action steadied her a little.

'Okay, Stephen. Just relax. Imagine that you're back in my office lying on the couch. I want you to feel the seat with your spine and to press back against it... That's right... Now let the tension drain out of those muscles and feel it falling away through your legs and feet.'

Stephen appeared to be complying remarkably well under the circumstances. But then the poor man was exhausted. She remembered back to their first hypnosis session; he'd been in the grip of insomnia then too and it had been ridiculously easy for him to achieve a trance-like state. She hoped that would prove to be the case this time.

'I want you to count backwards from seven, Stephen. Nice and slowly... Breathe in deeply on seven and exhale on six... Slow, deep breaths... That's it. You're doing very well... The same for five and four...'

She reached over and picked up his wrist. It was limp already.

'Take us both back to the day of the fire, Stephen... Let Edward tell us the rest of his story... He's waiting for you because he

383

wants you to know what happened to him. It's his gift to you, Stephen, and there's nothing to be afraid of... Go back with him now.'

She watched his eyelids flicker.

'...You are Edward Houghton again and witnessing your pottery going up in flames... There is a young boy at the third floor window... You look up at him and...'

CHAPTER THIRTY-TWO

The boy sank out of view. His mother immediately stopped screaming and began to wail.

'Help him,' she sobbed when she had drawn breath, 'someone help him. He's nowt but a child.'

'It be too dangerous to go in there, duck. The ceiling will be falling in, like as not.'

The man had been one of the last to put down his pail and was obviously not given to over-caution. Edward could see where his forearms had been singed smooth of hair.

'Happen someone had better do summat and do it quick.'

Edward could feel everyone looking at him.

'Is there no back way out?'

'You think your father wasted his brass on that? That bastard would' a had us pissing in pots at our wheels to keep from building latrines if he could'a got away with it.'

'Hold your tongue, George, 'member you need a living.'

'It's that poor mite needs that.'

'Jawing's wasting time. Someone will have to go up for him.'

Edward felt it was up to him to take control. He pointed to a muscled man who seemed to be less affected by smoke and exertion than his companions.

'You. Wrap yourself in wet cloths. Some of you others wait at the door and if he seems to be in difficulty then you can go in and rescue him.'

The man Edward had selected reached for the pump handle.

'It mun be true all bosses keep their brains up their arses. Nat here's got a wife and four kiddies to provide for. You get him killed and you'll have them to account for too.'

Edward could not conceal his shock at the man's words. No one had ever spoken to him like that in his life. Wharburton's earlier sentiments concerning his authority were laughable now.

'I reckon there's only one fit to go in there. Someone who's got no one to miss 'em if they don't come back out.'

'There's only one like that here.'

'And it be his potbank, too.'

'No fitter, I reckon.'

Edward's gaze swept around the sea of angry faces crowding in on him. The weight of his father's expectations to live by his code had been nothing compared to this. Through the grey smoke lacing the air of the courtyard, he could see Emily Smallthorne. She must have come down to the pottery to check on the outcome of his meeting with the government commissioner. Her expression was unreadable but he could guess at her thoughts. The child should never have been working in the potbank in the first place and then he would not be up there, trapped in a burning building.

'What you waiting for? Clay sticking your boots to the floor?'

Edward felt a shove in the small of his back. He turned to see an elderly woman, her hair tumbling around her smoke-smeared face. Her lips were set in frozen disapproval and she was glaring at him with a look of hatred that made him shudder.

Could he do it? Could he go in there, rescue the boy, and get out alive? Even Jonathan would decline to place a wager on the odds of him succeeding. But the chances of him remaining standing here unscathed were beginning to dwindle too. One or two of the men on the edge of the crowd were clutching thick wooden moulding pins. He remembered the savage lust he had seen on the faces of the men at the dog fight in the yard of The Potter's Wheel; it would take little to provoke an equivalent display of violence now. After all, with their livelihoods already gone up in smoke, they would be sure to feel that they had nothing to lose.

Edward flicked another glance up at the window. He had been concerned with balancing the scales of truth earlier; now it was lives he had to weigh up. His and a small boy's. The men around him might beat him to within an inch of his life for not attempting a rescue and, if they did not, would his conscience demand of him that he wish they had finished the job?

With shaking limbs he pulled his coat off and flung it to the ground.

'Fill that dipping basin up, man,' he instructed one of the workers standing by the pump.

The crowd stepped back and cleared a passage as the overflowing vessel was handed to him. He tipped the contents over his head and shoulders. The cold water made his nerve-endings prickle but cleared his head somewhat. With rivulets dripping into his eyes from his wet hair, Edward swallowed his terror and ran towards the smoke billowing out through the door of the Moulding Room.

He had barely advanced more than a yard

inside when he had to stop. It was almost impossible to see. And to breathe. The acrid smoke caught at the back of his throat and he retched. He pulled off his stock and tied it over his mouth and nose. He felt the uncomfortable sensation of being smothered but was at least able to suck in air without coughing. But his eyes were still smarting. He blinked hard a couple of times and looked at his tear-blurred surroundings. The place was unrecognisable in its charred and smouldering desolation. And it was hot. Unbelievably hot. He wondered briefly if this was what it was like working in one of the bottle ovens. The sinister crackle of still-consuming flames brought him back.

He wiped his streaming eyes with one of the loose corners of his stock and tried to get his bearings. It didn't help that he hadn't really known the layout of this room before it had crumbled in on itself. But he knew that the boy was upstairs and that the staircase leading to the upper floors was in the far corner. But first he had to get there.

He edged forward, his arms stretched in front of him like a blind man. The smoke was so thick that he could easily stumble up against a burning rafter that had dropped down from the ceiling. He was equally in danger of falling over something. The floor of the Moulding Room was a jumble of pottery shards, smashed moulds, the smouldering remains of wooden shelves, collapsed work benches, and tangled and broken machinery. He thought that it would be safer to move to the side and hug the wall on his way around. But after only a step or two, a buckled and broken water pipe hanging like a hellish snake hissed a blast of steam perilously close to his ear.

This was madness. He would never be able to save the child. Surely it was better that he give up now before they both perished? He looked back towards the doorway and had to stiffen the muscles in his legs to stop himself from running towards it. He would attempt a passage across the centre of the room and if he could not make it to the bottom of the stairs then he would retreat. With honour. No one could say that he had not tried.

He could hear his own breathing clearly. It was ragged and shallow, as if his lungs were refusing to inhale any more of the poisonous air. A terrifying thought flashed across his mind: if the fire and smoke did not render him incapable, would it be the noxious substances used in the pottery process that would force his throat to close and deprive his brain of life-giving oxygen? Mr Wharburton and Emily Smallthorne had both warned him about the perils of exposure to lead and other contaminants, and he imagined they may be more virulent when heated. He was no chemist but he was sure that he could taste something that was slowly numbing his tongue.

A shape loomed up ahead of him through the smoke and he paused before taking another small step forward. It was a brick plinth reaching halfway up to the ceiling. Probably a corner of one of the racks of shelving. He heard it tick ominously in the heat. Then there was a crack like a miniature internal explosion and it teetered and crashed to the ground. Edward leapt sideways and winced as a piece of it thudded into his shin. A cloud of choking dust thickened the atmosphere.

His stomach clenched as he wondered how much longer he had before everything collapsed around him and he was buried under the crumbling fabric of his own factory. Many of those waiting in the courtyard for his return might think that most fitting. Would Emily? Would there be anyone who would mourn his loss? The thought brought a sob to his throat. He could not bear it if he were not remembered. Or even worse, to have his name cursed with jeers and hatred as his father's was.

He was halfway across the room now – he could tell by the dimming of the light coming in through the doorway. To go on or back? He took a step forward. And then another. His fear was so great that he wanted to run – in either direction, it mattered not which – but he knew that haste would be a greater enemy even than the fire and if he were struck down on the way out then, when his body was recovered, everyone would know that he had been a coward.

Step by painful step, Edward reached the bottom of the stairs. The smoke in this corner was not so thick and the smashed windows on either side offered the relief of a little clean air. The fire itself had not yet reached here but, judging by the short amount of time it had taken to burn and corrupt the rest of the room, it would not take long. He removed the covering from his nose and mouth. He would need to be able to breathe without restriction if he was to be able to make the effort required to climb the stairs. Already heat – and the thought of imminent death – had exhausted him. He reached his hand out unthinkingly and leant for support on an undamaged bench by his side. The skin of his palm seared and puckered almost immediately. Edward bellowed out a cry of pain and then had to bend over double in order to replace the air in his lungs. The smoke was creeping ever closer and infecting this corner. He had come this far and now he had to get to the boy.

Edward ran up the first flight of stairs but was staggering by the time he got to the top of the second. The atmosphere was clearer here, but hotter. He took a moment to peer out over the banister rail and check that he still knew where the doorway was. And that he had an unimpeded passage to it.

His chest was heaving as he reached the third floor. Fingers of smoke clawed up from below. A door was in front of him. He went to grab hold of the doorknob with his undamaged hand and then stopped himself. It was brass. He had to take precautions against any further self-inflicted injury. He cursed himself for not realising that he might need his stock again; he had let it drop to the floor as he'd started up the stairs. He stood in impotent indecision for a moment and then pulled his shirt tails free from his britches and wrapped the loose material thickly around the doorknob. He twisted it and pushed but nothing happened. He wondered if the wood had swollen in the heat and was gripping the frame. He took a deep breath and shouldered the stubborn door. It was unyielding. Not even a fraction of movement or groan from the hinges. It suddenly came to him that it must be locked. But why? He had not even been aware that there were keys to the internal rooms.

He looked around him. There was nothing to hand that he could use to break the door down. He had no option but to retreat back down the stairs and look for something there. His heart sank as he retraced his steps across the landing. Every second was precious and he was wasting them by not thinking ahead. His father had always said that would be the undoing of him. An evil devil at the back of his brain made him smile; his father, if he was looking down at him from Heaven and was not in the other place where he deserved to be for presiding over the construction of such a death-trap, would probably be noting all of his mistakes in a fat ledger in order to recount them when they met again.

Edward wondered if the heat and exertion were addling his mind. How could he make a joke at his own expense at a time like this? Maybe this was what being conscious of the fragility of life did to you; made you laugh at the absurdity of everything that has gone before.

He ran down the stairs until he was once more on the floor of the Moulding Room. With a shock he realised that the fire was no longer creeping ever closer but had now taken wings on the air coming in through the smashed windows. He could see the orange glow like a demonic sunset not ten feet away. Trails of sparks were skittering up to the ceiling.

He looked around him for anything he could make use of. There was a sooty lump the size of a man's head that he thought might have formed the pedestal of one of the potter's wheels. Next to it was a singed apron. He picked up the cloth and wrapped it around the stone. He could feel the heat radiating into his chest as he carried his heavy burden back up the stairs. His progress was agonisingly slow and he felt sick with the effort and lack of air. He had reached the top again when an explosion from something giving itself up to devouring flames made his eardrums buzz. He had to get into the office. And now before it was too late.

Summoning up all his strength, Edward lifted the chunk of masonry above his head. He launched it at the lock. A noise like the crack of overhead thunder echoed around the hollow building. Twice, three times, he had to repeat the action until the external lock mechanism finally sheared away.

CHAPTER THIRTY-THREE

Edward pushed the door inwards and lunged forward into the room. A desk and chair were close by one wall and shelves containing stacks of ledgers were ranged along the length of the others. He doubled-over in a coughing fit for a moment and wiped his streaming eyes.

He forced himself to stand upright and take another look around. There. He had missed it the first time. A child's foot was poking out from under the desk. Edward crouched down on creaking haunches. The boy's wide eyes looked back at him from his deathly white face. He was panting shallowly. Edward tried a smile of reassurance but felt that he did not possess enough of it himself to adequately convey the message, so reached out his hand instead. The boy grasped it and Edward hauled him from his hiding place.

'Can you walk?'

'Reckon so, sir.' The boy's voice was thick with tears. And fear.

'Come on then. Quickly now.'

The boy stood up and appeared to be about to say something more when his legs gave way and he slumped onto the floor.

Edward cursed the God that was making all this so difficult for him and scooped the boy up in his arms. He staggered out of the room and across the landing. Was it his imagination or could he smell burning close by? Not the acrid tang of charred wood but the bright energy of living fire. He hoped not. Three flights of stairs in his weakened physical condition whist carrying an inert boy was enough for any man without asking him to outrun a fresh outbreak of flames.

He stepped carefully down the first of the stairs. He could not see his feet over the hump of the boy's shoulder and did not want to miss his footing and plunge them both downwards to rest at the bottom with broken necks. Although, he thought bitterly, that might be preferable to feeling his skin scorch and his hair frazzle in the moments before being consumed alive by flames.

He paused to catch his breath. The boy had gone limp in his arms. Edward looked down at his face. The skin was waxy and the eyelids hardly moving.

'Do not make a mockery of me, boy,' he breathed into the child's ear, 'I do not want to have risked my life only to be transporting a corpse.'

Some of his urgency must have communicated itself to the boy because he shifted slightly in Edward's arms. He gripped him a little more tightly in gratitude and proceeded to move forward once more. The further down he went, the more evidence he came across of the fire's relentless hunger; the smoke had started his eyes streaming again and he could hear the crackle and spit of the flames as they licked around yet another meal.

He made it somehow to the landing. One flight negotiated and two more to go. Here the staircase turned back on itself to hug the corner of the Moulding Room. He turned to his right to recommence his descent when the wood beneath his feet suddenly creaked and tilted. Had one of the supports gone? He stepped sideways to avail himself of the solid protection of the wall. Solid? Nothing was that anymore in this shifting world of corruption. Another two steps...

The toes of his right foot were groping for the next tread down when he felt a sickening lurch convulse his whole body. Edward jumped back onto the landing he had just left. And not before time as, with terrifying slowness, the flight of stairs below him collapsed and dissolved like a poorly constructed pyre. Showers of angry sparks shot up past him and flames roared in satisfied lust.

An evil fist of soot and ash rose up from the void to meet him. Edward knew he had to think quickly; the boy was barely breathing now. He looked down over the remaining banister. He could just see the doorway backlit with the light from the courtyard. But there was no way to get there. They were trapped. He gently laid the boy on the landing and peered over to see if there was any way he could get down. There was a drop of at least fifteen feet. Broken legs or impalement on a piece of debris seemed to be the fate that would await them.

Edward gasped in one breath after another until his lungs felt as though they would burst. The strain made him feel sick. Then he raised his hands and cupped them around his mouth.

'I have him!'

Could his voice possibly reach above the roar of the fire and out into the courtyard? He tried again.

'Come and fetch him from me!'

For what seemed like the longest moment of his life, there was no response. Then Edward felt, rather than saw, a quality of movement below him. He had to trust that more than one of them had come to his aid; he would have to drop the boy and they would need to catch him. He kept up a meaningless chatter of words so that they could follow the sound. The effort was exhausting.

'I am here. Above you. Call back to me so that I know where you are.'

He heard three distinct voices in the response and knew that he and the boy were to be given a second chance. He lifted his charge over the banister rail and dangled him down. Slowly he let the boy slip through his grasp until he was clutching him by his wrists. His damaged hand was excruciatingly painful. He knew he should put his faith in those below but could not seem to let go.

His shoulders were screaming and the muscles in his arms growing so weak that he felt sure he must drop him before he felt the weight of the boy's body lessening. They had raised themselves up somehow to bridge the gap and had him. He let go. The boy was safe. Edward wiped his smarting eyes and looked down. Four men had formed a sort of human tower and the top one was now passing the boy into his mother's arms. Edward wanted to shout at them for bringing a woman into such an inferno with them but knew, as soon as he thought it, that they probably would not have been able to stop her even if they had tried.

'You next, gov'ner,' he heard someone call.

He was just about to gather his strength to climb over the banister and drop himself down when he heard the mother cry out.

'Praise be to God, he is alive. My boy spoke to me, he said: "Max. Get Max.".'

'We only saw 'im at the window but happen there was two of 'em.'

At the man's words, Edward lost all thought for a panic-stricken moment. He could hear the fire taking hold again. There were only the stairs he was standing on and the floor above left to burn. No one. No one could expect him to attempt that journey again. And on the strength of the mutterings of a semiconscious boy. He had done what he came to do and he had to get out now. The men were still below; they would break his fall if he jumped. But what if there was someone else up there? He knew that it would not be remembered that he had saved one child, just that he had been too afraid to go back for another. He would be branded a coward until the day he died.

He had wasted too much time and the smoke was thickening once more, the flames whooshing up out of the remains of the fallen staircase and sucking in all the air from around him. He felt as lightheaded as he had under the effects of the ale in The Potter's Wheel. The memory of his impotent fury at what he had witnessed that night was enough to galvanise him. He had to do something: standing in the middle of a burning building wrapped in indecision was fruitless. He turned away from the men below and the prospect of the safety that lay in their arms, and started to climb the stairs once more. His legs would not move as quickly as he wanted and once or twice he staggered and nearly fell. He was almost too weak to reach the top. It was only the desperate thought of failure that kept him going.

Edward was finally in the office once more. He looked around again. How could he have possibly missed another child up here? Or was it a child? Had the boy been referring to a pet dog perhaps? He should have stopped to ask. Surely it was a sin to risk the precious gift of life for an animal. He called the name he had been given anyway, between shuddering breaths. He ripped the front of his shirt open in an attempt to give more freedom to his lungs. Yet all the while he fancied that he was wasting his energy; if indeed there was another soul clinging to life up here then he doubted he would be able to hear any response over the sound of his heart thudding in his ears.

He skirted the room for a second time. There was nowhere left for a boy or beast to hide. As he lunged to look beneath the washstand, he knocked against a coat rack and it clattered to the floor. There, tucked away from view, was a slim cupboard. He wrenched the door open. Inside there was a shelf on which stood a bottle of what looked like whisky and, beneath it, a small boy.

Edward reached in and pulled him out. The child's head lolled back on his shoulders and his sightless eyes stared accusingly at his would-be rescuer. With a sob of recognition, Edward saw that it was the very same boy he had witnessed being beaten by Crossly. He held him in his arms and the tears streamed down his face. 'I am sorry... forgive me... I am so sorry...' he muttered over and over again. The child was his responsibility. He had been breathing his last whilst he, Edward, had been debating whether to save his own life. He should not have even given it a thought. It was monstrously selfish to have been so preoccupied. What weight did his life carry anyway when put on the balance scales against that of a ten year old?

Sickened by grief and desperation, Edward lay down beside the boy's corpse. He had nothing left to give. Not even for himself. Houghton's pottery would be the death of him, too.

CHAPTER THIRTY-FOUR

Vivien stilled her hands in her lap. What she was about to say would at the very least save Stephen's sanity and, if her theory was right, could even save his life. The coroner's report she had read on the plane coming over was the key to it all.

'Edward. I want you to listen carefully. I know you are feeling exhausted but I want you to put all your remaining energy into concentrating on my voice ... can you hear me, Edward?'

'Yes...'

His voice was strangled as if he was having trouble breathing. Vivien had to stop herself from imagining the horror of the situation he found himself in.

'...but you are faint as if from some distance ... my God, if you are on the floor of the Moulding Room then you must get out now.'

His fear was almost tangible; Vivien could

feel it invading the space around her.

'Don't worry about me, I'm safe. I'm not in the building with you but you can speak to me all the same. It doesn't matter how; just accept that you can.'

'What is your name? Do I know you?'

'I'm very familiar to you but not in a way that you'll have any memory of. And my name is Vivien.'

'It is damnably hot in here.'

'I know. But it'll soon be over.'

Vivien picked up Stephen's wrist and checked his pulse. It was barely discernable. She had to get on with it.

'I know you are haunted about how those two little boys got caught in the fire. You think it's your fault and your responsibility ... but it isn't.'

'This is my pottery and they work here for me. I cannot wash my hands of what has happened to them. The blood of this child will be on my conscience forever.'

'It doesn't have to be that way, Edward. What I am about to tell you will free you from that burden.'

She so hoped that she was right. The poor man deserved to be released from the hell he was putting himself – and Stephen – through.

'Let me take you back to when you first ran up the stairs to the office. You were surprised to find it locked, weren't you?'

'Yes. But now I think that maybe the boys found a key – perhaps in the desk drawer – and were playing a game.'

'No, Edward. The lock was on the outside, remember? It was someone else who locked them in.'

'I do not understand... I am tired... I cannot think...'

'I'll do the thinking for you, Edward; all you have to do is listen. It all started earlier in the day when the workers were having their meal. The two boys–'

'Max and his friend.'

'That's right. Afterwards, the boy you saved told his story to the coroner and I'm going to tell it to you now in much the same words. The two boys weren't hungry and were alone in the Moulding Room making small balls of clay in their fists and throwing them at each other. Your foreman caught them at it. The younger boy managed to run away and hide but Max wasn't so quick. Crossly took off his belt and started to beat him.'

'...Crossly...'

'But he didn't stop. He was so enraged by seeing you with the government commissioner–'

'Then I must take responsibility for the poor boy's flogging, as well as his death.'

'Edward, it wasn't your fault. None of it was. You couldn't stop Mr Wharburton coming to inspect your pottery; you were obliged by law – you should know that better than anyone. And, more importantly, you can't take responsibility for other people's actions. What Archibald Crossly did, he did of his own volition. Anger and envy made him what he was; you put neither of those things inside him. It was his God-given nature.'

'And what, pray, is my nature that I knew this man to be the bully he was but declined to remove him from his position for fear that such an act would tie me to the running of the potbank forever?'

'That's what you're about to find out, Edward. I'm going to tell you just the sort of man *you* are – not your father, not your brother, but you – as witnessed by your own actions.'

'I heartily wish you would because I scarce know it myself.'

'But first I have to continue with what led up to your part in all this. According to the coroner, Crossly later confessed that he didn't know what came over him and only stopped the flogging when the boy collapsed on the floor under the blows. At first he thought he was pretending to faint to escape further punishment but then he realised that he was dead.'

Stephen's rate of breathing increased rapidly and Vivien paused for a moment to give Edward time to recover from the shock.

'He picked Max up and carried him upstairs. Then he came back down to the Moulding Room to hunt for the other boy.'

'To beat him too?'

'No, Edward. By then he was more concerned with saving his own skin. He didn't want there to be a witness to his brutality. He found the boy hiding under one of the benches and dragged him upstairs and locked him in the office.'

'With a corpse?'

'It's a horrible story, Edward, but it's one you have to hear. Immediately after the fire, everyone thought it had been a stray spark from the kilns that had started it – even Mr Wharburton said so. But it wasn't. It was Archibald Crossly. He set fire to the Moulding Room in the hope of covering up his crime.'

'The man is the Devil incarnate.'

'But he didn't get away with it. The little boy you saved was able to tell his story, and Crossly was arrested. He was sentenced to hang, Edward.'

'That is the best of everything you have told me.'

'No, the best thing of all – the reason I am telling you all this – is that if you hadn't have acted as you did then none of the truth would ever have been revealed and Crossly would've escaped justice. Don't you see...? You could have done nothing to prevent

Max's death – Crossly had already killed him before the fire – but the one life that there was to save will be forever in your hands: you sacrificed your own life for the life of another. A child. There is no action in the world more honourable or noble than that.'

A smile appeared on Stephen's lips. Vivien reached out and held his hand.

'You can die in peace, now, Edward.'

Vivien sat in silence for a while. It was for her own benefit as much as it was for Edward to assimilate the end of his story. Her own words had affected her deeply. When she thought she could speak again without her voice betraying her emotion, she let go of Stephen's hand and sat back in the car seat.

'Stephen. I want you to describe for me what is happening to Edward now. Is he still in the burning building?'

'No. His body died when the smoke became too much for him. He's ascended to a place where nothing can hurt him anymore.'

The Bardo plane. Vivien almost clapped her hands together in triumph. She had done it. She had enabled Stephen to release Edward and move on.

'Tell me what it feels like?'

'Calm and restful and free from everything that has gone before. I'm floating.' Stephen laughed. 'There's that light again.

But it's brighter than before. And I'm not alone. There's a child here with me.'

Who was it? Max? Dmitri? Now she had got to this moment, Vivien was almost too afraid to ask. But she had to. She had to know: she needed closure, too.

'Is he the same boy as before, Stephen?'

'Yes.'

It was Dmitri. Vivien felt her heartbeat in her chest. Her mouth went dry and she licked her lips.

'What is he doing, Stephen?'

'He's walking towards the light ... now he's so close to it that it's like he's on fire... I can't tell where he ends and the light begins. And now he is part of the light. He's turning towards me. He is waving and smiling. He's so happy.'

'And how do you feel, Stephen?'

Stephen smiled.

'Me? I've never felt such peace.'

Vivien focused as hard as she could on the man sitting beside her. She wasn't going to make the same mistake again and put her needs and feelings before his. She had made a promise to him to end this session gently and she owed it to him to do just that. Asking him questions about Dmitri would only worry him and shatter his new-found serenity. She breathed deeply and hoped that some of it would rub off on her.

'I'm glad you're so relaxed and at ease

with yourself, Stephen. I want you to hold on to that feeling and let it wash through your body until you can sense it penetrating every single particle of you and to know, that once your very being is soaked in it, that it will never leave you. It is part of you forever.'

Stephen smiled once more. A warm happy smile that made her think of the little boy he once was, playing hide and seek in the apple tree on the day of the perfect picnic. Her eyes filled with tears.

'Very well done, Stephen. You have discovered everything you possibly can about yourself now. I led you through the journey but it was one you took alone. You exhibited a courage that few men have, Stephen, and you should be very proud of yourself. I am.'

She watched his chest rise and fall as he took deep, life-affirming breaths.

'Now count backwards from five for me. Slowly. On each count you can feel more and more of the world around you; the pressure of the headrest on your neck; your thighs pressing into the seat; the feel of the clothes on your skin. When you reach five, all your sensations are alive again and you will wake up feeling relaxed and refreshed.'

Stephen was still for a moment longer and then he began to wriggle as if to find a more comfortable position. Eventually he opened his eyes and turned to her.

'That was amazing, Dr Blake.' His voice was soft and full of awe. 'I feel so different. I can remember driving here but it's as if I can't remember why; what made me. The man who would've thought nothing of driving off a cliff and probably would've been thankful for it, has gone. I can never thank you enough. But why didn't you tell me all that stuff earlier? You know, what you found out about what that monster Crossly had been up to.'

'Because it was important for you to find out as much of the story as you could for yourself. For Edward. He had to live through the moment of discovering the truth so that he could forgive himself. He was proud, stubborn, and somewhat misguided in his opinions but he was prepared to accept the call for courage when it came and was selfless in his actions. The sacrifice had already been made, Stephen, and the price paid. That was Edward's message to you.'

But what about Dmitri's message to her? He had sought her out one last time and had waved – to her, she was sure of it, not Stephen – before walking into the light. But what had happened to him then? A thought struck her with a power that felt like a physical blow to her stomach. If Dmitri had indeed been preparing to go to his next life, was it connected to Stephen in a far more visceral way than she'd ever imagined: was

410

Dmitri about to become Hélène's child? It was a fantastic idea but, after all that had happened here tonight, it didn't seem absurd. Six months ago, she would never have believed that a patient could have walked into her office and be experiencing the trauma of unresolved past lives. Six months ago, her son was healthy and happy and daily filling her life with joy. She wished with every fibre of her being that she could know the truth of where he had gone after he'd left the Bardo plane. Except that wasn't possible; no one knew the secrets of what happened after death. Her mother's words at times like these came back to her: *you have to learn to live with uncertainty, honey: it's just not possible to know the answer to everything. You'd drain the excitement right out of life if you did.*

She lifted her hand to her face and caught sight of her watch. It was exactly midnight. She had done what she came here to do.

'Happy birthday, Stephen,' she said. 'I think this truly is going to be a birth day for you in more ways than one. Now, it's about time we got you to the hospital; Hélène has had you away from her for far too long.'

She shifted in her seat and swallowed hard.

'Would you like me to drive?'

If Stephen could display such courage to face his demons then she could, too. He smiled sweetly at her and nodded. Vivien

411

switched on the ignition. The cold engine stuttered into life. She had to drive again some time and it might as well be now. There could hardly be a better reason to go forward into the future.

Vivien pulled up on the brightly lit fore-court at the front of the hospital.

'Your wife's in there waiting for you.'

She could feel Stephen's body next to her, thrilling with excitement; it was no longer fear or apprehension, just an eager antici-pation. He opened the car door and got out, then bent back down

'Thank you, again, Dr Blake. I would've been a basket-case without your help – nearly was, in fact.'

'You were never that, Stephen. Just a confused man burdened with a trauma that was not of your making and that you could never have found the key to on your own. The point is – and I want you to remember this in the days to come – the reason why it affected you so deeply was because of your sense of responsibility and not, as you thought, because you behaved irresponsi-bility that day on the school trip.' Vivien reached out and touched his arm. 'Your baby will be very lucky to have you as a father.'

Stephen smiled and then ran to the door of the hospital and disappeared inside.

This Large Print Book, for people
who cannot read normal print,
is published under the auspices of

THE ULVERSCROFT FOUNDATION

... we hope you have enjoyed this book.
Please think for a moment about those
who have worse eyesight than you ...
and are unable to even read or enjoy
Large Print without great difficulty.

You can help them by sending a
donation, large or small, to:

**The Ulverscroft Foundation,
1, The Green, Bradgate Road,
Anstey, Leicestershire, LE7 7FU,
England.**
or request a copy of our brochure for
more details.

The Foundation will use all donations
to assist those people who are visually
impaired and need special attention
with medical research, diagnosis
and treatment.

Thank you very much for your help.